THE SIEGE OF KA'AN
Book2 in the New Roman Empire series

I0554109

THE SIEGE OF KA'AN

Book 2 in the New Roman Empire series

Roger W. Kramer

THE SIEGE OF KA'AN

DOUBLE DRAGON

PROLOGUE

Toka moved away from the downward strike of the sword. Through the slits of his helmet, he could see his attacker stumble forward, as he had expected, to hit the shield of his opponent.

"I thought I had taught you better!" Toka laughed as he used his shield to help his friend stay upright. "Keep your balance at all times."

The man stepped back and raised his sword. "I will not be so easily fooled this time."

The swords clashed together and they separated. Warily, they circled each other and looked for an opening.

"Shall I show you my final lesson for the day?"

"I will teach you a lesson, little man."

The boy smiled to himself. His neighbor was the sword instructor in this region, but had long ago conceded Toka was equal or above his own skill level. But the boy had to be better as he would eventually take over as the Supreme Master of the Land, once the current master was dead. Not that the neighbor expected such an occurrence any time soon. The old warrior seemed to be ageless.

"Silvius, you make me laugh." Toka stepped forward and feinted towards his opponent's head. With a smile, the man prepared to defend against the standard overhead downward strike. The sword never made it as the shield came up into view. Silvius lost sight of the sword and tried to step back and find his opponent. Toka had raised his shield to obscure his opponent's view and shoved with all his strength against Silvius. While Silvius was off balance, Toka reversed the overhead strike and brought the sword up under the shield and struck out at his leg.

It would appear that his trick would work, until Silvius pushed back and caught him off balance. The sword never made it to Silvius' leg as Toka was pushed over backwards. Screaming in triumph, Silvius watched the boy fall. But Toka continued to roll and came back up and planted his feet for the rush he was sure would come. Silvius didn't disappoint him. With all his momentum going forward, he didn't have time to block the thrust of the sword to his stomach.

As it was, the wooden sword bounced off the protective slats tied around the man's ample waist.

Silvius swore as he felt the hit.

Toka screamed in triumph, "Ah, ha!"

"How in the Gods' names do you think of techniques like that?" Silvius spat out as he threw his own wooden sword down on the ground.

"I just think about what you wouldn't expect and then do it."

"I have never seen a fighter fall to the ground and get back up like you do."

"I've had a good teacher."

Silvius thought he was being paid a compliment and then laughed to himself. He had to agree with the boy. His grandfather was the master of dirty tricks in hand-to-hand combat. It was always an honor to practice against him or his grandson. Even a teacher could learn new tricks, as he had been taught here today.

Pulling off his helmet and body armor, he took a cloth and wiped the sweat from his brow. The twin suns had warmed the day and waves of heat were rolling across the fields. A slave brought them a jug of water and began to pick up the weapons from the practice field.

Sitting on the ground and looking out over the Middle Sea, Silvius glanced at the young boy who had so easily beaten him. Feeling a lump in his throat, he had to keep a tight rein on his emotions. He genuinely felt sorry for the young man as Toka had lost his mother and father just a few months ago. Silvius had also lost members of his family in the plague that had struck the city of Ka'an. Shaking his head at the thought, it was a miracle the sickness had been contained in the city alone and didn't strike the Seven Ruling Families of the Plains.

Another slave brought them some bread and fruit. Leaning back against a small tree, Silvius grabbed a bunch of grapes and began to pull the round, sweet spheres off the vine and throw them in the air, then catch them with his tongue. Already, Toka was snoring in the light shade keeping them from the worst of the twin suns' heat.

Looking at the grapes gave Silvius a thought.

Soon, they would begin the Mid Sun Passing. Usually, two suns would be visible in the sky, except when the planet passed between them. When such an event took place, only one would be visible. During this time, the snows on the mountains would melt and heavy rains would cover the land and protect them from the heat of the suns. It was the best time for growing crops and the grapes, which would be used to make his favorite beverage, fermented grape juice.

Toka sat up with a start and Silvius dropped the bunch of grapes. "What?" Standing, Toka looked over the crops. A slave was screaming the boy's name and he took off in a dead run. Silvius had a bad feeling of foreboding and ran after the boy. Unfortunately, he was right.

***

The tear rolled down the boy's face and fell to the earth. He brushed away the tears that followed and held his breath as the pain of his loss threatened to overwhelm him. It was the first time he ever had to bury someone close to him.

The slave had found the old man this morning, slumped over in his favorite chair. A cup of Ka, Ja root tea had slipped from the old man's fingers and shattered against the rough wood floor.

Granther had been the old man's name. He was the boy's last living relative. In his grief, he didn't hear the slave walk up behind him and interrupt his thoughts.

"Master Toka...the grain has been loaded onto the wagons. Do you have any further orders, sir?"

It took a few moments before he was able to answer. Too much had happened in such a short time. First, his grandfather's death and then, a scroll from the new King of the Roman Republic. His thinking was sluggish and he fought to find the right words. "Yes, Hilidia, please take the other workers and go to the House of Leim. The Matron of the House will protect you."

"Will you be along soon, Master?" the man asked.

8

It was still strange to be called by his father's title. Toka shook his head in the negative and dismissed him with a wave of his hand. He needed time to be alone.

Indecision seemed to plague the man, he felt he must say something. "I am sorry to visually witness your loss, Master, and the other workers asked me to convey their sadness at the passing of Granther into the Death World. He will be sadly missed by us all as he was more a friend than a master."

Even through his sadness, hearing the slave's concern warmed him inside. Toka sighed. He would miss them, as Hilidia and the other slaves had been like family to him as well. Absentmindedly, he reached into his toga and pulled out a scroll. "This is a message for the Matron Leim. Follow the main road to the east. When you reach the keep of Leim, I order you to give the Matron Leim this scroll. Then follow her instructions without question."

The man looked surprised. "You are not coming with us, Master?" Master Toka didn't reply as he sank within himself and tried to work through his grief, so the slave turned to leave.

The head slave's gait was slow and deliberate. He suffered from severe headaches and would get dizzy at times. The attack of the wild boar had surprised him. Knocked to the ground, his head and neck had been crushed and mauled. If not for the quick sword thrust of the master, he would be dead. Hilidia smiled at the thought of his salvation and the killing of so worthy an adversary.

They had eaten well that night. They had always eaten well while under Granther's care. As Hilidia approached the wagons, he called his son to him and walked off to the side. Whispering a message in his son's ear, Hilidia slipped a knife into the boy's hand and then hugged him.

Master Toka could hear the shouts of the slaves as they began to move down the road to Cera. He hoped they would be safe. Even within his own sorrow, he felt fear for the families who helped him work this land. However, the rumors of the advancing Barbarian army were too numerous to ignore. He had to get the workers to safety. He chuckled to himself. The workers...he had never shared his father's belief in the keeping of slaves. Most of the children he had grown up with and he considered them more as friends than just slaves.

He had helped work the land and labored beside them night and day to bring in the harvest, even working long after the slaves had gone to their rest. He didn't begrudge them a bit as this was his land and he felt he should be the one to set the example and work the hardest. That, too, was now at an end and the future was clouded and unsure. He didn't know if he would ever make it back to his home, where he could sit against his house and watch the twin suns set behind the mountains and reflect off the waters of the Middle Sea.

The scroll he was sending to the House of Leim would give his slaves their freedom. On the other hand, he would answer the king's call to arms to defend the city of Ka'an from the Barbarian Horde threatening the New Roman Empire. Taking his grandfather's breastplate, shield and sword, the young man filled his sack with grain and a few extra pairs of clothes. With a glance at the horses, his face broke into a knowing smile and he grabbed an extra shield and sword.

Before leaving, he stopped one more time to look at Granther's grave.

"I will be back to see you again, Granther. I will not let the savages destroy what you fought to protect your whole life. May your journey to the Death World be without incident. Tell my mother and father that I love them." Wiping the tears from his eyes, he turned and looked at the twin suns in the sky. He would have several hours before nightfall and the horses were well rested. Tying off the reins of the packhorses to each other so they would follow in a single line, he grabbed the mane of his mount and threw a leg over its back and started on his way.

Toka glanced down the road the workers had taken and was amazed they were already out of sight. He must have spent more time at the grave than he thought. The movement of the horse was gentle and soothing. He hadn't slept well the night before and dozed for a bit. His horse, Thunderhooves, knew the way and kept plodding along. The boy could, and had in the past, fall asleep at the drop of a hat, but the faithful steed was used to it.

Toka woke, slumped over the neck of the horse. Thunderhooves had known it was time to stop and Toka glanced around. The long shadows of the trees denoted this fact. Patting Thunderhooves on the neck, he slipped off his back. He then pounded stakes in the ground to tie the animals to so they could graze. Once finished caring for them, he pulled several sacks off the packhorses and dragged them off to one side. Picking up limbs from a dead tree, he made a pile and stuffed moss and leaves underneath it.

Pulling a small tin box from his pocket, he blew on a small coal and watched as it grew hot again. Carefully, he bent down and placed the moss on top of the coal and blew again. When it burst into flames, he hastily pulled his hand back. The leaves soon caught fire and he sat back with a look of satisfaction on his face.

"Josf," he called out, "would you like something to eat?"

A bag on the ground began to move. "Can you untie the top of the bag please?"

Toka laughed and untied the knot. A young man crawled out and stood up. "How did you know I was in there?"

"You snore," Toka said.

"I do not," Josf muttered. "My father told you I was in the bag." He was indignant he'd been found so easily.

Toka shook his head in laughter and went back to tending the fire. "I asked if you wanted anything to eat."

"I'm starving," Josf said as he came to sit down across the fire from his master. Toka looked at Josf, who was the son of the head slave and his best friend. He noticed his friend was dressed in rugged clothing and looked like he was ready for a long journey. Underneath the rough homespun shirt, he could see the slave's muscles ripple as he tended the fire.

"What do you want to eat?" Toka asked him.

"Forgive me, Master Toka," the slave said as he jumped up. "I have forgotten my place. I will prepare us something."

"Josf," he called out, "come and sit down." His friend jumped at the sound of anger in Toka's voice. Reluctantly, he walked over and sat back on his heels; ready to meet any demand his master would have of him. "Sit," Toka commanded him, and the man did.

"Josf," he started, "we've been friends ever since we were old enough to remember. When I sent your father to the House of Leim, I also sent along a scroll. The scroll gives you and your family your freedom so you're no longer a slave. You do not serve me or my family any longer."

Josf broke down in tears. "Have I not given you good service, Master? Will you leave me in the wilderness to fend for myself?"

Toka went to him. "You and your family have always given good service to my family, my friend. Listen to me," he said gently, "you are my friend. I wouldn't leave you by yourself."

Josf seemed in shock. "What will I do with myself? I own no land and don't know a trade. I will starve to death. Oh, Master, please do not do this...I beg of you."

Taking Josf in his arms, Toka hugged him. "The land you grew up on is yours. I have given each of you a section of it. If you want, you can take one of the horses and follow this road to the House of Leim. You should be able to catch up with your family in a few days."

Josf sat for a moment. "And what of you, Master? Where will you go?" Toka sat back and looked into the flames. "I will go to the city of Ka'an.

The new king has sent out a decree to the Ruling Families of the Plains. He has ordered all men, women and slaves of twelve and older to come and defend the city."

"Defend it from what?"

"The Barbarians are on the move again. From the messages to the Families, it would appear the savages are less than a month's ride away. The cloud of dust on the horizon indicates to me anyway they are much closer than the new king realizes, so we must make haste to get to Ka'an before they attack." Josf could only sit and look at Toka for a long moment. In less than half a day, his family had been thrown out of the system they had belonged to for generations. On top of that, his master was going to war. "I will go with you, Master." Josf announced suddenly.

"My name is Toka," he said softly. Walking to the packhorse, he pulled two items from a bag and walked to the fire. Reverently, Toka placed the bundles on the ground and began to untie the knots. As he moved the cloth aside, the firelight glittered off a shield. The other bundle revealed a sword.

"This was my father's shield and sword," he said softly. "I want you to have these weapons."

Josf was overcome with emotion. "You really want me to come with you...Toka? And you want me to fight, too?"

"Yes, my friend. We will need every able-bodied man to defend the city." Josef sat quietly, as if not sure he understood all the changes that happened in the last hour. The twin suns had disappeared behind the mountains and darkness began to fall upon them.

Turning to another pack, Toka reached in, produced a bird and began to pluck it. When he was done, he speared it with a sharpened stake and then propped it up over the fire. He kept quiet and let Josf think for a while. A moon passed overhead and shed light until it disappeared over the mountains. Five slower moons moved over the mountains and followed the first.

Turning the bird to make sure it cooked on all sides, Toka sat back and pulled his sword from its sheath. Taking a soft cloth with oil, he began to rub it down and remove any signs of rust.

"Will you teach me how to use the sword, Master Toka?"

"We will begin in the morning." Toka's grin was hidden in the darkness. His plan had worked. The smell of the bird was drifting on the night breeze and he felt his stomach growl. Josf slipped a knife from his pocket and began to slice off chucks of meat and placed them on a leaf. Quietly, he placed the food beside Toka.

"What is the purpose of oiling your sword?"

"Get yourself some meat and sit beside me. Then I will show you why."

Josf did what he was told and returned.

"If you look at the surface of the blade, you can see small pits where the rust is beginning to weaken the metal. When you oil it, this protects it from the rust, for even blood will damage a sword if left on too long. You want the blade to be as clean as possible. When you cut through another person, if there's rust or a knick in the edge, the sword can become stuck and allow the other person to strike at you, or leave you exposed for attack from another quarter."

Josf shuttered at the thought of cutting into another human being. Toka acted like he didn't see the movement and continued.

"You can use the shield to defend your body from the sword of another, arrows or a javelin thrust. I have a few tricks I can teach you to use the shield to block the opponent's view. Then you can strike from underneath and take off a leg or stab him in the gut."

Josf stopped eating as Toka continued describing the horrors of battle and looked as if he would throw up. Perhaps it had been a mistake to come with the master.

But then Josf remembered his father's order. He would follow this order until it was his turn to take the journey to the Death World.

Later that night, rolled up in a piece of woollen cloth, Josf thought about the words of Master Toka, now just Toka. He could remember when Toka had been born and even though Josf was a few years older than the Master, the two had hit it off almost immediately. At the showing of the new baby, Toka had cried at everyone except for a young boy, who held the small bundle in his arms. A boy called Josf. Whenever the baby couldn't be quieted down, the master had called for Josf to rock the boy to sleep.

As Toka grew in age and stature, the two boys became inseparable and would have been considered brothers if not for one being a slave and the other the son of the master.

Both of them shared mischievous adventures that should have gotten them killed, but by the grace of the gods, they had been spared. Like the time Toka decided he would learn to jump from tree to tree like a squirrel. Taking a running leap off an outcropping of rock, he flew through the air and grabbed what looked like a stout handhold. The branch held for a moment and a smile graced his youthful face. It was soon replaced with a look of horror as it snapped in two and he began to fall toward the ground.

Clutching at anything, his weight tore a path through the upper part of the tree. With a scream of pain, his journey stopped at a branch thick enough to stop his plunge toward death, but at the expense of several layers of skin and a few broken bones.

Using a rope, Josf had helped lower the pathetic looking human squirrel to the ground. Taking some Ka, Ja root, he cut out the black heart and put it between his young master's gum and cheek to help with the pain. Then Josf ran to find his mother, who would discreetly help bandage the young master's wounds. It was a task the slave had to perform many times and she kept the boy's secrets close to her heart. Boys were meant to be boys and getting cuts and broken bones were just a part of the path to manhood. She wasn't sure if the older Master would have shared the same viewpoint, but what he didn't know, wouldn't worry him.

Then Toka reached the age where he was required to learn how to run the land and handle a weapon. The two boys' time together was severely limited, but even after a long day of sword practice, Toka found occasions to wrestle and share time with Josf, who in turn, was being schooled by his father to someday become the leader of the slaves. Two different paths, but one solid friendship.

In the dying embers of the firelight, Toka looked over at his friend and thanked the gods Josf was with him. It would help with the loneliness and fear of being on his own for the first time on the way to Ka'an. Chocking back a sob at the memory of Granther, he turned over and finally fell into a restless sleep.

CHAPTER ONE

King Attalee rolled over in his bed and reached for his sword. Something didn't feel quite right and it unnerved him. Ears and eyes strained to hear, to see anything in the darkness filling his room. Usually, he slept soundly at night, but this night, something woke him up. He controlled his breathing and kept as silent as possible. Was there someone in the room with him, creeping up in the darkness to slit his throat? He tried to push that image from his mind, as Attalee had been taught a thought could kill a man before ever a fatal blow could be struck. Despite his apparent unease, he smiled at the memory of the lesson.

Before going to bed, the king had leaned his sword against the table and he slowly moved his hand toward it, wanting to feel the familiar grip within his grasp. He had a small knife in one hand, in case he needed to fend off an attack, but he would feel much better with his sword. Slowly, he moved toward it, trying to control his breathing, but it sounded loud to his ears. He could even hear his heart beating in his chest as his unease increased.

The king's fingers touched the edge of the table and could feel a small pouch of coins and knew the weapon was just to the left of it. In the dark, he grabbed the sword and vaulted from the bed. Such was the rush of his adrenaline, he was halfway across the room before he realized he still hadn't been attacked. The pouch fell open and a gold coin rolled out and fell to the floor.

As Attalee stood in the darkness and prepared to fend off an attacker, he heard the coin hit the floor, roll and finally fall on its side. He stood for a moment and then began to laugh to himself. He now understood the source of his feelings of unease, silence. The silence is what had woken him up. For the last few weeks, he had been hearing the sound of trees being felled and siege equipment being built. Pulling a small cover off the lantern, the room was bathed in light. It only took a moment for the king to put on his armor and strap his sword around his waist.

The two soldiers casually guarding his door were startled to see the king emerge in their midst and in the dead of night. Attalee smiled to himself at their startled expressions. Walking past them, he bounded up the stairs two at a time and onto the top of the wall that surrounded and protected the city of Ka'an.

He was met with a spear in his face. "Be at peace," Attalee whispered to him and the guard instantly dropped the weapon when he realized he was facing the king.

"Sorry, my Lord," he mumbled and shrank away in fear.

"Not to worry. You were just doing your duty. Keep up your vigilance, for it is needed."

"Thank you, my Lord," the man said as he immediately straightened up and with renewed energy, resumed his watch.

It's amazing what a few kind words can do for morale, he thought as he played with his ear. Attalee caught himself and forced his hand down. A nervous habit he had, but he didn't want his men to know or even suspect the king wasn't in full control of the situation.

What had his instructor taught him? The men in one's fighting force take heart in one's attitude they can win, even against insurmountable odds. The army of over one hundred thousand barbarians against his own mere forty-five thousand men, women, slaves and even children was an insurmountable odd.

Yet morale was high among the troops and it was a test of self-control for Attalee not to worry that ear. In private, he had about pulled it off until General Cae had mentioned how red it was looking and perhaps he should see the healer, Caiisa.

He could see in the moonlight of the seven moons, the colonnades highlighted against the night sky. *The twin suns would be up in three hours,* he mused.

What action should he pursue? He really only had a gut feeling to go on, but something was wrong, terribly so.

The night air was dank with moisture and he could feel it creeping down from the mountains and over the wall as the earth slowly cooled. The fog permeated his clothes and he suddenly shivered.

He tried to see out over the Plains of Sorrow, but the only thing visible was the all-consuming darkness. It was like peering into the depths of a deep well and he had the sensation of falling into its oppressiveness.

It had been raining for the past month and the rivers were swollen and overflowing their banks. The one that started at the base of the glacier and ran down through the center of the city had flooded many from their homes and the mud made it hard to move troops and weapons. General Cae had built

21

walkways across the flooded plain, but it was still hazardous going to the wall. If a person fell into the raging torrent of mud, they had little chance of being saved. This was the reason why Attalee and the General had been sleeping in the wall instead of the king's quarters.

Walking along the wall, he came to the statue of Jupiter standing guard over the entrance to the city. Looking up at the likeness of the God, he prayed for his city and his people. Attalee found it hard to believe less than a cycle ago, the Gods and Romans had fought off a creature from legend; a monster called the Abomination. They had fought and mortally wounded it, but Jupiter, the king of the Gods, sensed it was pregnant.

The creature had gotten away before they could kill its babies, so everyone would have to be vigilant against the return of the Abomination or its children.

The events of the last few months passed through his mind's eye and he was almost overwhelmed.

Feeling a robe being placed across his shoulders, Attalee jumped, startled by the touch in the darkness.

"You will catch your death out here if you aren't careful," the general said to him in a tone just above a whisper.

Attalee looked gratefully at the man and pulled the robe around his body. General Cae was always trying to look out for him and Attalee appreciated the gesture. It had been almost two months since he had met Cae and their first meeting hadn't been a pleasant one.

When King Attuicus disappeared, Jupiter had delivered a scroll to the men of the King's Council stating Prince Attalee was to ascend to the throne. General Cae had left to escort the new king to Ka' an, a journey of several months. With the general away, one of the Councilors, Eliam, had tried to take over the city. Cae's next in command, Major Raki, discovered the traitor's plan and Eliam had slipped away before he could be arrested.

If the truth be known, even Cae had opposed Attalee as the new king. He thought the boy was too young to assume control of the Republic, but Attalee had surprised him. On the road to Ka'an, Cae had come to know Attalee and soon, even he had to agree the boy was the best choice. One of the problems with the current Senate was their egos and the pursuit of money, which seemed to be at the root of all disputes.

Attalee cared little for money or prestige, but he did have a deep love for his country. One thing the king and general didn't agree on was the Barbarian horde camped outside the city.

General Cae's opinion was they were savages, whereas King Attalee thought of them as a brother or distant relative. The Barbarians actually named themselves the Quranians and had a spoken history they called the "Oral Tradition". This story told the history of humankind's creation from the beginning of time and how the human race had been split apart.

Violent earthquakes pulled the continents apart and destroyed the first civilizations of Pon. Families were separated and many of the people lost or forgot the Oral Tradition.

Now the Quranians were all that remained of the people who had an history from the beginning of time and Attalee knew if the Barbarians were killed off, the link with the past would be severed forever. Attalee had sent a message to Chief Messa of the Quranians requesting a meeting in an effort to try and head off the upcoming confrontation. But any thought of negotiation had been cast aside when the savages had arrived on the Plains of Sorrow.

Chief Messa the Fifth had poles erected at the front gate on which were placed the severed heads of Roman citizens found hiding in the surrounding villages. The gesture had angered King Attalee and the Roman people. United as one, they looked forward to avenging the cowardly murder of their friends and family at the hands of the Barbarians.

***

"What's wrong?" Cae asked him.

"I'm not sure," Attalee whispered back.

Attalee strained to hear activity out on the plains but the only sounds were the wind playing through the grass and the men behind him. The king stood for so long, Cae was sure he had fallen asleep standing up. The general had been woken up less than half a rotation ago and rubbed his eyes. Feeling the fatigue in his muscles, he stood beside Attalee and waited. And waited. General Cae shifted uncomfortably, but Attalee didn't seem to notice. He stood with his head turned slightly towards the plains.

"Damn the gods, what are they doing…?" Cae muttered. Attalee held up his hand in a signal for silence. "I wonder if they have retreated," Cae said. Cae smiled to himself as the hand gesture became more animated.

Leaving the king to his vigil, General Cae went down behind the wall to check on his troops and noted with satisfaction that almost all forty-five thousand men and women had been silently assembled and now stood in ranks.

**

King Attalee felt a hand on his shoulder and turned to see Captain Dav Vad of the United Universe Forces. He smiled at the look of concern on her face. "I came as soon as I heard something was wrong."

He patted her hand. "The silence is what woke me up. The air has a feeling of foreboding to it and I had to come here and try and figure out what the Quranians are doing."

Dav shook her head. "By my display," she said, looking at her wrist, "it would appear they are just standing in formation, just out of arrow range."

Attalee looked at her in surprise. At times, he forgot about the nature of this visitor to Chosen. They had met on the road to Ka'an and Dav told them the story of how her spacecraft had been hijacked by the Gentle One, who diverted the ship to the here and now.

The Gentle One had sent Dav on a mission to find King Attuicus. She had been placed on the surface of their planet at a point several months travel time away from Ka'an, and had walked here.

Along the way, the captain had rescued Chenee, a HighBorn of the House of Xyer.

At the thought of Chenee, Attalee felt his body begin to respond in a physical way. He had fallen in love with the young woman and was sure she felt the same. He tried to arrange his toga to hide his growing erection.

As he looked out into the darkness, he sent his heart out to her. The memory of his and Chenee's first meeting had been a mysterious one. Chenee claimed to be a HighBorn of the House of Xyer. He eventually realized she was lying and was actually a spy for the Quranians, but he had allowed Chenee to believe her disguise had fooled him. Attalee had hoped he could convince Chenee that he wanted peace and he had even defended the Quranians in front of the Senate. An innocent act that in retrospect, could have broken out in civil war if he had not been backed by the Roman military.

In the end, Attalee had to confront Chenee about her being a spy. Chenee had expected to be immediately executed, but Attalee had surprised her, whispering how much he loved her and wanted them to marry. Unfortunately, years of warfare and fighting had built a wall of distrust and prejudice that even his tearful pleas of love and fidelity couldn't break through and though Chenee loved him in return, she had returned to her father's camp.

"Dav," Attalee whispered, "there is one thing I've always wanted to ask you. Is the Roman Empire still in existence in your time?"

"It still exists, but now, it's just considered the country of Italy." Opening up her wrist pad, she showed him the maps of the planet Earth. "Show

26

me a map of the early Roman Empire," she ordered. "Begin with a progressive scan of the rise and fall of the area the Romans once controlled." A map appeared and began to show how the Romans had conquered most of the known world and then been beaten back to rise again. It finished with the map of Italy in her time that covered most of Western Europe.

Attalee had watched in amazement as thousands of years' worth of information scrolled across the screen. "I wish I could read all the history from the time our ancestors left Earth until now."

"No problem," she said. Pulling a small chip off the display, she placed it behind his ear and tapped it once. Immediately, the text transferred into sound, traveling from his jaw to his ear. It was a history of the Roman Empire. "Just touch it when you want to stop and start it."

"I can start writing it down and placing it on scrolls," he exclaimed.

"You don't need to do that! I can print it out for you in Latin and you'll have it all laid out for you. One nice thing is the pages are recharged by sunlight and last indefinitely. So you don't have to worry about fire or water, like you do with your scrolls."

Attalee grinned. "If you don't mind, I would like to write it out. I remember it better."

Dav began to laugh. "There's over a million scrolls of history contained there, Attalee. You'll be writing without end for the rest of your life."

"A million scrolls," he said wistfully, "would be a dream come true."

"If you want to write them down, go ahead, but I have some small hand- held devices you can use to read the information. When they begin to lose power, just lay them in the sun and let the batteries recharge."

"I have no idea what you just said to me," Attalee laughed.

She had to laugh with him. Taking a small plastic square from her pocket, she held it up. Dav had already placed all the information from the chip onto the hand-held. "Push on this button here and it will turn on the screen." It lit up and the history of Rome began to scroll before his eyes. This oval spot here is a converter that takes in the sun's energy and turns it into power, which is stored in a thing called a battery. The battery will recharge itself and then supply the power to the screen.

Attalee was amazed at the device Dav was showing him. "This little thing has millions of scrolls in it?"

"Actually, it now holds the entire history of the human race from the Oral Tradition to the recorded history of my time. I would say there are billions of scrolls on it. If you were to print them out, the scrolls would fill every house in the city of Ka'an and you and your people would spend your entire lives writing and still not see a fraction of the information contained on that disk."

This was just too much for Attalee to imagine.

"You can just get the highlights and then do a more in-depth study on the items that interest you."

"Thank you," Attalee said. He wanted to hurry down to his room and start reading right now, but duty required he stay on the wall. It was something for him to look forward to.

Dav left him to his reading and went to find General Cae.

**

Captain Dav Vad tried to peer through the fog and see the face of General Cae. It was too dark and she reached out until her hand touched his cheek. Cae flinched at the touch and then relaxed as he realized it was her. They were so tense, so ready for battle. She smiled to herself. How many battlefields had she stood on and had to spend hours waiting before the fighting started? The time seemed to stretch into infinity. He reached up and gently took her hand in his. Kissing it, he returned it to his cheek. Softly, she patted his grizzled cheek and then let her hand slide down to the armor-covered shoulder. Wistfully, her hand stayed there as if to protect him from the upcoming battle.

The general wouldn't want her help and he had survived worst battles, she thought, but still, she worried about him.

Just a few days ago, the two had been eating at a table that overlooked the merchant's square. Owners were out in front of their shops, calling out to perspective customers to come and sample their wares.

Taking a pitcher of wine, Cae poured each of them a glass. Breaking a round loaf of hard bread, Dav passed him a piece. The vendor brought them a bowl of hot, spicy meat and picked up the hundred dinar note the general had left on the table.

Dav was looking at him. "You seem more worried than usual today."

"I'm not sure how I can get everyone trained in time," he muttered and took a drink from his cup.

"What do you mean?"

"It would appear that most of the Barbarian soldiers are equipped with swords or clubs. We don't have the time to train the volunteers to use a sword to counteract this threat."

"You don't need to train them how to use a sword. An untrained person is actually better off if they use a spear or don't have a weapon."

Cae grimaced. "Is this more of your dark humor? Someone armed with a sword will always defeat a person without one."

Dav dropped her bread. "Do you want to make a wager on that?" Her voice was neutral.

Cae shook his head. "I've seen you in your suit. You're too fast. Without it though, I could run you right through…"

She stood so fast, the stool fell over with a loud crash. Dropping her armor to the ground, she pulled the suit off, right in front of everyone, which brought cheers of approval from the men in the eatery. Cae could only sit in stunned amazement. Soon, she had her overshirt back on and walked out into the open.

"Let's see what you got, General Cae."

The crowd turned toward him with a look of expectation on their faces. "What do you mean?" He was flabbergasted.

"You said you could run me through with your sword. Here I am! Unarmed and without the help of the 3S."

30

Cae chuckled. "You're serious? I don't want to embarrass you in front of this crowd."

Dav didn't answer and stood with her arms crossed, a faint smile on her lips. Their eyes met across the space and he felt his blood begin to boil when he noticed the look of disdain on her face. Obviously, she didn't know he was an expert swordsman. But here she was, taunting him in front of all these people.

A smile graced his own lips. Perhaps he should teach her a lesson. As he stood, his sword came from its scabbard in one smooth motion. Warily, he approached. Dav was tricky and he knew her to be a master of various fighting techniques. By the gods, she was about a hundred years older than him.

Keeping the sword in front of him, he moved in from the right to keep the weapon between them.

Dav watched his approach, never changing her stance or expression. Cae stopped. Gauging the distance between them, he made a half-hearted thrust. Dav knocked the sword away and punched him in the jaw. Cae fell to one knee and looked at her in surprise.

"You shouldn't leave yourself open like that, General Cae."

He spat out some blood and stood again. "You want me to kill you, huh?"

"You can try, but you won't even come close."

With a shout, he sprang toward her, his sword cutting down from overhead so fast, it was a blur.

Instead of backing away from the blow, Dav spun in closer, out of the path of the sword. Too late, he tried to check the swing and paused, which gave her time to grab his wrist with her left hand.

All in one motion, Dav spun so her right shoulder was locked into his armpit. Reaching with her right hand to grab his armor, she stepped to the right and leaned forward to pull General Cae off balance. Then his feet lifted off the ground and he was sailing through the air and landed hard. The air rushed out of him in one gasp.

Dav didn't stop there as she twisted around again until his elbow was hyperextended. Wincing in pain, Cae dropped the sword and tried to get up, but Dav had his wrist and arm locked so he couldn't move without breaking his elbow.

Cae looked around at the crowd and saw the horrified looks on their faces. Looking into Dav's smiling eyes, he yelled out, "I've never quite fell head over heels for a woman like that before...! Will you marry me?"

Dav let him go with a laugh and the rest of the crowd joined in.

Cae could only look at her in amazement. She had taught him a lesson he would never forget. They returned to their table and finished eating.

***

With a smile on his face, General Cae was thinking about that lunch when he went down the steps behind the wall and called the twelve centurions in charge of the cohorts. *She never did answer my question,* he mused to himself and one of the soldiers interrupted his thoughts. The senior centurion saluted. "Pilus Prior Raki reports all men and women are battle ready, General."

Cae returned the salute and whispered to his trusted aide, "Have the first legion man the wall. Quietly. Keep the other legion in reserve."

"Yes, sir." Raki turned to leave.

General Cae thought about the troop structure he and Attalee had made up. They had forty-five thousand troops divided into twelve legions of thirty-five hundred men. Each legion was broken down into ten cohortes of three hundred and fifty men. Then the cohortes were made up of three manipuli of one hundred and sixteen men, which was further broken down into two more centuriae of fifty men. In the last Barbarian war, he had discovered moving a large army to be almost uncontrollable. With the organization broken into smaller groups, he found he could control the situation much faster.

The centuriae had trained to fight each other and the general smiled at the thought of the companies competing against the other. Morale was high within the ranks. Looking out over his "men", he saw one stumble and a woman caught his arm. That was another idea of the new king. With the plague decimating half the population of Ka'an, the army had to rely on the women of the Republic to help defend the city. In addition, the slaves of Ka'an had been given their freedom to aid in the defense.

There had been grumbling within the ranks at first until they had practiced against the women. Even he had been surprised at the ferociousness with which they fought. The barbarians would be shocked as well, or so he hoped.

***

Councilor Eliam, or former councilor, stood on the mountaintop and looked at the battle formations displayed before him. Back when he had been the trusted aide of King Attuicus, the councilor had been hidden behind the persona of an advocate for the poor, mistreated slaves and the downtrodden.

When King Attu had disappeared and General Cae had gone to escort his replacement to the city of Ka'an, the council had sent a scroll to all the ruling families to send men and slaves to help defend the city against the Barbarians.

Eliam had burned the scrolls and substituted one of his own. His sources in the city had broken the code General Cae used to send messages up and down the signal line. He had a different message sent up the line, one giving the order to have the council members put to death.

Eliam spat on the ground. How he hated General Cae and Major Raki. If the major would have followed orders, the council members would now be dead. But the major was a suspicious man and followed the councilor to his home.

Major Raki had discovered that the persona of Eliam had all been a lie, and uncovered his treachery. Eliam had barely made it out of Ka'an before the major had come to arrest him.

Now he was being hunted as a traitor to the Republic. Not that this mattered to him.

For years, he had secretly made plans to take over the city of Ka'an and destroy the power of the Senate and the ruling families. Then he would hold all the power and he would rule with a cruel fist and destroy any who stood in his way.

During a council meeting, he had heard the savages were marching on the Romans. This would be his opportunity to have his two enemies destroy each other, then he could pick up the pieces.

Unknown to the rest of the world, he had a passage to the other side of the mountains. This was where he trained his vast army, who would eventually help him rule the country. This little war would help him achieve his goals a great deal quicker than he had anticipated.

He could have closed off the tunnel and built his empire on the other side, but he realized men needed an enemy to stay united toward a common goal.

Most of the rabble he'd collected was just barely at the intellectual level of a child, but he didn't want them smart. Just well-trained and deadly with a variety of weapons. The less intelligent the men were, the easier it would be to use them to destroy the Roman and Barbarian armies. Then he would have to find something else for his men to focus on and this worried him a bit.

For now, he would just work on destroying the armies and capturing the city. Then the blood would flow for weeks from under the wall of Ka'an.

***

Sorti Ne woke up screaming in the darkness of her stateroom. The Control, sensing her increased respiration and adrenaline surge, turned the lights on and sent out a distress signal to the executive officer.

"What's wrong?" a disembodied voice requested from over her head. "I'm not sure. I had the nightmare again where I was being smothered under a mound of puppies."

The executive officer chuckled. "Sounds like an oxymoron."

"You're a moron, Carl," she snapped. Looking at the chronometer, she groaned. Time to get ready for her watch.

Ignoring the fact Carl was watching her, she threw the blanket from her legs and walked nude to the Autosalon. It washed her hair and made up her fingernails with a multicolored design. Slipping a uniform over her head, she pressed out the creases and prepared to go on duty. She didn't really care how long Carl stayed on the monitor and watched. Everyone knew he was a pervert.

Jumping into the shuttle, she began the half hour trip to the bridge. The Control automatically prepared her dinner. A tray with rice cakes, a bowl of fruit and a beer appeared beside her. Thick slabs of cheese with mustard topped the rice cakes. Grabbing one, she slipped back into a seat.

Absentmindedly brushing crumbs off her chest, she tried to figure out why she kept having nightmares about puppies. It did sound like an oxymoron. Smothered by puppies. A small autocleaner scurried across the floor and began to vacuum up the crumbs. With a squeal of protest, it finished and returned to its recharging area, only to be sent back again as Sorti Ne took another bite.

The beer tasted bland. *It must be time to make another batch*, she sighed. The twelve hours on watch, twelve hours off rotation was getting a little old. For the last two months, the ship had been orbiting a planet called Chosen. It should have stopped at Aqua, a retirement planet, but they had been hijacked and the captain sent on a stupid mission to find some King Attu.

The proximity alarm sounded, indicating the shuttle was approaching the bridge. Standing, brushing the last of the food away and giving the autocleaner electronic heart failure, she prepared to step on the bridge.

Carl Jenkins, Executive Officer of the *New Beginnings Colonization Ship*, was bent over the monitor, reviewing the star charts he'd been creating. The man was still trying to find out where they were and was working on a plan to get the ship home.

"Chief Engineer Sorti Ne on the Bridge. I have the deck and the Control. I relieve you, sir," she announced in a loud, clear voice. "I stand relieved," he replied automatically.

Climbing into the captain's chair, the Control began to pop up screens all around her to review orbit stability, hull integrity and engine status. All the displays showed green. Tapping a button on the arm of the chair, the screens minimized into a small dot, just in case she needed it.

Carl usually went below immediately, but today, he came over and sat down on the engineering couch. "I have an unpleasant task to perform, Sorti Ne. I have to put you on report for falling asleep on the job."

Sorti Ne looked at him for the longest time and the man squirmed under her gaze. "Do you really want to go there, Carl?"

"My job as acting captain is to maintain regulations and procedures."

"Did you read that in one of our personnel reports?"

Carl's face began to turn red. When Captain Dav Vad had reported aboard, Carl had let it be known he knew things about her which could only be found in her personnel file. This had upset the captain, causing her to cry. The Control had alerted the rest of the crew she was suffering an emotional episode and might require assistance. Sorti Ne had never forgotten his insensitivity at asking how Dav's family had been killed in the Yang Zen Massacre.

"There are only two of us here, Carl. It isn't like we have two hundred crewman to watch out for here. Back off!"

He looked at her grimly. Sensing he wasn't going to let it go, she began to punch some buttons and a screen popped up beginning to run displays of the previous watches. The central theme of all fifty was Carl leaning back in the captain's chair and snoring loudly.

Occasionally, a bottle of home brewed beer would fall to the ground and shatter. The mess was quickly cleaned up by the autocleaner while Carl slept on.

Carl left the bridge without saying another word and she smiled to herself. Two hundred years of herding ships across space had taught her how to deal with the "Do as I say, not as I do" head up their asses officers.

Kicking off her shoes and sitting back in the chair, the Control came back online.

"Good morning, Engineer Sorti Ne. I hope the Lieutenant Commander hasn't upset you?"

"I can take care of myself," she snorted in disgust.

"It was a most interesting display of one-upmanship on your part. May I keep a copy of it on file to review for future reference?"

Sorti Ne laughed. "For a computer, you have eccentric tastes in recording human behavior."

"I am not a computer, I am the Control. I have the processing speed of a computer, but can learn the commonsense of a human and…"

Sorti Ne cut it off. "I've heard this lecture before."

"I was just informing you that I was offended by your remarks."

"My apologies, Control. What would you like to talk about tonight?"

"I am interested in how you learned to control the multidimensional portals."

"I can't answer that."

"I am sorry. Is this considered to be top secret?"

"No, it's just I can't describe how it's done without spouting a chain of formulas you already have in your memories. You could make the jump if necessary."

"I do not have access to those files and it will only be granted if all personnel have left the ship or become incapacitated. What I am more interested in is your feelings when you touch the power well and send us on our way."

"What does it feel like?" Sorti Ne frowned. "It feels like giving birth." The Control was silent.

"I guess I do not understand."

"You can't! You're not human."

"I have been programmed with over one hundred emotional responses." You're still just a machine, acting out your programming."

"So are you…"

"No, I am not. I am flesh and blood. Don't even try to bring yourself up to the level of a human being."

"It was not my intention to consider myself your equal. Forgive me. I wish to clarify something. You are also acting out your programming. My argument is it matters little how the body or machinery is taught to learn anything, we are both programmed."

"Control, you're out of your circuits on this one. Does insanity run in your family's hard drives?"

"That wasn't very nice, Engineer Sorti Ne. You are attempting to perform a delaying tactic and have not answered my question. In debating competitions, this is a sign of weakness and a lack of belief in your own statements. Do you concede the point?"

"Do you see me waving a white flag? Let me roll up my sleeves here and get down to a serious debate."

"Very well. I would like that, Sorti Ne."

Sorti Ne smiled to herself. They had spent many hours like this, locked in philosophical debates. The Control was right about her. It wasn't the fact she believed what she was saying, she just liked to argue.

At the end of twelve hours, both had come to an agreement that no matter how an object was programmed, theoretically, it could experience emotions.

Carl had a sullen look on his face as he accepted responsibility of the Control and the bridge. Without a word to her, he took his seat in the captain's chair and brought up the readouts.

"Good night, Control."

"Good night, Engineer Sorti Ne."

Walking off the bridge and into her shuttle, she thought it had been a fun watch. The Control was learning how to argue more effectively and soon, she would be able to argue to a stalemate. Carl never talked to the Control, other than to bark out orders. He was missing out on the experience of getting to know her.

To know her…she was thinking of the Control as female. The trip back was going to take an hour because she always stopped by the engine room to check on everything, even though they were in standby mode. Climbing onto a mountain bike, she started the "Tour De Lunar mode" and was soon pushing herself to make it up a crater wall at over thirty klicks per hour. Her personal goal was to make it to the top before the shuttle arrived at the engine compartment. She lost by sixty-three seconds. *I must be slipping in my workout regimen,* she muttered.

Grabbing a towel to wipe the sweat from her face, the doors opened into a vast chamber that took up one-third of the ship. In her presence, the Control opened the panels and displayed the schematics of the drive.

"I didn't see this reported to the Bridge Control. Why is the port ventricle showing a red line?" she asked.

"It was hit by a meteorite, sir. Repairs are underway as we speak."

This was a different Control than the one on the bridge and she didn't feel as chummy with this one. "I think it's your job to keep that from happening."

"That is true, sir. My success rate is ninety-nine point nine to the seventh trillion power.

"Point conceded," Sorti Ne replied. Looking at a remote shot, the robots were welding and reshaping the damaged area. "Keep me informed on progress," she ordered.

"As always," it sounded exasperated.

Shaking her head, Sorti Ne climbed back into the shuttle. That Control sure had an attitude. *I wonder where it got that from? No one I know is sarcastic,* she thought and had to laugh at her own play on words. Slipping back into the chair, she took a nap as the shuttle headed back to her stateroom.

A jolt indicated the shuttle had stopped and Sorti Ne automatically walked through the portal and felt her feet slip out from under, as her body tumbled down a long tunnel. Gravity was low, so she bounced from side to side, trying to find purchase on the smooth walls. Suddenly hitting bottom, Sorti Ne felt like she was being smothered in puppies.

Clawing her way out from under the pile, wave after wave threatened to overwhelm her and it really started to piss her off.

"Sorti Ne," her name was being called. "Damn it, Sorti Ne…wake up!" Fighting to open her eyes, she found she was still sitting in her chair and as she sat up, she hit the image of Carl. It fizzled as her head came in contact with the telefield. Climbing from the chair, Carl watched her progress across the room. "I'm going to put you on heavy sedatives during your sleep cycle. I think the stress is getting to you."

"I'm sure this will make my file, too."

Carl didn't answer. Cautiously, she palmed the portal open and it revealed the entrance to her stateroom. An automed unit was waiting for her. The Intravenous needle arm extended out and as she lay on the bed, Sorti Ne felt a pinch in her shoulder and in seconds, was sound asleep.

***

Chenee looked at the wall and she could see King Attalee looking at her. Their eyes met across the distance and they seemed to be frozen in time. Finally, he turned away and her shoulders sagged in grief at what she had lost.

***

The general and the king were looking over battle plans and discussing strategy. A knock on the door interrupted them. General Cae opened it and took the message.

"Dav respectfully requests our presence in her workshop. She has something to show us."

Attalee sighed and put his sword and armor back on. "What I wouldn't give for a chance to sit down for a sip of wine."

General Cae smiled in agreement. It had been a few stressful and tiring weeks training the troops. Walking across the ramps, Attalee looked down at the mud and water. The rains had slowed the advance of the enemy, but also limited their own access and flexibility in moving troops to the wall.

Dav was sitting outside the building and smiled as they approached her "laboratory", as she called it. "Thank you for coming." She opened the door and gestured them in. As General Cae walked past, she playfully pushed him and laughed as he stumbled and acted like he was going to fall down.

King Attalee whirled around to catch him but the General had regained his feet. "Are you alright?"

"I think I stumbled on a rock or something," he mumbled sheepishly. Attalee looked at the perfectly flat floor and then at Dav. When he saw the grin on her face, he decided to drop the subject and instead, turned to look at what Dav had built.

It looked like a large crossbow mounted on a stand.

"What is this? Cae asked as he too looked over the weapon.

"In your day, it was called a Scorpio, but this one has a few modern updates. It's set up to shoot the heavy iron lance you see loaded in the slot here."

Dav pointed the end of the weapon toward a stout beam and pulled a lever. There was a loud snap that startled both men, but it was forgotten as

44

they watched the lance fly through the air and imbed the tip several inches into the wood. Dust and hay fell through the rafters from the impact.

"By my calculations, this lance will travel through three or four human bodies, if grouped close together."

General Cae nodded. It would be an excellent weapon to help repel the Barbarians if they were able to breach the wall. "How many do you have made so far?"

"We have five right now, with another twenty in the beginning stages. I need more help with fabricating the parts. Men or women with blacksmith experience would work well."

Attalee looked deep in thought and was pulling on his ear. "I think I know a blacksmith we can ask to help. His shop is close."

Dav suddenly remembered the shop he was referring to and placed a comforting hand on his arm.

When the king had first arrived in Ka'an, he had taken a tour of the city and looked over the battle plans and defenses. The sound of metal being shaped had intrigued the boy and he had gone into the shop. On a whim, he'd bought Chenee a sword, he knew she'd been taking lessons from Dav. Her old practice sword was one taken from the leader of a group of thieves, who no longer needed the weapon.

***

The thief had lost his head while trying to capture Chenee and take her as a sex slave. The girl

45

had successfully killed most of the men with her bow and arrows and was tricked into a one-on-one fight with the leader. While her attention was on him, Chenee had been grabbed from behind and roughly thrown to the ground.

Dav had intervened, killed the rest of the men and rescued the girl from the degrading life as a plaything for men. Afterwards, Dav found the girl was going to Ka'an, but was guarded about her reasons. As they became friends, Chenee finally confided she was sent as a spy to help defeat the Chosen.

Dav had become her friend and wouldn't choose sides with or against her. Her secret was safe. It was the first time Chenee had anyone, besides her brother, befriend her. Chenee's father, on the other hand, would beat her until she lost consciousness and more often than not, the villagers would have to pull him away as he kicked and trampled the girl.

With Dav, Chenee felt more self-confident and wanted to be like her friend. Just as strong and sure of herself, but she was just an enemy spy, and a crippled one at that. Her mother had died giving birth to Chenee. The toes on one foot had fused into a sharp point and as the baby traveled through the birth canal, there had been massive internal damage. Her mother had bled to death before Chenee had even taken her first breath.

Her father had blamed the baby immediately and refused to have anything to do with Chenee until she was older. Her brother was kind and trained Chenee in how to use a bow and a staff to defend herself. When he died, her father had taken out his grief by beating her. During the beating, he was screaming it should have been her who died and not her mother, nor her brother.

Escaping to the woods for months at a time, she found a hermit that lived in a large cave by the Middle Sea. He taught her how to use Ja, Ja root for medicinal purposes and how the color of the flower would indicate its use.

The white flower indicated the strongest medicine, which was strange to her as the heart of the root was as black as the moonless night. She knew her father used Ja, Ja root all the time. Usually it was for a person in extreme physical pain, but Chief Messa had no obvious wounds. His wounds went deeper than skin, they affected his heart and his mind. The loss of his wife and son almost caused him to lose his sanity.

As chief of the Quranian people, he had watched as their lands had been encroached by the Roman scum and when they fought back, their defeat had been humiliating. They had beaten by a young boy who had taken command of the Roman army when their general had fallen with an arrow in his throat.

So he was in pain alright, deep emotional pain. The Ja, Ja root helped him to forget his people were slowly starving to death and there was little he could do to stop the Romans.

Then the Gods finally smiled on the Barbarians. A plague swept through the city of Ka'an and killed over half the population. The once proud Roman army was decimated and a gleam came back into the chief's eye. Now they would have a chance to right the wrongs the Chosen had inflicted upon the one true people.

With the help of his childhood friend, Battle Master Thom, he began to plot on how to take over Ka'an. Messa had been surprised when Thom had shown him the plans for a new weapon. The catapult was capable of throwing stones over far distances and could be used to break through the walls of the city. Messa and Thom had spent many nights over the fire, planning and discussing ways to move the catapults and troops.

The rope used to make the tensioning device had been made from the hair of their people. All had sacrificed their proud manes to help with the war effort. Thom just wanted to take the hair ropes and build the catapults when they arrived on the Plains of Sorrow. Chief Messa disagreed. The Romans could burn the forest down and they would be left without a source to build their weapons.

The Quranians built fifty of the catapults and began to move toward the Roman capital. The Roman bridges hadn't been built for the extreme weight of the weapons and they had to tear the catapults apart, move them across piece by piece, and put them back together again. The journey of a month turned into six and gave the Romans time to refortify the city.

Thom had to admit the sight of fifty catapults with over a hundred thousand men spilling onto the Plains of Sorrow had been a grand event. Hopefully, it would strike fear into the hearts of the damn Chosen.

The chief was proud of his men and walked through the camp, calling out to them by name and patting them on the back. Thom was heartened by this as the man had been chewing more of the Ja, Ja root than normal and at times, acted like another person. Like the time they had come across a small town and found a few Romans.

A blacksmith, terrified to the point of being frozen, had been challenged by Chief Messa to defend his land. When the man had just stood there, Messa had plunged a sword into the blacksmith's stomach and almost cut him in half. A scream from the wife and child had drawn the chief's attention. It had been many a sun since he had a bed mate. Tying the child to a stake, he took the Roman woman as his concubine and tortured the girl to make the woman behave.

At first, it was the treatment of the girl Thom had found offensive. Messa would step on the rope and urinate on the girl. Even though the nights were growing cooler, the girl had no clothes and was fed very little. Usually, she slept curled up around the stake that kept her in place. Thom had walked in Chief Messa's tent to find him putting firebrands on the woman's back as he savagely raped her.

The smell of burning flesh had sickened him. Doubting the sanity of their leader, Thom thought about invoking the ritual of the Challenge. When a member of the tribe thought the chief was wrong in his decisions, they had the right to challenge him in combat. Chief Messa the Fifth had killed his father to become the current leader. But the morale of the troops was high. They had more food than they could eat in twelve lifetimes and they were finally getting a chance at striking back at the enemy.

Now wouldn't be a good time to issue the Challenge.

CHAPTER TWO

When the blacksmith had been killed by Chief Messa, the murder had been witnessed by another member of the family, a young boy named Rian. As the attack on the village had unfolded, he was in the woods and hadn't been found.

Watching his father's murder had shocked him and it was several hours later before he realized he'd been running away from that awful place. The sound of death was far behind him and he could finally sit and cry over the loss of his father. But inside, a terrible anger had begun to build and he vowed to one day kill the man who had taken his father from him.

Finding an abandoned house, he took food and blankets and headed into the mountains to try and make it to Ka'an. Staying up in the mountains made travel slow and hazardous and by the time he reached the walls of Ka'an, the savages were already guarding the only way in. He would have to stay outside and survive until his oath could be fulfilled.

By chance, he'd found a cave and realizing he was hungry, went to look for food. Rian found the body of a dead man with a crude knife still in his hand and a bag of corn meal tied to his belt. In the grass, he tripped over an axe. Seeing the body, the boy had an idea and tried to plunge the knife into the corpse's heart, but the blade stuck in its breastbone. Feeling his own chest, he moved to the left and plunged the knife in to the hilt.

This is how he would kill the man who murdered his father. He practiced again and again until there was a gaping hole in the corpse's chest. Returning to the cave, he tried to find the rocks to make fire. He'd seen his father do it that way, but he couldn't find any of the right rocks. After finding some roots, he trudged back to the cave and expected to spend a cold, damp night in the darkness.

The smell of smoke greeted his arrival and fearfully, Rian hid. Maybe the dead man had come back to life and was waiting to cook him up for supper. Maybe even to take his heart to replace the one Rian had destroyed. Creeping up to the entrance with the crude knife at the ready, all he could see was a fire and two rabbits ready to be cooked. Checking the muddy floor, he noticed only a paw print. Nothing human had been in the cave since he left. How the fire and rabbits appeared he wasn't sure, but with the acceptance of a child, he was glad they had.

Skinning and gutting the two rabbits, he ate and then laid down for the night. As the air grew cool, he wrapped himself up in the odd assortment of cloth blankets he had found, but a cold wind seemed to flow past him and into the depths of the cave. Then two bodies curled up against him and kept him warm. His mother had told him how the gods would give each person a guardian to watch over them. "Good night, guardians," Rian whispered as he fell asleep.

***

52

"Captain Dav Vad, this is Yin, over. We have encountered an indigenous young boy. What are your orders, sir?"

"Maintain contact with the boy and keep him safe. There's no way we can get him into the city at the present time, over."

Yin looked at Yang and whined. "Roger that. We will keep the boy in our care and continue our surveillance of the Quranian army, as per your previous order."

"Roger that, Yin. Dav out." Dav turned off the connection to the two German shepherd dogs.

***

Caiisa, Most High Priestess of the Goddess Athena and Guardian of her temple, sat at a table used by the wounded and sick patrons looking for healing from Athena.

She smiled to herself at the memory of how she had risen from a lowly miller's daughter to this position of power and influence. Wherever she went, people would shower food or money on Athena's temple. So many goods, in fact, Caiisa had to turn away payments and instead, just asked for the healed individual to pray for the well-being of the Gods and to give the food and money to the poor. Some of the women were repeat customers, requiring treatment for diseases of the genitals and from being beaten by the men who sought sexual favors from them.

This had stopped after Caiisa had sent the Warrior to visit the men and deliver a scroll from the Priestess stating this type of conduct wouldn't be allowed in the future. Only one man had gone against her wishes. The sword of the Warrior had sliced him completely in half and his body had been left in the street as a warning. Even though the family of the man had appealed to the Senate and the king, the former condemned the practice, whereas the latter wholeheartedly agreed with and championed the killing. It wasn't a lesson that needed to be taught again.

***

Various men and women had joined her as healers and were learning to develop the power of healing with a touch. A gift of knowledge the Priestess had learned from the Goddess Athena and started Caiisa on this grand journey to Ka'an.

Sitting back against the cool stone wall, she closed her eyes and remembered the moonless night her father had requested she accompany him into town. Climbing from the cart, four men had clubbed the old man and began to rip her clothes off. Struggling and screaming for her life, none of the villagers wanted to get involved out of fear of injury or retribution from the thieves.

All except Thudder, the boy who slopped the pigs and was known as the village idiot. A boy almost seven feet tall and muscular. At first appearance, he was someone to be feared. Then he would fall into the pigs' fecal matter, which was a source of amusement to the townsfolk.

As she was dragged by her hair, the leader began to whisper what was in store for her. As a virgin, she'd never heard of the unspeakable acts the man was telling her of and she screamed again.

Thudder had materialized out of the blackness of the night and saved her life, but was stabbed in the stomach by the leader. The town healer was drunk and said Thudder would die. In desperation, she took him to the abandoned temple of the Goddess and requested Athena heal the boy.

Shockingly, the statue had come to life and told Caiisa that she had the power to heal Thudder with a touch of her hand. Pulling the knife out and with his blood pouring through her fingers, the Goddess showed her how to focus the energy and repair the wound in Thudder's stomach.

It had been an exhausting lesson and Caiisa collapsed on the floor. During her recuperation, she asked the Goddess what she wanted in return for giving her this ability.

"This isn't a gift I have given you. As the Goddess of Knowledge, I've just made you aware of your own power."

Caiisa was impressed. The Goddess could have demanded anything from her, but had been completely honest with the girl.

There was one request. The Goddess needed a Priestess to reopen her temple in the mountain fortress of Ka'an.

"I don't expect your answer tonight, my child. Go and think it over. If you will go for me, I will have an escort and attendants at the crossroads in the morning."

Thudder had thanked Caiisa for saving his life and she in turn, did the same. Her tiny hand was swallowed in his as he tried to speak, but couldn't.

Caiisa had left the temple and healed her father. After thinking about the opportunity, she packed a bag and made her way to the crossroads. On the way, she saw Thudder slip face down in the pig offal and the townsmen screamed in laughter.

Hopefully, she would see him again one day.

At the crossroads, a man of massive stature and covered from head to toe in armor had been waiting for her. An attendant told Caiisa to sit down while the tents were packed away. The metal man intrigued her and she tried to get information from her attendant. The woman informed her he was the Warrior Athena had assigned to escort her to Ka'an.

As they traveled, she was never alone with the Warrior and Caiisa never saw him without his armor. She only managed one brief glimpse as the wind blew the opening to his tent open a bit and it was only from the back. But what a back! The man had huge muscles that rippled as his armor was put on and his attendant tucked the long mane of black hair into his helmet. She had fallen in love without even knowing if he was a man or a God. Caiisa romanticized about him during the day and dreamed about him at night as she lay in her bed.

Her attendants weren't human and she assumed the Warrior wasn't either. Since he had been sent by Athena, Caiisa was sure he was a God. Even so, he had been defeated by a very special woman named Dav. On the way to Ka'an, their passage was blocked by a rockslide and they had to turn and follow an animal trail up into the mountains.

Then the way had been blocked by two women. The warrior had made the sign of truce but the woman had shook her head in the negative. Even when he signed again, she again responded in the negative. Regretfully, he had pulled his sword and advanced. Caiisa thought the woman was insane to actually think she could fight the Warrior. As the sword descended down on her, Dav had the same thoughts.

The clash of swords was deafening and Dav was driven into the ground six inches. The 3S was screaming into her ear that it was reaching critical overload status. The suit gave her the strength of ten men, but the warrior was even stronger, and eventually Dav had to use the art of the gentle way to deflect the blows. Slowly, she was driven back by the Warrior's strength and speed.

Using the two dogs to hit the warrior from behind, it pushed him forward and off balance. Using all the power of the 3S, she brought her sword down on the thinnest part of his blade and broke it in two. The Warrior's sword had exploded and thrown them both through the air. Dav had been far enough, but the Warrior had stayed where he fell and even Caiisa hadn't been able to heal him.

The Goddess Athena appeared and helped the warrior to his feet and fixed the sword.

"Take what you want and leave us alone," Caiisa had screamed at them.

Dav and Chenee had been mystified.

"We aren't thieves," Dav had stammered.

"The Warrior gave you the sign of truce and you responded in the negative."

Dav had been shocked. The waving sign was the signal to get out of the way in her culture. But she wasn't in her culture. She was on the planet Chosen with a totally different way of thinking.

Apologizing to the Warrior and to Caiisa, she'd asked to accompany them to Ka'an. Caiisa had been mad, but eventually agreed. She later became good friends with the two women.

***

That had been months ago. She didn't trust the HighBorn Chenee when they had first met and as it turned out, she was justified in her feelings when the savage returned to her father. She had learned to like the girl and would miss her.

"Priestess," an aide called to her. "We have a child who cut her arm on a sword."

Turning to look at the injured, her healing power was already flowing to cut the blood flow. The child's face, once tortured in pain, was now starting to ease and she even smiled. The blue light from her hands was seeking out the damaged tissue and knitting it back together.

The cut closed quickly until only a faint scar was visible. "There you go, little girl." Caiisa looked at her mother. "How did this happen?"

"There was a stack of swords for the soldiers getting ready for the battle. She slipped in the mud and cut her arm."

Caiisa smiled at the girl again. "You're alright now, sweet child."

"Thank you," the mother gushed. She reached into a bag and took out a few coins.

"No payment. Please pray for the Goddess and for the health of our city."

"I will," she began to cry in relief and walked away.

58

Caiisa turned back to heal the rest. A dark shadow covered the entrance and she looked up expecting to see the Warrior. Instead, Thudder stood towering over her. "Good day, Thudder. Why are you here?"

"Come. Defend city," he mumbled and looked uncomfortable.

The Warrior had walked up behind Thudder and was waiting to see if the man was a threat. Caiisa hugged Thudder and the Warrior backed off.

"I never really had the chance to say thank you for rescuing me a few months ago."

Thudder just stood and looked at her. "Come and eat." She took his hand.

He stumbled forward and then turned to stand in front of the statue of the Goddess Athena. Caiisa remembered how he had stood in front of the same statue in the city of Millerstown. *What had the Goddess said?* Thudder would come and talk to her every night. *What was that about?* Just like the feeling she had about the HighBorn Chenee, something didn't seem quite right.

***

Attalee could remember when he had first seen Chenee. It had been during the trek to Ka'an, a trip he'd not wanted to take. General Cae arrived at his house and made a startling pronouncement to his mother, the Matron Ceran. Prince Attalee, from the obscure but noble House of Ceran, was to ascend to the throne as king of the New Roman Empire. A young boy of only seventeen revolutions of the Mid

Sun Passing, he had been thrust into the position of the most powerful person on the planet Chosen.

While men had been known to gamble everything for the chance to gain the power of this office, Attalee was just the opposite. He was more comfortable sitting among his scrolls and researching the history of the world around him.

From his earliest childhood memories, he could remember the finest scholars traveling from Ka'an to train him in the art of war and government. He had assumed it was to eventually take over the leadership of his House. How wrong he had been, Attalee thought as he scratched his chin and smiled to himself.

His mother had sent him away to be escorted to Ka'an by General Cae and a group of handpicked, battle-hardened soldiers. On the two cycle journey, they had arrived at the main crossroads, dirty and tired from their urgent, forced march to get to the capital ahead of the Barbarian horde.

At the crossroads, they had come across an odd assortment of travelers. Their attention had immediately been drawn to a man of mammoth proportions, dressed head to toe in armor and carrying a sword that would have taken two men to wield it. The Warrior had the crest of Athena across his breastplate and when he had signaled truce, they quickly returned the sign.

A woman stepped from a tent and Attalee had felt his breath catch in his throat. She was the most beautiful woman he had ever seen and he couldn't help but look at her loveliness. Trying to remember he was a gentleman of nobility, Attalee had tried to look away, but found himself unable to.

When the woman smiled, the suns became twice their normal brightness. Bright red hair tumbled playfully from the gold comb atop her head and flowed along a graceful neck and onto her shoulders.

As if in a daze, he shook his head to clear the ungentlemanly thoughts and was grateful two other women had pulled aside the flap of the tent and stepped out. Glad to have something else to draw his attention, he turned his gaze upon them.

The first woman had caught General Cae's eye. She was dressed in Roman battle armor and carried a sword across her back. *The second was a HighBorn, from the house of Xyer,* Attalee thought. The red band along the bottom of her stegatta denoted she was the Matron of her House, but she stood behind the Roman warrior.

He tried to think of what he knew about the Noble Family Xyer, which was very little, as the family was cut off from the rest of the Empire for extended periods of time due to the heavy snows that closed the only pass through the mountains. They were the closest family to the Barbarians and also known to be highly skilled mountain climbers.

Attalee smiled to himself. He loved to climb just about anything within reach—a tree, a building or some of the smaller ravines near his home—but he had nothing like the forty thousand foot mountains surrounding the Xyer family. He would like to learn what this HighBorn could teach him about the skill.

General Cae had approached the alleged Roman warrior and found out she was Captain Dav Vad, an other worlder. It was a story they would have to hear and did. But Attalee was intrigued by the HighBorn and went to introduce himself. She was very backward and shy and with a shock, he realized half her foot was missing. *Was it a new wound or had she been born that way?* Most Roman families would have taken the deformed child out and left her in the wild, so it must be a new injury or sustained when she was older.

Even though she was disabled, Attalee found something he liked in the girl. She was different from other HighBorn women he had met before. HighBorn girls were always too full of themselves and focused on their future status as Matrons of their households. But here was a girl who, at a young age, was Matron of her own house. Yet she was shy and unassuming in personality. It was a change from what he expected and Attalee warmed immediately to her.

The thing that struck him as odd was the Matron seemed to be looking at his soldiers and sizing them up. Odd for a Matron, but he laughed to himself. He was sure he would do the same thing when he was in charge of the family estate. As the new king, he was now in charge of all the family estates. It was hard for him to think of himself as anything more than just a land owner.

General Cae had discovered the captain was reluctant to tell of her origins, so they had all retired to a log and listened to the amazing story of how a woman from four thousand years in their future had been brought to the planet Chosen to find King Attuicus.

The captain was in the United Universe Force when she had been injured and forced to retire. On the way to the retirement planet, her ship had been hijacked by the Gentle One. In turn, the Gentle One told her the story of how he had moved the humans to this planet to keep them from fighting. Alas, to no avail. The only being that seemed able of keeping the peace was King Attuicus, but he had disappeared and the Gentle One needed Dav to find the former king and restore peace in the Republic.

To help prove her point about being from the future, the captain demonstrated a suit from her time period, a 3S or *superior strength suit*. It made her ten times stronger than the normal human. She had defeated the Warrior in battle, a slight misunderstanding over the hand signal for truce.

Attalee was happy the group would accompany them to Ka'an, especially the HighBorn Matron. It was nice to have someone of his own status with them, it helped take his eyes off the beautiful creature, Caiisa. He soon realized the Matron Chenee felt he was making advances toward her. In anger, Attalee told her that he was only trying to extend the hand of friendship to her and at least for the time being, his intentions were honorable.

Chenee had been taken aback by the anger and didn't understand. It was common for her people to sleep with whoever they wanted as long as they were back in their mate's bed by nightfall. Then Chenee remembered she wasn't among her people. Her job was to spy on the Chosen and learn how to destroy the city of Ka'an. The only problem was she had fallen in love with Attalee and couldn't stand the thought of life without him, but she feared her father's wrath even more and had eventually returned to her people.

***

General Cae stopped at a trench to relieve himself when a sound reached his ears. It sounded like a moan and in the night air, it was terrifying. Tying off the opening in his pants, he raced to the wall and found King Attalee still looking over the plains. From the top of the wall, the noise was louder and even more terrifying.

"What is it?" he demanded.

Attalee replied without looking at him. "It's their battle hymn. They sing to open the gates to the Death World so any men who fall in battle will be able to enter."

"You think they will attack today, then?"

Attalee's shoulders seemed to sag. "Unfortunately…"

The moan began to rise in pitch and Cae was startled to see a pebble vibrating on the ground as the energy of a hundred thousand voices rolled over the wall. The sound gave General Cae the chills and he shuddered involuntarily. It was as if he could hear the gates to the Death World opening.

As the twin suns crept up the back of the mountains, Attalee and Cae could start to make out the force displayed before them. It was an impressive sight. The Quranian army was lined up along the length of the wall, just out of arrow range. All the catapults were loaded with rocks and a man stood by to unleash the missiles.

General Cae could see Battle Master Thom standing on his platform and their eyes locked together across the battlefield. "I will not let you take this city," Cae shouted at him, even though he was sure the man couldn't hear him.

Thom was the first to look away, but then he held his hands up as if to say, *This is the finest army in the world. Romans, your destruction is at hand. We will trample you and your city into dust.*

General Cae snorted in disgust and then laughed. Attalee looked at him in surprise.

The Quranian battle song began to build in tempo as the solders beat the ground with their feet. As the very earth began to tremble, Attalee and Cae looked up at the columns and arches on the wall. Dust began to scatter in the wind as the vibrations continued and Attalee whispered something to General Cae. After a moment of thought, the General hurried away with a smile on his face.

Soon, the wall began to fill with Roman solders standing at attention and looking out over the plains. Trumpets began to sound and from somewhere close, the sound of the harp.

Attalee began to sing out in a loud, clear voice, "We are proud of our Republic—together, we stand in her defense. Arm in arm, we stand against her enemies, we stand together in…"

The soldiers began to sing along and their voices echoed throughout the valley. The Quranians were surprised and quieted down as the Romans began to sing their battle hymn.

"How dare the damn Chosen interrupt our sacred song?" a person muttered. As one man, the Quranians began to sing to counter the voices of their enemy. As the sound filled the valley, the very mountains seemed to shake with fear. As if on cue, both sides finished their songs at the same time and a deathly silence fell over the battlefield with both armies watching the other.

The sound of the catapults letting go was thunderous in the silence and Attalee watched in horror as the rocks tumbled through the air.

"Vacate the wall," he screamed at the troops. He felt rather than saw a rock hit a column nearby and with a sickening groan, it and the arch began to topple. Grabbing a soldier who had frozen, Attalee pushed him down the stairs as a two ton arch fell across the opening. The impact shook the ground and caused them to tumble down the steps. The man's body helped cushion the king's fall, but Attalee heard a sickening sound of bone breaking and saw the man's head resting at an odd angle.

Sadly, the king disengaged himself from the tangled arms and legs and looked out through the doorway into the courtyard. The troops were now scrambling to get out of the way. Screams pierced the air and Attalee began to tremble with anger. Mindless of the falling columns, he walked into the courtyard and began to grab soldiers as they ran by and ordered them to retreat to the Upper City. A column looked like it was going to fall on the king, but at the last moment, it hesitated and then turned and struck the ground less than a foot from him.

He ignored the danger and was slowly able to get his troops reorganized and away from the wall. The ground was littered with broken columns and arches. As he watched, the catapults hit the last few columns. They collapsed amid the cheers of the Barbarians. The once proud face of the Ka'an wall had been forever changed.

"Retake the walls!" General Cae screamed out. "We need to help our men and women out from under the rubble."

The troops were looking at the General in shock.

He screamed again, "We are under attack! The columns are all down and the only thing you have to fear is that the Barbarians may overwhelm the wall. Put your fears aside and remember, we are not only protecting the Republic, but our families as well."

The men still looked uncertain, so Attalee grabbed one centurion by his armor. "Are we Romans, or are we cowards?" he screamed in the man's face. Fear left the man's face and his features hardened.

Angrily, he pushed the king away and screamed at his men, "Come on, you filthy animals...you want to live forever?" Pulling his sword, the centurion ran toward the wall. Seeing the fear leave their leader's face, his men pulled their swords and followed him up the stairs to tend the wounded.

General Cae was glad to see his veteran legion already manning the wall, forming the new troops into a defensive position. Even though they were coming under heavy fire from the Quranian archers, the veterans were using their shields to build a movable wall to protect the defenders and the wounded. Very few of the arrows were causing any damage and the Roman archers began to respond.

***

Thom watched with satisfaction as the columns began to tumble and a cloud of dust filled the air so the whole wall was obscured from sight. He and his men screamed with delight at the destruction. The sunlight began to glint off their weapons as they held them up in the air and prepared to attack. A Roman solder, trying to dodge a falling column, tumbled over the edge of the wall and fell among the Quranians. He was still alive when he was dragged away and pulled into the crowd. His mutilated body was then loaded onto a catapult and sent back into the city of Ka'an. The Roman solders screamed in rage and promised to avenge their fellow countryman's death.

Thom looked at the statue of Zeus on the wall and noticed it hadn't been damaged by the catapults. Even now, the rocks were hitting and bouncing off it. Thom rubbed his eyes. Hadn't the statue been sitting yesterday and now stood with its arms folded across its chest in defiance? No matter, he would show even the Roman Gods they needed to respect him.

The Quranian troops surged toward the wall, oblivious of the rain of arrows and rocks falling down upon them. Ladders were placed against the wall and men yelled with blood lust as they climbed toward the defenders of the city.

***

General Cae gave the signal and his troops began to pour out on top of the wall. The Romans grabbed the ladders and tried to pull them up or twist them to throw the attackers off.

This defense was overall effective, but several of the savages actually made it to the top of the wall unopposed and they began to form up into a defensive formation until reinforcements could arrive.

General Cae seemed to watch the battle unfolding in slow motion. *The enemy was just too vast and the wall too long to hold off the enemy. Ka'an will be lost.* Pulling his sword, he ran toward the Barbarians.

The savages roared as they caught sight of the general. Then Romans seemed to spring out of three sides of the wall and the Quranians had to stop and regroup to assess the new threat.

The attack pushed the men back to the edge of the wall as General Cae's elite force came into play. Some of the men tried to climb back down, but most were slaughtered and their bodies used to knock more men off the ladders. As quick as they had appeared, the Romans disappeared back into the wall. General Cae shook his head as if to clear his eyes.

Another group of Quranians had broached the wall and Cae gathered his men together to repel them. Cae walked to the back of the wall and watched as Major Raki directed his troops on horseback to race to that section. Slowly, the major and the troops would creep up the stairs and along the back edge. Then they would all attack simultaneously from three sides and push the Barbarians back down their ladders. Then, as before, they would melt back into the wall, leaving the enemy with a surreal fear that some evil force had aligned with the Romans.

King Attalee had rallied a group of archers. The Roman bow had greater range and power and they slowly began to take a toll on the attackers. He had also stationed a line of soldiers with their massive shields to stand in front of the archers and protect them, whereas the savages had no such protection.

***

Thom recalled his archers and moved them to where the catapults could smash through the shields and his men could get a foothold on the wall. He had watched in disgust as his troops would take a section and then be overrun by a group of Roman soldiers. He spit on the ground and cursed his team leaders.

***

General Cae called up the next legion of soldiers to relieve the defenders and then realized the centurions had been changing them every hour as he had ordered. But still the Quranians continued their seemingly inexhaustible assault.

King Attalee saw General Cae and ran over to him. The general had a bad cut on his leg and was covered in blood from head to toe. As Attalee shouted his name, Cae turned and looked wildly at the king. In fear, Attalee took a step back from him.

He reminds me of a cornered animal that will fight to the death. Glancing over the general's shoulder, he noted the position of the suns and estimated they had been fighting for six hours.

"General, you must get that wound looked at and you need some rest," Attalee shouted to him above the roar of battle.

"I won't rest until I've wiped this scum off my wall!" he screamed in rage and stormed off to repel another attack.

Attalee could feel the fatigue in his own body and he wondered if he had the stamina the general was displaying, knowing he too would continue to fight until he dropped or was killed. A signalman next to the king was sending an urgent message along the line.

He looked in horror as the message came through. The Barbarians now commanded the top of the western end of the wall. Major Raki's force was too far away to launch a surprise attack and the Roman troops were already engaged in their own battles along the wall. Battle Master Thom had seen a weakness and exploited it.

Even now, the Quranians were lining up in formation to march on the king's position. Attalee's heart felt heavy and a feeling of certain defeat began to settle over him. They had lost.

Thankfully, General Cae had already seen the threat and was directing a counterattack. The Quranians swarmed unopposed up the ladders and a loud cheer went up as they realized they had taken a section of the wall.

***

Thom smiled from his tower and sent a runner to direct the right flank to climb the wall. Over one thousand men were already there in battle formation. Chief Messa pounded Thom on the back. "You're going to win, my friend," he shouted in excitement.

A group of Romans were seen carrying a weapon onto the wall and pointing it at the Quranian troops. It looked like a large bow set on a pedestal. More of the new weapons began to arrive and Thom directed the archers to keep the new weapon pinned down, but General Cae had anticipated this and set up a wall of shields to protect the Romans.

The Quranians roared and started attacking directly at the new weapons. Then the Scorpio let loose an iron shaft and a Quranian screamed in terror as it penetrated his shield and then passed through three men before impaling itself in a fourth. The battle formation stopped and began to crumble as another shaft flew through the air with the same results.

***

The confusion gave General Cae enough time to move thirty-five hundred men, one legion, into a defensive position. With the Scorpio and the archers causing fear in the Quranian ranks, Cae felt he had a chance to repel the invaders. More Scorpios were set up on the wall and the ground behind it. As the iron shafts began to fly through the air and run completely through their men, it took a psychological toll on the savages. As the charge broke and ran, men started to climb down the ladders as others were still trying to climb up.

The ladders began to crumble under the combined weight of so many troops and Thom screamed in rage when he saw his men running in terror and even leaping off the wall when they could find no other way down. Then General Cae's legion hit the Quranians hard. They outflanked the Barbarians at the rear and cut off their escape. One man stood his ground and battled the Romans from three sides as he tried to let his men make it back to the ground.

Even General Cae had to admire the ferociousness of the Barbarians. But even he couldn't stand against the might of the Scorpio. Finally, the team leader threw down his sword and ordered the rest of his men to do the same. There was no way they could get down the ladders or overrun the Scorpio weapon. Five hundred men were taken prisoner and after having their arms tied behind them, they were marched away behind the wall.

***

Major Raki and his men quickly pulled up the ladders to hold off another assault. Thom had personally arrived at that section of the wall and watched as his men were taken prisoner. He shouted words of disgust at his men, especially the team leader, Tymbo.

"Tymbo," he shouted out, "you are a coward. When this battle is over, I will kill you myself, if you are fortunate enough to live through Roman torture." Tymbo trembled as he heard Thom's words and he looked very frightened. Thom raised his voice so the men around could hear. "The Chosen will pull your fingernails out and chop your fingers off at the joint. Red hot pokers will be shoved up your ass into your gut and you will die a long, horrible and painful death. May your soul rot in the Death World, little mouse!"

Tymbo had turned white and looked as if he would faint and literally peed himself. He had heard of unspeakable torture methods the Romans employed while interrogating prisoners. Perhaps it would have been better to have died in battle. But it was too late. His arms were tied behind him and he was being led away. Thom laughed at the look of sheer terror on the team leader's face. Even though Thom doubted the Romans would torture the team leader, he wanted to make sure no more of his men would give up so easily .

In Quranian tradition, it was a form of dishonor to die while being tortured and his men would fight to the death rather than face such an event. Thom ordered his men away from the wall as night began to set. The Roman defenders cheered when they saw the savages leaving.

***

General Cae immediately had the legion on the wall replaced and ordered them to get some rest. Gratefully, the men and women retired to their homes to sleep and see their families. It helped the soldiers realize what they were fighting to protect. It would make them fight even harder to save the city the next day.

The General staggered his way to the bottom of the stairs and gave the head watch leader some final orders. He sank to the ground against the wall and was fast asleep. A women helping tend the wounded placed a blanket over him to keep out the chill of

74

the night. Later on, she told the healer where to find him and as Caiisa went through the wounded and healed all she could, she placed her hand on his head and abdomen to close his wounds. His breathing became easier and with a sigh, Cae slipped into a deep and peaceful sleep.

***

Caiisa was helping the healers put bandages on the table and noticed the color slowly returning to her hands. A few weeks had passed since she had fought off an attack from Hades, the God of the Death World. Her being a healer was preventing people from dying and it was effecting his power. Power he wasn't willing to share.

Hades began trying to kill Caiisa. A regrettable plan for him, as even the God of the Death World was taken in by her beauty.

The healer first noticed little spider legs crawling out of the corner of her eye. When she would turn and look, she could see nothing. She started to have dreams about the legs and woke up screaming in the night.

As she lost weight and her appetite, Caiisa's ability to heal others vanished. Being so sick, she couldn't even heal herself. Calling on Athena to help her, she had been amazed when the Goddess didn't respond. Her friends had come to pay their last respects when it seemed Caiisa was on the threshold of the Death World.

The Warrior jumped into his suit as Caiisa sat up in her bed. "No…!" she screamed. "I will not let you have them!" Throwing the covers from her legs,

Caiisa rolled off the couch and began to fight with the air. As if a veil had been lifted from his eyes, the Warrior could see what the Priestess was fighting. It was a tentacle creature from the Death World, literally trying to suck the life force from her soul.

He had seen these creatures wrapped around the dying before, but this one was the most hideous he could recall. Caiisa was grappling with a tentacle as big as a tree trunk. Pulling his sword, the Warrior struck down at the space between the suction cups. The creature howled in pain and withdrew from Caiisa.

She was thrown roughly to the ground, but rolled away and looked for a weapon to defend her temple. An ornate spear given as a gift to Athena, lay on the ground. Picking it up, she turned to do battle and gasped as she noticed the room overflowing with the tentacle creatures. Caiisa had been thrown clear and her Warrior was in the middle of them, trying to fight his way to her side.

Had the damn things been here the whole time? Slowly draining the life force from her patients? An anger began to build in her and she screamed, "In the name of the Goddess Athena, I command you foul creatures to leave this temple."

The creatures paused and then their leader began to melt and mold itself into the figure of a man. "Who dares give the God of the Death World an order?"

"It is I, Caiisa, Priestess of the Goddess Athena. I command you to leave my temple or you will be destroyed."

The God began to laugh. "You are interesting, human. But I have come to take what is mine and I will not be stopped."

"These are my patients and until I say they are beyond my help, they will remain with me."

Hades shook his head. "You are causing too many problems, human. The fates decide when a human must pass into the Death World. I suffer each time you change their hour of death. Be generous in your opinion of how I make humans' passage as gentle as possible."

Caiisa began to laugh. "My opinion of you is lowered every time I see your work. If a person is suffering from a disease where their body wastes away before my very eyes, you prolong their illness and seem to get a perverse pleasure out of it. You let them continue to suffer until their body can barely hold onto their soul, rather than making their death swift and painless.

"The last few weeks, you have been trying to convince me that I was sick so you could try and take more souls to the Death World. Now that I know who you are and how you can trick people, I will do everything in my power to keep anyone from taking the passage to your world. If I am unable to save their lives, at least I will make their passing as gentle and compassionate as possible. Therefore, you will gain nothing from their suffering."

Trembling with rage, the God advanced as his hands turned into tentacles and began to reach for her. Hades stopped as the Warrior stepped between them and held his sword at the ready. He had already proven his sword could cut the God and cause pain and injury.

"If it wasn't for the pitiful excuse of a man standing between us, you would have no hope of defeating me."

Stepping around the Warrior, she screamed, "Come then and fight. I no longer fear you, God of the Dead!" Holding up the spear, Caiisa prepared to defend her temple.

Realizing his ploy hadn't worked, he made a gesture to the other creatures in the room. Melting into a misshapen glob of mucus, he began to seep into the ground. "We will meet again, Priestess," he spat out.

The Warrior prepared to step forward and attack, but Caiisa grabbed his arm. "As far as I'm concerned, from this day forward, we are at war with the God of the Death Word and I don't intend on losing."

The Warrior put a hand on her shoulder as a sign of his agreement.

The God of the Dead will not find me so easy to fool in the future, she vowed to herself. She had committed herself to the Goddess and her healing. If the God of the Death World wanted to fight, so be it. Hades would soon learn he has confronted the wrong human.

After the battle, Caiisa turned and went to step down onto the earthen floor but instead, stepped into a snowdrift. Staring down at her foot in amazement, she heard Athena's laughter and slowly looked up at the Goddess.

"It is hard to get used to being transported by folding space," Athena said gently.

"I kept trying to call you," Caiisa whispered as she took a moment to compose herself. Involuntarily glancing around them, she took a step back when she noticed they were standing on the edge of a cliff that overlooked the world below.

"Don't be frightened, my child. You are in no danger here. I will catch you if you fall."

Caiisa was still looking over the edge and trying to control her fear. Athena took the woman in her arms and peace flowed through Caiisa. "Is that better?"

"Yes," the healer said. "Why didn't you come when I called you?" Athena looked as the snow was being blown off the mountain tops and into the crater, eventually becoming rain that would feed the crops.

"I had to wait so I could get you alone. Until the Gods can regain our power, Hades is the strongest of us all and will stop at nothing to destroy us if he can. I had to take you to a place where Hades can't reach. Stone.

"If we are touching the ground, he would be able to reach us and cause mischief for you and I."

"What should I do?" Caiisa asked.

"When the time comes, you must kill the God of the Death World and either take his place or appoint someone to the job."

Caiisa just stood and looked at her. Then she burst out, "You want me to kill Hades? It can't be done."

"It can be done. The fewer victims you send to the Death World will cause his power to falter and wane. He is strengthened with human souls and must be stopped."

Caiisa nodded and looked at Athena. The battle lust was still strong in her. "If I get the chance, I will kill him with my bare hands."

Athena smiled. "That is exactly what I need you to do, my child." With a smile, Athena folded space and they were back at the temple.

Taking her place back on the pedestal, the Goddess stood and looked at Thudder. "I promise, my son. It will be as it once was before." Thudder looked confused and stood without speaking.

Caiisa frowned and walked away. What was Athena saying to Thudder and why was she calling him son? An old man was suffering a heart attack and needed her assistance, so she would have to think about it later.

Then the call came for her assistance. Too many had been wounded to bring the men and women to the temple.

Caiisa was shocked at the amount of destruction and death the first day had wrought on the city and its inhabitants. The Warrior helped her walk over and around the carnage as she tried to heal Roman and Quranian alike.

CHAPTER THREE

Supreme Land Owner Toka stopped his horse and looked out over the road to Ka'an. It was choked with a mass of humanity fleeing the Barbarian horde with all they could carry. Old men and women stumbled under heavy packs, falling down to be ignored by other Romans hurrying to get to the safety of the city.

He and Josf would climb down and help everyone they could and he was about to start ordering the citizens with carts to begin carrying those walking when a young man had pulled his sword, stepped in front of a man's two horses and threatened to kill them if he didn't stop.

This had shocked everyone, including Toka. Who was this young boy threatening another citizen? Intrigued, he had pushed through the crowd to watch as the boy climbed up on the cart and gave a speech about the proud Roman heritage of helping each other and how their lack of respect for others wasn't a good way to carry on the tradition. He had ordered the carts to ride on one side of the road and the walkers to stay to the other side. Also, no carts were to pass that point without being full of people. Then when the carts made it to Ka'an and delivered their occupants and personal belongings, they were to return and pick up more refugees.

Even more surprising to Toka, General Cae was with the young man and after setting up an orderly procession, they rode off toward the city together.

Scratching his head, he lined up with the walkers and helped in any way he could. It was almost nightfall before they made it to the city.

After several weeks of getting organized and joining the military, Toka asked for directions to the villa of a HighBorn. The guard looked at him and laughed. "What would a HighBorn want with you, little boy?"

Josf had cringed at the outburst he was sure to come from his former master.

"I am Supreme Land Owner Toka," he stated softly. "I don't believe the HighBorn will have a problem seeing me."

The guard had looked surprised and decided to err on the side of caution. "My apologies, my lord. Would you like an escort?"

"No, thank you," he paused. Taking a coin out of his pouch, he handed it to the guard. Gratefully, the man took it and turned to push the lowborn out of the way so his horse could make it quicker to the upper city.

Soon, they stopped at a large house that covered most of the hill it was sitting upon. Large marble columns lined its exterior and it had an open, breezy architecture. It was beautiful and modern looking to a boy from the plains.

A servant came to the archway and noted their dirty clothes. Inquiring why they had stopped at this house, the servant not so gently suggested they return to the lower city to find accommodations with the common men and women of their stature.

"I am here to see the HighBorn of this residence," Toka announced.

"That will not be possible." With a rude glance, the servant expressed his distaste for the men before him. Obviously, they had been on the road for many months and hadn't had the time to visit a bathhouse.

Climbing off the horse, Toka came to stand by the man. "Is the HighBorn of the House present or away?"

"That is none of your concern."

Looking at Josf, Toka smiled. "We have come far and are in need of rest and a bath. My friend and I will be in the guest house if you need us. When your employer is ready to see us, I expect you to let us know."

Toka was already pulling a pack off his horse and heading to the guest house. He walked like a person who knew where he was going. The servant was put off by the man's demeanor and thought it best to consult with the HighBorn of the house. He had made it quite clear several times the boy wasn't welcome and would now have to be removed by force. This was something he would enjoy.

The servant reported to his superior, who sent the message up the chain of command. In no time at all, the HighBorn was seen to be headed to the guest house with a small group of personal bodyguards.

When the door of the guest house burst open, Toka and Josf were happily soaking in a large bath and enjoying the feeling of being clean for the first time in months.

"I demand to know why you have invaded my house and taken advantage of my hospitality without being invited."

"You are Councilor Toka?" he asked.

"Yes I am," he sputtered as the guards began to pull their weapons and move toward the two men. "I would like to know who you are before we mix your blood with the water of my bathhouse." The original servant was looking on with open excitement at getting to see the boy and his friend cut down for their barging in on a HighBorn's property, without an invitation he might add.

"I think you will forgive me for not standing to introduce myself. I am Supreme Land Owner Toka. You were a friend of my father's."

The councilor took a step back. Here was the son of his best friend and a namesake to boot.

"My father and I visited you when I was very young and you told me then your house was to be my own whenever I had need."

Councilor Toka began to laugh. "So I did, young Toka, so I did! I never expected you to take advantage of it in quite this manner."

"I am sorry for the misunderstanding, Lord. I did try to gain an audience with you, but your..." Toka's face tightened as he tried to think of a word that would describe the snobbish servant, instead he bit his tongue, "servant, wouldn't let me talk to you," he finally finished.

"I am sorry." Councilor Toka frowned. "Since the new king has freed the slaves, they have become a little unruly. Most have stayed on as servants and we are required to pay them. Unfortunately, we must also put up with their attitudes as well." The elder Toka dismissed his personal guards.

Toka looked around. "I never did agree with keeping slaves myself." With the guards leaving them alone, he climbed naked from the bath. Taking a cloth to dry off with, he sat down on a low couch. "I don't expect to be staying with you long. I'm going to volunteer for the defense of Ka'an, so I'll probably be living with the other troops in some type of building close to the wall."

The older Toka laughed. "King Attalee has decreed we open our homes to refugees and soldiers, so you are welcome to stay here with me. I'll have one of the servants show you to a room." He motioned for a man to come to his side. He was the same servant disappointed by the turn of events. "Take Supreme Land Owner Toka to the guest room next to my own. Also, inform the Matron of the House we will have visitors for dinner and I expect her to be dressed appropriately."

"Yes, sir." He rolled his eyes as he walked away.

Councilor Toka saw the look and his face turned red in anger. "You could always volunteer for the army if you find the work here distasteful, especially to a man of your obvious talents."

The servant grimaced and then gulped. "That will not be necessary, sir." Turning to the two men, he lifted a hand to indicate they were to follow him.

"Thank you, Councilor Toka."

"I'll see you at dinner this evening," the councilor announced and turned to leave.

***

The last memory she had was of a stinging sensation in her shoulder as the automed injected her with a shot. Opening her eyes in the dimly lit room, she turned her head to look at the chronometer. It indicated she had only been asleep for a few hours, which was medically impossible. The drug had a twenty- seven hour cycle time before it left a person's bloodstream. Stumbling toward the doorway, she prepared to head to the bridge. The door opened to reveal the long, dark tunnel she had fallen into in an earlier dream.

Panicking, she stepped back and hit the panel to close the door. *I'm not awake then and I'm trapped in the same dream from before...or have I not woken up at all? Am I still in this dream and can't get out? How could that happen?*

It sure as hell didn't make any sense. Sitting down on her bed, she tried to logically think it out. Frowning, chewing on her lip and idly wrapping a strand of hair around her finger, she sat and thought. Then a smile played across her face. If this was her dream, she should be able to do whatever she wanted.

"I want to be encased in a 3S excavation unit," she ordered. The suit began to form at her legs and soon covered her body in a rigid titanium hull with multiple arms attached front and rear for digging and climbing.

Looking at the displays, she used her chin to hit a toggle. A faceplate snapped into place and there was a slight hiss as the suit became airtight.

Now she was ready. An arm swung out and pushed the button for the door to open. Lights around her suit automatically kicked on so she could peer into the dark tunnel. Stepping out, Sorti Ne felt the sensation of going from full gravity to zero. Arms shot out and explosively anchored their tips into the rock as she began her descent. The lights revealed the space where the hull met the rock. It looked as if the two substances had melted together.

Atmospheric data was flowing across the screen: point zero, zero three gravity and zero percent atmosphere. Thumbing the excavation suit forward, she watched as the sides of the tunnel began to move by. It showed signs of having once been sedimentary rock. With the walls being a smooth as they were, could this have been created by running water? Radiation isotope readings placed it trillions of years before humans would have been around, at least on Earth. Another mystery to look into later. Then Sorti Ne laughed. This was all a dream.

It was funny to think this was actually real.

As she traveled deeper into the tunnel, the darkness seemed to swallow her up and bile began to form in the back of her throat. She hated confined spaces and claustrophobia was beginning to set in. An auto Ralph bag deployed, just as she lost her rice cake and cheese dinner. A vacuum cleaned off her face and wiped it with a moist towel.

This dream was getting way too real. *This dream?* With a thought, the tunnel began to expand or did she grow smaller? Sighing in relief, it was bigger now.

The alarm sounded as an arm went to set an explosive bolt and found no purchase. The lights swiveled to follow her gaze, the tunnel had ended.

Cautiously, she stepped out and played the light across the cavern. Screaming at the sight of the creature, Sorti Ne was trying to backpedal so fast, the arms became entangled and locked up. An explosive bolt detonated by her leg and blew if off below the knee. The pain was overwhelming and the 3S cinched down on the leg to cut off the blood supply and flooded her system with morphine.

Oblivious to the pain, Sorti Ne could only sit and look at the horror that lay before her. A great mass of clear protoplasm, covered with oozing, pus-filled sores. The floor was thick with the infectious goop of the creature and it almost made her sick again. The auto Ralph bag popped back up and she disarmed it. Pieces of her leg and blood were scattered in the vacuum and beating against her faceplate.

What the hell is this thing? It didn't appear to be alive. It almost reminded her of an egg, but the yoke in the center was shattered, as if it had been stabbed.

First things first. She had to take care of her leg. *I want my leg to grow back.* The blood and leg reversed its outward motion and condensed back into a whole group. The explosion turned inward and returned to the anchoring bolt arm. Moving the arm out of the way and testing the leg, she couldn't tell it had ever been blown off.

Whew! Thank God this was just a dream.

The creature wasn't moving, so she slowly walked towards it. There was a large gash where some sharp object had cut through the outer layer and into the yoke or brain zone. It still looked like an egg yolk to her, so she would continue to call it that.

A sample of the creature indicated it was a type of flesh, but also an energy source at the subatomic level. It was incredibly complex and alien. Walking around the back of the corpse, she saw seven small yellow spheres deeply embedded within it. With the shadow from her lamp, it looked like one of them moved. She chuckled to herself. This place was really creeping her out.

Then it moved again. "Shit," she muttered, pulled back and ran towards the tunnel.

The carcass exploded as seven yellow balls ate their way out of the creature and jumped onto Sorti Ne's back. As their combined weight drove her to the floor of the cavern, she felt like she was being smothered by puppies.

If not for the faceplate and the vacuum of space, her scream would have echoed all the way back to her stateroom.

***

Attalee needed help getting down the stairs behind the wall. He stumbled his way across the courtyard to where the prisoners had been herded together. A chair was brought out for the king and he sank gratefully onto it. He closed his eyes and seemed asleep.

Gathering his internal strength, he said softly to the guard, "Bring the Quranian team leader to me."

The guard called out, "Bring Tymbo here."

"Yes, sir." The order was relayed.

Hearing a scraping sound, he opened his eyes to see four guards having to literally drag the team leader. The man's eyes were wide open with terror and he was sobbing uncontrollably. The guards dropped him unceremoniously at King Attalee's feet. Tymbo looked up and then shrank away from the boy sitting in the chair.

Attalee was covered in blood and his once proud gray and scarlet cloak was tattered and dirty.

This must be the torturer. Look, the blood of his victims still covers his clothes. Tymbo began to wail louder at the prospect of the torture he was sure would soon be forthcoming. "No, no, please I beg you. Spare me and my men."

The king looked taken aback by the man's comment and frowned. Then he ordered, "Cut this man loose."

A guard stepped forward and cut the rope that held his hands together.

The team leader rubbed his wrists to get the circulation back into his fingers. Now that his hands were free, he would have a chance to fight before the torture began. Hopefully, he would be killed before they could tie him up again.

"Bring another chair and some food for my guest."

Soon Tymbo was seated in a chair across from the king and food was set on a tray across their laps. A manservant brought a bowl of water to each man. The Quranian frowned until he saw Attalee place his hands into the water and then wipe them off with a cloth. *What a waste of water.* Grabbing the bowl, Tymbo drank it down, oblivious of the water running down his shirt. Ignoring the cloth, he wiped his mouth on a sleeve.

A tray of fruit was brought next and the man looked at it suspiciously. "It is not poisoned," Attalee said as he took a piece of fruit from the tray and began eating it. Knowing the king spoke the truth, Tymbo greedily ate the food, his eyes never leaving the king. Attalee ate his food slowly and likewise watched Tymbo.

With a belch, Attalee wiped his mouth with his sleeve and sat back in his chair. "Are you the senior man among the prisoners?" he asked Tymbo. Tymbo stiffened in his seat and Attalee could see him swallowing hard and clenching his jaw. Sweat broke out on his forehead and upper lip. He began to tremble so hard, he dropped the grapes he was eating and almost fell out of his chair in a faint.

"By the Gods," Attalee swore, "what is wrong with you, man?"

Tymbo fell to his knees, pleadingly, "I do not want to die. I do not want to be tortured. Please…spare me…please…" he sobbed.

"Ah, now I see," the king whispered as he bent down on one knee. "I am not sure who told you that I was going to torture you, Team Leader Tymbo, but that person wasn't correct."

"You aren't going to kill me?" he asked in disbelief.

Attalee looked him in the eyes. "As king of the New Roman Republic, you have my word that not a hair on your head will be harmed as long as you don't engage in mischief or try to escape."

"I'm not going to be tortured?" he asked again.

Attalee had a look of disgust on his face. "I have given you my word, Quranian. I don't treat prisoners of war in that manner."

"Why did you call me here then?"

"I need to know if you are the highest ranking officer so you could be put in charge of the other prisoners. Mainly, to allocate their daily food rations and most importantly, to maintain order. As you well know, we have an unprovoked war to attend to and even though it would be easier for me and my men to just slaughter the whole group of you than to guard you, I won't and I repeat, will not allow you to be harmed.

"So it is your responsibility, Team Leader Tymbo, to keep your men in line. Don't attempt to escape or cause mischief, and you and your men will be set free at the end of the hostilities. Please bring your wounded to the gate so they can be seen by our healer. Do you understand your responsibilities.?"

The man began to weep uncontrollably in relief. "I understand and thank you," he buried his head in his hands.

"Take him back," Attalee ordered. As soon as the prisoner had been taken away, Attalee sat back down and then slumped over in the chair, fast asleep. Carefully, his men carried him to his room and the attendants stripped him of his bloody clothes. They washed the blood and grime from his body. He didn't stir once during the bath, so deep was his exhaustion. Attalee was snoring softly as the attendants closed the door to let him sleep. Two loyal guards blocked the door and sent away the senators trying to see the king.

***

Major Raki ordered his men to help General Cae to his room also. The soldiers were lucky they had disarmed the general before attempting to move him, as several were bruised from the encounter. Cae told them to leave him alone. He would sleep where he was needed, which was at the wall in case the Quranians attacked during the night. In any event, he was to be notified immediately. Leaving a squad of solders near the general, Raki wanted the general to have a force of men ready and waiting. Now it was time for the major to try and get some rest.

The general was one of the few men who could come out of a deep sleep, instantly take in the situation and start yelling orders. Major Raki hoped someday he could learn to do this, but it seemed it was an instinctive ability rather than a learned one.

***

The Warrior and Caiisa came to heal the wounded Quranians and to determine which men were beyond hope. There were over five hundred men to keep under guard and Raki had two Scorpios set up outside the gate to the slums to quash any thought of them trying to escape.

The prisoners had seen this weapon in action and they shrank back away in fear from the gate. Tymbo made his way through his men and passed on the message he had been given by the Roman king.

Major Raki had ordered the dead Quranians be wrapped in sheets and lowered over the wall. The bodies disappeared during the night.

***

Roman solders arrived with food, jugs of water and blankets. Handing them through the bars of the gate, Tymbo made sure each man received his share. Even though the men were grateful for the food and water, they curled up in their blankets. It was obvious they were badly demoralized. They had to be wondering what was in store for them now. The men were no longer in control of their own destiny.

The team leader took his blanket and shuffled off to find a corner to sleep in. He didn't care what he ate or where he slept. He was just happy to be alive. Someday, he hoped to get back home to his wife and children. He knew deep in his heart he wasn't a warrior or a leader of men. Tymbo was just a simple hunter, albeit with the right family connections to Chief Messa, which was the only reason he had been picked as a team leader.

No matter what family connections he had, he was a dead man. Tymbo was starting to hope the Romans would win the war.

As he sat among the men, he thought about his botched attempt to take the wall. He contemplated how miserably he had failed. When the war was over, he knew Chief Messa would behead him and set his head on a stake as an example to the rest of the team leaders. Maybe the men could have been rallied into a counterattack, but then he shook his head. The men were all like him, they weren't warriors either. A mouse fart could send them into a rampaging panic that not even the Great Chief Messa or Battle Master Thom could stop.

He chuckled to himself. "A mouse fart."

"What did you say?" a man close to him asked.

"Oh nothing...nothing," Tymbo said as his mind slowly began to become unhinged. "Just loving life and enjoying these lovely quarters we've been given." His laugh turned maniacal. A Roman guard outside the gate shivered in the night air as the laughter echoed through the slums.

***

Chenee made her way through the wounded. Most of the men who had been able to make it back to the base camp had simply dropped from exhaustion and slept where they had fallen. She cleaned and bandaged their wounds as carefully as she could, but some still cried out in their sleep as the Ja, Ja root water was poured into their wounds and the acid began to eat the bacteria away.

Taking crushed goldenseal, she would pack the deeper wounds to stop the bleeding and place a clean bandage over them. For the severely injured men, Chenee would cut the heart out of the Ja, Ja root and slip a piece between their cheek and gum to let its narcotic effect help ease their pain or their death. There were hundreds of men with injuries and she worked through the night. As the twin suns broke over the mountains, she finished with the last wounded man. Sinking gratefully onto the ground, she curled up in a blanket and went to sleep, dreaming of Ka'an and King Attalee.

***

The next morning, Thom walked among his men and despaired at how exhausted they looked. He was aware Chenee had worked on the wounded during the night. At least she was doing something useful. Damn the girl for withholding information on how to destroy Ka'an. Not that he could blame Chenee. Her father had sent Chenee with the hope she would be killed by the Romans.

Instead, the girl had succeeded in getting information and was returned by the Roman king with a message of peace. When his daughter had returned to their camp, rather than being overjoyed she had the news he wanted, the chief had pulled Chenee off her horse and then ground her face into the ground still wet with his urine. He had berated her in front of the whole tribe and told her she was a failure.

But a spark of suppressed anger was ignited in the girl and she stepped in and grabbed the chief's sword. Chenee proceeded to tell Chief Messa how he had failed her as a father and how he was failing their people as the chief of the Quranian people. Deep down, the chief knew her words were true. He had found himself powerless to respond. Chenee told him if he ever touched her again, he would die and from the look in her eyes, Chief Messa the Fifth believed her.

***

Thom called his team leaders together. "The men will rest today and we will prepare to re-join the battle on the morrow. Now leave me. I have much to think about."

He returned to his tower, looking out over the battlefield and then at his map. The catapults had been highly effective against the columns, but being spread out, they were largely ineffective against

96

personnel. As battle master, he had to think of a way to use his weapons more effectively. They had the superior numbers, so why had they not been able to take the wall when they had overwhelmed an entire section?

True, the team leader had been incompetent, chosen only because he had family connections to Chief Messa. *Still, we should have been able to capitalize on taking the wall and keeping it as a staging area for more troops.*

Tymbo should have waited until there were several thousand men on the wall before attacking, as had been his orders.

Instead, the idiot had led his forces in a headlong rush, which strung out his soldiers and allowed the Romans to outflank and then surround him. But, most importantly, the Romans had been able to cut off the troops coming up the ladders. This is where the problem was most clear, but what could he do to counteract this threat?

The statue on the wall was leaning towards him, a smirk graced the God's face. He shook his fist in anger and shouted his defiance. How he hated the smug look on the statue's face. Turning his back on the damn thing, he tried to figure out what to do.

You were a fool, Tymbo, he thought as he spat on the ground. Of course, in the face of the new weapon, he would have panicked too. But he wouldn't admit his fear to anyone. Tymbo had failed.

Now what was he to do. *Think, Battle Master Thom, think.* He pounded the table in frustration. The catapults were ineffective against personnel, because they had been spread out. Um...

He looked at the map again and began to move the rocks that represented the catapults into a new formation. *Yes, it might work,* he smiled and pulled on his beard. Calling the team leaders together, he discussed his new plan and they all agreed it was a good idea. He sent them back to tell the rest of the men and to prepare to move the catapults.

The top of the wall was filled with broken columns and arches, but his idea to break through it had been ineffective. The wall seemed to be made out of a think, hard quartz and the rocks didn't even seem to have any effect on it. Not a crack, or a scuff mark. So they would have to go over the top to take the city. Hopefully, the Chosen would be terrorized into submission, but he doubted it would work. The Romans would have to be utterly destroyed before they would submit to Quranian rule.

Well, he would do everything in his power to make them surrender, even if he had to expend every last one of his men to do it. They would be victorious in the end. Thom shook his head. *No...I will be victorious in the end.*

He would wipe the smile off that damn statue's face.

***

The Romans awoke to find the Quranians hard at work moving the catapults to new positions along the wall. Realizing the Barbarians weren't going to launch another attack, General Cae gave the men and women the day off and rotated the legions on guard duty every two hours. Word was passed down the ranks to prepare for the battle to resume in the morning. While the soldiers rested, their families worked through the day to make new arrows and sharpen their swords.

Attalee and General Cae climbed to the top of the wall and watched as the catapults were moved to five strategic points, so he ordered his troops to move in position to protect the wall at those sites. Cae rubbed his chin and looked over the battle plans on his map.

"What are you thinking, General?"

"When the savages were trying to use the ladders to attack, they used the catapults to try and keep our men off sections of the wall so they could climb up them. Fortunately for us, the catapults were spaced too far apart and we could employ the shield defense to protect our archers and take the ladders from them."

"So you think the tighter formation of the catapults will be more effective against the shield defense?"

Cae nodded.

"Will Thom try another ladder attack at the catapult locations?"

"No," Cae said deep in thought. "The ladders are too easily upset by the wall defenders and only a few men can climb at a time. I would bet my next week's pay, he'll try to build ramps up the wall so he can use the overwhelming force he has at his command."

Attalee looked at him in mock surprise, "Next week's pay? You mean you're getting paid for all this?"

Cae began to laugh and then looked embarrassed. "To be honest, I rarely ask to be paid.

I just love my job so much. Where else could I work only a few hours a day and have weekends off with pay?"

The general and the king looked at each other over the table with grave serious looks, then they both started to laugh rather boisterously. The strain of the battle the day before had finally come to a head.

Attalee had to wipe his eyes with a cloth. The looks the soldiers walking by gave them sent them both into another round of laughter. Finally, they had to catch their breath and Attalee waved the cloth in surrender. "Cae, you are hilarious. Let's take our act on the road and entertain the masses. We could probably make more money than we are now."

Leaning on the table, Cae chuckled. "Do you think we could find two men crazy enough to take on our jobs right now?"

"Not with the pay we're getting," Attalee said and they again broke out in gales of laughter.

Gasping, Cae held up his hand. "Enough of this joking, we have a bloody battle to plan here…"

"Alright, alright," Attalee said, trying to catch his breath and holding his side. "So you think the Quranians will try to build a ramp up the wall?"

"That's what I would do," he wiped his own eyes.

"What if we put our archers off to each side of the impact zone and hit the ramps builders in a crossfire?"

"The catapults will cover an area that will reduce the effectiveness of our archers."

"How about the Scorpio?"

"We can use it, but I think we will still be at a disadvantage."

"I wonder if Dav would have any ideas."

"Maybe," Cae said, but he was still deep in thought. He stared out into the night sky and went quiet.

***

That damned statue of Zeus was standing on the wall, looking at the battle master with a bored smile on its face. Why, the damn thing was actually yawning.

Thom spit on the ground and kicked dirt toward the wall as he tried to ignore it. The team leaders watched the battle master as he occasionally looked at the figure on the wall and shouted out a curse or raised a hand in anger.

Thom was pleased the catapults were being moved so quickly. The men's morale improved as he walked among them and complimented their work. He had tried to speak to Chief Messa about his plans, but the old man was too busy playing with his woman prisoner. Deep in a Ja, Ja root daze, the chief was taking coals from the fire and laying them on the woman's skin as she tried to crawl away from him.

Messa would grab the tether tied around her throat and pull her back to him, laughing at his victim's screams of terror. Sexually aroused, he grabbed her hips and savagely plunged his limp member between her legs.

Thom had walked in as he was riding the woman and the smell of burnt flesh was strong in the air. Even though this was a Roman woman, he still felt pity for her. *What kind of beast has the chief become?*

He wasn't the only one having second thoughts about the chief. Even the men were grumbling when the chief pulled the women along behind him like an animal everywhere he went. Equally disturbing was he always made the woman walk around nude, even on the coldest mornings. She hadn't taken a bath since she'd been captured and the smell from the tent was atrocious.

"Chief Messa," Thom said loudly. The chief turned toward him and the battle master was shocked at the look of insane glee in the chief's eyes.

"Would you like to have fun with my pet?" he asked, chuckling.

Thom shook his head in the negative. "I need your council, Chief Messa. We're planning another campaign tomorrow and I would like your advice, sir."

The chief's features turned dark. He hated being disturbed when he was having so much fun. Sighing, he threw the coal back into the fire and kicked the woman out of the way. "Come on then," he screamed in resignation. "Let's go see what you've messed up now."

The battle master didn't like the chief's tone of voice and the fury of emotion threatened to overwhelm him. For the first time in his life, Thom despised his boyhood friend. While good men were out on the battlefield dying, the chief was more interested in torturing a poor, defenseless Roman woman.

102

Thom was beginning to realize his chief and the Supreme Ruler of the Quranians was a coward. This realization hit Thom like a sword in the gut and he once again thought about issuing the Challenge.

Then Chief Messa surprised him. "You have done well, Battle Master Thom." The chief clapped him on the back. As they walked among the troops, the chief would call out to the men by name and ask them how they were doing and inquire about their injuries. Messa seemed to have a perfect memory when it came to his men and could recall something as simple as a strained ankle two years ago, or the exact date and time of another man's birth and how many children he had.

It was a trait that endeared him to the people and they began to cheer as he passed through the camp.

Thom's loyalty was torn. He knew the chief was on a path to self- destruction and would probably take his people with him, yet Thom truly loved his old friend. Deep in his heart, Thom knew he couldn't issue the Challenge.

Messa seemed reenergized by walking through the camp and seemed like his old self again. *If I can just keep him out of that tent, maybe the chief would take an interest in life, in his people, like he did in the old days.*

They climbed the ladder to the tower and looked over his map. "I think you have a much better attack plan here than before, Thom." The chief pounded him on the back so hard, he thought it would break. He prepared to leave.

"Would you like to join me for lunch, Chief Messa?" he asked hesitantly. Messa stopped for a moment and looked at him and frowned. "My bones are hurting me, my friend. I need to get some more Ja, Ja root and I need to attend to my pet. Perhaps another time…"

He tried to hide his disappointment by turning his back to the chief and acting like he was studying the battle plans. In a short while, Thom could hear the woman's tortured screams and he kicked the table in frustration. What did he have to do to get through to that man? *This whole damn campaign is resting on my shoulders now…*

***

"Battle Master Thom, we meet again!" Thom glanced up to see the former Roman Councilor Eliam looking over his shoulder at the battle plans. Thom turned the animal hide over.

This caused Eliam to smirk. "I see you've made good use of the catapults I gave you."

The savage sat and looked at him. "You betrayed me and went behind my back!"

"Now, now, Thom. Don't get upset at your old friend Eliam. I knew you were busy with the battle plans and were surrounded by your men. I had to pass the information along somehow. I couldn't just ride into your camp in full Roman armor and expect to make it to you, so your chief was the next logical choice."

"Yet here you are in broad daylight and within sight of the wall."

"I have betrayed no one but my homeland, Thom. Until I could escape the city, I had to keep my plans and identity secret. Now that everyone knows I'm a traitor, I no longer need to sneak into the camp. I can ride in and ride out as I please."

What a cocky bastard he is. This was an enemy who couldn't be trusted and Thom would make sure his men kept an eye on the councilor's comings and goings. Any man who would turn on his country, for whatever reason, was someone who should be killed when his usefulness was over. It would be good to get rid of him, but he still might have information Thom would need.

Eliam watched as the emotions played across Thom's face. If he made one wrong move, the savage would be dead. But the man's body relaxed as he decided he might still have use for the former councilor.

"What do you have for me?" Thom asked.

Eliam smiled. The savage was stupid, but Thom still needed him.

"Remember what I told you about building the ramps up the wall?" He bent over and began to draw in the dirt. "There is something else you can try, but it will take a little longer. You build a tower in the shape of a giant ramp and then tilt it over and let it fall against the wall. It will allow you to hit one section with all your forces."

Tom looked at the plan. "We'll go with the first idea you gave us. We're running out of time."

***

Eliam sat back on his heels. Building the ramps up the wall would actually take longer and cost the battle master more casualties, but Eliam wasn't going to let him know that now. He wanted the

105

Quranians to lose as many men as possible. Then he would destroy them all.

"If that's what you want to do, then I'll leave you to it. I'll stop back in a few weeks to see if there's anything else I can do to help."

Thom forced a smile. "I look forward to your return."

Eliam had to suppress a laugh. Taking his rag dipped in vinegar, he held it under his nose. Unlike the chief, at least the battle master took a bath occasionally and didn't smell of rotting animal flesh. The barbarian still smelled of sweat and human stink. Climbing on his horse, he kicked it in the sides and took off toward the northeast passage.

***

Dav was seated at her workbench in the shopkeeper's storeroom. She smiled as King Attalee and General Cae walked in.

"Well, I have two visitors to see the mad scientist," Dav said with an evil laugh.

Attalee and Cae looked at each other. "Mad scientist?" Attalee asked. Chuckling, she explained, "I'm making reference to kings that keep men in the dungeon to work on making new and terrifying weapons to be used against their enemies."

"Oh," Cae said as he shook his head. "Why would anyone do that?"

"I'm not sure if it happened or not, but that's how it was portrayed in the stories I heard when I was growing up," she explained.

"It sounds like a terrible thing to do to a person," Attalee said with a touch of distaste in his voice.

"I agree," Dav said. "So what brings you two here today?"

"We need some advice," Cae looked embarrassed.

"You do?" she asked, brushing a strand of hair behind her ear so she could hear him better.

Cae took out a scroll and laid it on the table. He showed her the layout of the catapults and explained what he thought Thom was planning for the next Quranian attack.

"You think he'll attempt to build ramps up the wall?"

"I believe so," he grimaced.

"What will they build the ramps out of? Wood or stone?"

"With their skill with woodworking, I think they'll probably be made of wood."

Scratching her nose, Dav thought about the problem. "You already had the solution earlier, General Cae. Get me some lamp oil, a cloth and a wine bottle."

Cae frowned. He had never asked for these items. "How will these items help us?" the general sputtered. He had expected her to come up with another terrifying weapon, like the Scorpio.

"I know it doesn't sound like much, but it will be very effective against the ramps and the people building them." Attalee and Cae looked at each other and shrugged. "Trust me," Dav said as they left the shop and walked out into the sunlight.

"Have you been busy?" Attalee asked Dav as they walked along the street toward the wall.

"If I may use one of the general's expressions, 'By the Gods', yes I have been busy. Can't you see the dark circles and bags under my eyes? I haven't slept more than a few hours the last few weeks and I'm starting to feel like a mad scientist."

"You look pretty good to me," Cae said and then grew embarrassed again as Attalee threw him a smile.

"Flattery will get you anything you want, dear General." She took his arm in hers.

"Would you two like to be alone?" Attalee put a hand over his mouth to try and hide his amusement.

"Yes," General Cae said.

"No," Dav said at the same time and then they laughed together. "Later, General, after I show you my new weapon." She punched him playfully on the arm.

"Alright then," he looked dejected. "I know how it is with you captains. All you think about is war, war, war. Divide and conquer, weapons of destruction and the whole bit."

Dav stopped and put her hands on her hip. "Now wait a minute. You two came looking for me, for advice I might add, on a weapon, not the other way around. There I was, working hard at my table…"

"Sleeping…" Cae whispered and received a dirty look from Dav.

She continued, "When I was rudely interrupted and you forced me to come with you."

108

"Forced you to come with us?" Attalee asked. "Is this another one of your stories?"

Dav tried to look hurt, but couldn't keep from laughing. "I never can stay angry at you two. You always act so innocent."

"You actually think it's an act?"

Dav started to laugh at them and both the general and king tried to look hurt. "Come on, you two. I don't have all day to stand in the street and banter with you. We do have a war going on."

"Why wasn't I informed of this?" Cae demanded of Attalee. "I thought it was the Senate's responsibility to tell you."

"I'm always the last one to know." Cae looked sad and sighed.

"You are such a fraud," Dav said and she started to run as Cae chased after her. "Ah, young love," Attalee shouted and began to chase after her too.

CHAPTER FOUR

Chenee watched as the catapults were moved into new positions. The little girl she had rescued from the front of her father's tent was following her around as she checked on the wounded and changed the men's bandages. The girl was no more than twelve summers old with long, black hair.

After cleaning the child and dressing her in some furs, the girl had lain in a fetal position for a few days. She would shy away from Chenee when she brought food, but eventually, the child's hunger overcame her fear and when she realized the woman was trying to help her, the girl began to follow her like a lost wolf pup looking for its mother.

Chenee had been disgusted at what her father had done to the child and from the comments she overheard some of the soldiers making, they too had been appalled. It became important to her to keep the little girl away from her father's tent so the child wouldn't hear her mother's screams of terror and agony. The realization her father had lost his mind began to sink in.

The Quranian people were starting to splinter into small groups with different loyalties. Most were still loyal to Chief Messa, but Battle Master Thom was also attracting a much smaller, but loyal, following. Then there was still a large faction distrustful of both men and if the chance arose, they would slip quietly off into the woods and return to their semi-nomadic ways.

They hated having to stay in one location for so long and tension was thick in the camp. Fights were beginning to flare up over small disputes and several men had even killed each other. She could only sit back and watch as her father and Thom led their people down the path of self-destruction.

Chenee knew her people couldn't win this battle and in the end, they would be defeated. In the worst case, they would be utterly destroyed and wiped from this planet. Chief Messa should have listened when she told him the Romans wanted peace.

Instead, he had turned on her, as he had all her life. Chenee knew her mother had died soon after her birth and whenever she'd tried to learn anything about her, she'd received nothing but a stony silence from her father. Her older brother wasn't permitted to talk about their mother and only made vague references or said he couldn't remember.

A distant aunt had told Chenee her mother was a HighBorn of House Netter, one of the Ruling Families of the Plains, and her name was Jaffna Chenee Netter. The House of Netter was one of the few Roman Families who traded with the Barbarians. The young Messa had met and fallen in love with the HighBorn and she, in turn, returned his affection.

It had caused quite a scandal on both sides of the border when the HighBorn had run away with the Barbarian. Chenee had been shocked to learn she was half Roman. It helped her understand why her father hated the Romans so much. It was funny how everything had come full circle now that she was in love with a Roman! Was that why he had struck her when she first returned to him? Had he suspected she'd fallen in love with a Roman, like he had in his youth?

Her aunt had also told her that her father's abuse was because of her mother's death. The guilt was a heavy burden for a child to bear and it haunted her dreams.

Afraid to sleep, she would lay awake at night, and try to visualize what her mother had looked like. The aunt said they could have been twins. Her people had always whispered her features were different from the other Quranians and her skin was much darker. It would explain why she was shunned as being different, an outcast. The thought depressed her. She was tired of not being wanted by her father or her people.

Chenee had few friends when she was growing up and spent most of her time in the forest or with the hermit.

The hermit was considered by all to be a future seer and people would travel for many days to ask him a question. Usually the answer would only bring more questions and it was frustrating in that he would only answer one inquiry. He'd taken Chenee under his wing and taught her about the herbs in the forest and the delicate balance in nature. She was the only one who would receive answers to multiple questions. He would also ask her questions that didn't make sense. He acted like he had never been around humans before and wanted to know why they acted a certain way. It had puzzled her until she remember his solitary lifestyle.

The hermit lived in a cave and led a simple existence. Unlike most of her people, he didn't follow the migration of animals. Her question to him had been what her mother had looked like.

Grabbing his walking stick, the hermit motioned for her to follow. Hobbling painfully down the path to a small pond, he bent over to look in.

Wondering what he was looking at, she also peered down into the water and could see her reflection.

"Now you know what your mother looked like," he muttered as he walked away.

Studying her reflection, she concluded her mother had been very beautiful indeed.

One time, the hermit had taken her to the Middle Sea to collect Ja, Ja root. The plant grew in the water and sent its roots deep into the soil. The root could be dug up, cut off and used for various medicinal purposes. As far as she knew, it was the only plant able to survive in water. There were quite tasty fish as well, if one could find a place the Ja, Ja root hadn't branched out and overgrown the bank.

The plant could grow up to two miles from the Middle Sea and she saw stems that looked like tree trunks. In the early spring, Ja, Ja roots sprouted foot long stems of fragrant blossoms, yielding an intoxicating bouquet of smell and colors. The flowers could be harvested, crushed and the liquid squeezed to produce a thick wine. It had to be watered down though and would make anyone who drank it dizzy and happy all at the same time. Or it could be left as a thick syrup and used as a tea for illness.

The Middle Sea never froze in the wintertime because heat still bubbled up from the center of the planet and kept the water warm. The Ja, Ja root seemed to thrive on the rich volcanic soil and the hermit told her the area they lived in had actually been one large volcano in the planet's early days.

As she sat by the little girl, she felt a bit sad the hermit had disappeared when she was older. The time she spent with him had been among the happiest of her life. Well, one of the few.

She could still remember a talk about the mountains and how they hemmed everyone in like a bowl. He'd told her there wouldn't be enough food for everyone, and within twenty years, there would be mass starvation throughout the land.

Chenee asked if there was a way across the mountains and he'd chuckled. "All obstacles can be overcome if one is so inclined to try. Some obstacles are physical, some are mental. Someday, your race will overcome the mental obstacles and then the physical will melt away."

She had been puzzled by his answer and he had refused to elaborate. It would aggravate her when he would say something and then not explain his statement. Soon after, the Quranians started having problems finding food and tried to move out on the plains to find substance, only to be beaten back by the Romans time and time again.

The Quranians learned to terrace the mountainsides to grow their food but it never seemed to be enough to feed the exploding population. Chenee knew someday the hermit's words would come true and the population would outpace the land's ability to feed them.

Then the plague had struck the Roman city of Ka'an. Over half the population was decimated before the sickness had run its course. Chief Messa had sent one of his men to ask the hermit if the plague would strike the Quranians as well and Chenee had wondered the same thing. The hermit had said the plague was from the dirty living conditions in the city. As long as they stayed away from the Romans, the Quranians would be spared.

Chief Messa had ordered no further contact with any Roman and they had been bypassed by the plague, just as the hermit predicted.

With the Roman Republic in a weakened state, the Quranians could try to win back control of the land and the right to once again return to their semi-nomadic ways. A way of life they had been following for millions of years.

When Chenee had been told she was to be sent to Ka'an as a spy, she had been overjoyed at the prospect of helping her father. Their relationship over the years of her childhood had been stormy at best and she felt like he was reaching out to her in his own way.

Now that she had returned, Chenee realized he'd wanted the Romans to find out she was a spy and possibly kill or imprison her for the offense. No one could have predicted what had happened between her and Attalee. She hadn't been looking for love in Ka'an. On the contrary, she had been seeking a way to destroy the Romans. Instead, she had fallen in love with a young HighBorn who also turned out to be the new king.

Chenee laughed to herself and then was soberly reminded of her deception. It was sad to think about the lies she had told and the guilt was overwhelming. Attalee had been hurt by them and she felt a deep depression and sadness that consumed her very soul.

She herself had been hurt all her life by people. People she thought she could trust and Chenee had learned to hold any true feelings deep inside and not let anyone know she had been hurt. She had built an invisible wall of protection and wouldn't let herself feel anything. In the past, she had learned emotions were a bad thing. To experience emotions only invited pain and hurt, so she closed herself off and developed the ability to clamp down on her feelings, to utterly and completely control them.

On the outside, she always looked so happy, so confident. Inside, she was torn by indecision and self-doubt. Deep down, she really hated herself and her inability to stand up to her father. Hated her inability to be in command of her feelings of helplessness and her lack of control over all aspects of her life.

No matter what task she was given to learn, Chenee worked the hardest to master it to perfection. Many a time, her teachers had told her to slow down when she'd dropped from exhaustion, but she would just push herself harder. Never could she overcome the feelings of low self-esteem and the nagging self- doubt about her abilities. Failure wasn't tolerated in the Messa family and that fact had been ingrained into her very being from early childhood. It was also the reason why it had been so hard for her to return to her father. Chenee had failed for the first time in her life and it was a blow to her ego.

Even now, she didn't know why she had finally stood up to her father. It could have been all the pent up anger from the years of abuse.

Messa hadn't realized Chenee had given up the chance of true love with Attalee to return. Her rage had filled her and she told him exactly how she felt and was shocked when Chief Messa backed down. It was an empowering experience for Chenee to release all those years of anger and pain. To actually let herself feel emotions, to laugh, to cry when she wanted.

Never again would she allow herself to be hurt by anyone and not let them know. Never again would she feel guilty for being angry, or lie, or hurt another by telling lies. Someday, she would return to Ka'an and beg Attalee for his forgiveness. She had been wrong and deeply regretted her actions in the past.

It was time to look forward to the future, to heal the mental wounds caused by childhood and to become an adult. To become a feeling and emotional person.

Chenee sat down and unwrapped the cloth from around her foot. Some dirt had lodged between the skin and bone, causing stabbing pain as she tried to walk. The little girl, taking water and a cloth, began to help clean the dirt.

Grateful, Chenee sat back and watched as the child used a stick to dig the dirt out. Taking Ja, Ja root and putting it in a stone bowl, the child took a pestle and began to crush it, exactly as she had seen Chenee do it. Adding water to the fibrous powder and mixing it together, the child made a paste. She then used a flat stick to brush and push the mixture between the flap of skin and bone. Taking a clean skin, the girl wrapped it tight and used a cord to bind it. Then she stepped back to see what Chenee would do. The smile from Chenee was all the thanks the child needed.

Taking the girl's hand in hers, Chenee led her toward their tent. "Come, little child. It is time for your supper. I'll protect you." The girl looked up gratefully at her and smiled. The smile warmed Chenee's heart and she smiled back.

***

Toka had just finished his nap and was getting dressed when he was summoned to dinner by Councilor Toka. He and Josf started to walk to the grand hall. The smell of spicy meat floated through the air and his stomach growled in anticipation. The councilor looked up as the men entered the room and he frowned when he saw the slave. "You won't need your manservant here to wait on you. I have plenty."

"He's my friend, not a servant. He has come to help with the defense of the city."

"Is that so?" The councilor's face hardened. "Well, please sit and eat. My house is your house."

Toka could tell the master of the house wasn't pleased the slave had been allowed to stay. The new king had freed them and felt they should be treated as citizens of the Republic. Leaning back on the low couch, he rearranged the pillow and reached for a bowl of grapes. Josf looked uncomfortable, so Toka handed him a bowl and as he sampled the food, would pass it to his friend.

"You're going to fight with the Roman army," the councilor began. His toga kept slipping down as he moved and subconsciously, he pulled it back up

118

over his shoulder. The young Toka had never liked togas and preferred to just wear a long overshirt with a sword belt or armor to hold it closed. Togas were irritating because they always had to be readjusted over the shoulders and patted down with chalk to keep them whitened.

"I was very saddened by your father's death," the councilor said. "He was a great man."

Toka didn't know how to respond, so he sat quietly and chewed on a piece of the spicy meat.

Sensing the boy was uncomfortable, he changed the subject. "Have you met the new king?"

"I haven't had the honor. What's his name?"

"Attalee. Of the House of Ceran."

Toka sat up. "Attalee? We saw him on the road as we arrived. He was directing the refugees to form lines on their way to the city."

Councilor Toka chuckled. "Just a few days ago, Attalee held the threat of life or death over us and was kind enough to listen as we told him of the treachery of one of the other councilors. Luckily, Major Raki, who is General Cae's right hand, had seen the man's awful deeds and freed us. We had thought we were to be put to death!"

"That was very kind of him."

"It was, but I would like to see him stripped of the kingship of the Republic."

"Really? Why?"

"He's just a boy, with the outlook of a child. We need a leader with more experience and wisdom. His removal from the position wouldn't be a great loss."

Toka frowned and looked at Josf.

119

"There's a movement within the Senate to take back power from the boy king, but we're hampered in our efforts since Attalee is backed by the military."

"What you're suggesting sounds like treason."

The elder Toka began to laugh. "It's only treason if one gets caught." Toka shifted uncomfortably on his couch.

"If you're interested in helping, we could use all the men we can get."

"The Republic is at war and you're working to overthrow the government?"

"It's a minor pursuit. Just a game for some of us Senators. With the war starting up, we have so little to fill our time."

Toka took a drink of his wine to hide the look of distaste on his face. Personally, he had been impressed with the new king.

Councilor Toka began to speak of other matters and seemed able to talk for hours without saying anything. Meanwhile, plate after plate of food was brought in and set before them. After hours of wine and food, Toka begged his forgiveness and asked to leave and get some rest.

"My servants will show you back to your room."

"Thank you for your hospitality."

"I hope to see you in the morning."

"Good evening, Councilor."

Back in his room, Toka lay on the blanket and looked out the window at the stars, troubled by what he had heard.

***

Caiisa heard the voice again. "Halt!" it screamed in her head. Startled, she stopped as a large rock crumbled off a building and landed where she would have been standing. As she made her way through the wounded, the voice would keep her safe by directing her movements. Her eyes narrowed in anger.

"Damn you, Hades," she whispered. The God was trying to kill her. If not for Athena's warnings, she would be dead by now. She had been working hard to keep men and women from dying and it would appear her plan was working. The God of the Death World was becoming desperate and wanted her out of the way.

Whenever she saw one of the tentacle creatures, Caiisa would spear it until the slime faded from existence.

Athena had been by the temple to congratulate the priestess on her progress.

"Hades grows weaker every day," Athena crowed to Caiisa, the Warrior and Thudder. "You'll be able to kill him soon."

"Do I really need to kill him? Can't we try talking to him?

Athena looked at her. "You are so innocent, my child. I have forgotten those days of my youth when I looked at the world with such trusting eyes. He won't stop until one of you is dead. That is the way of the Gods. He and I both realize this is a conflict neither dares lose."

"Why does anyone have to lose? We can make peace with Hades and make it easier for people to die."

Athena's laugh drifted through the temple. "When the time comes, Caiisa, you must kill Hades."

"And if I don't?"

A dark look crossed the Goddess' face and then was replaced with a gentle smile. "You will, my child. He will give you no other choice but to kill him." Caiisa sat and looked at the Goddess. The dark look had frightened her and made her mad. Caiisa had the feeling Athena was doing something behind her back. Something that would affect them all. Could she depend on Thudder and the Warrior to help her if she had to disobey the Goddess?

"Now," Athena turned to the two men, "I want you to keep a close eye on my priestess. Make sure the God of the Death World is unable to reach her."

Walking over to Caiisa, Athena placed a knife in her hand. "If he is able to get to you, this is the only weapon that will kill him. A knife made from stone. Keep it with you always, for you never know when he might strike."

Taking the knife, Caiisa placed it in her pouch. Before she used it, Caiisa was going to talk to Hades first and try to get him to change. If he wouldn't, she be left with no other option than to use the knife.

"I must go now," Caiisa informed the Goddess.

"I understand," Athena said. "I'm sure all this talk of fighting has upset your delicate nature."

Nodding, Caiisa bowed and walked out.

When she was gone, Athena motioned the Warrior and Thudder to come to her. "If she is unable or unwilling to fulfill her duties, one of you must kill Hades and then I will rule the Death

World." The Warrior began to laugh. It was the first sound he had made since coming on this mission. Thudder began to laugh with him, even though he didn't know why.

***

General Cae dodged a rock from the catapult and worked his way across the top of the wall with his new weapon. Using his shield to fend off arrows, he threw the bottle down onto the ramp builders. He watched as it broke on one of the supports and oil splattered on wood and man alike. The burning rag from the bottle hit the oil and caught fire. Soldiers and builders screamed in terror as it ignited.

Retreating to get another bottle, he dodged another rock and then watched in terror as it bounced off one of the fallen columns and rebounded into a group of soldiers carrying the firebombs. Bodies were crushed by the rocks and the firebombs exploded and caught his men on fire. Quickly, he took his cloak off and tried to smother the flames as another rock bounced over the wall and almost took his head off. Dragging the wounded toward the steps, he helped get them to safety and returned to the battle.

All along the wall, he could see the smoke from their firebombs as they tried to burn the ramps. General Cae was sure the Barbarians would have attacked yesterday, but all they had observed was the enemy felling trees and dragging them to the wall. Their craftsman had notched the ends so they could be linked together and early in the morning, the godforsaken savages had attacked.

Dav helped General Cae put two ideas together to make a weapon to counter the ramp building. She had heard General Cae talking one evening about using bladders to drop oil on the enemy and then throwing torches down to start fires. Her invention, or reinvention, had all the components in one object. It was a weapon the Quranians hadn't counted on. Even now, the Barbarians were milling around in confusion.

The team leaders were screaming at their men to return to building the ramps while trying to stay out of the way of the burning oil. Two of the ramps had been reduced to ashes and a third was burning rapidly. The catapults were highly effective in keeping the Roman archers away from the ramp builders, but the Barbarians had little defense against the firebombs. The Scorpios had greater range than the archers and they were also taking a toll.

Thom had ordered ladder attacks against the Scorpios, but the Romans countered with their long shield defense and stationed archers as a counter measure. One of the team leaders started having his men carry sacks of dirt to throw on the fires. It seemed to help to blanket the wood and keep it from burning quite so easily.

Thom had his men use their shields to deflect the oil. They would then be open to getting hit by the iron lances of the Scorpios or arrows from the Roman archers. The casualties on the Quranian side were tremendous as the day wore on.

The smoke was so heavy at times, men on both sides had to leave their positions and retreat to get a breath of fresh air. Attalee directed the wounded to Athena's temple for healing and worked to make sure the men and women were relieved on a regular basis to reduce their exhaustion.

The catapults were very effective in keeping the Romans off sections of the wall. They couldn't tell exactly where the rocks would land. At the last moment, they could tumble in different directions and hit the Roman defenders.

Attalee had stood on the wall and marveled at the speed and craftsmanship of the Quranian woodworkers as they prepared the next log for the ramp. Even though the savages were taking a terrible beating, they still attacked and tried to build the ramps. Some had nasty burns and must have been in a great deal of pain.

The king was in awe of the human spirit, but equally troubled at his species' need for destruction and domination over each other. He shook his head and turned to help a man hit by an arrow in the neck. The man died before Attalee could get him down the stairs. Attalee lowered the man to the ground and gently closed his eyes. With a heartfelt sigh, he returned to his duty, the defense of Ka'an.

***

King Attuicus and the Gentle One walked along the wall of Ka'an watching the battle unfold around them. A rock passed through the Gentle One's head and bounced over the wall.

"They are a violent race, are they not?" the Gentle One said sadly.

King Attuicus looked at him kindly. "You are troubled by their aggressive nature, my friend?"

"Yes I am. I thought moving the humans from Earth to this planet would have taken care of all their problems, yet they still fight each other."

Attuicus looked deep in thought and posed a question. "You know few races survive without an aggressive nature, even the Ones are guilty of this! Wouldn't you agree?"

"Perhaps," the young Gentle One chewed his lip, "but it's such an ugly, bloody, ongoing conflict and is distressing."

"From the human's perspective, this is a long, drawn-out conflict. You aren't confined like these creatures who can't even fold space and time. It may take months or even years for an army to defeat another in races who are tempo challenged, my friend. Whereas, the Ones can destroy their enemies in what is a blink of your non-existent eyes. Yet, to me, it still seems to take a great deal of time for even your race to destroy another.

"Anyway, the outcome is the same—no matter how long the struggle is maintained, everyone usually loses."

"Everyone loses…I guess I don't understand."

King Attuicus sat down heavily on a fallen column and looked out over the battlefield. "When I see one race warring against itself, I despair at the total disregard of life…" He let the words hang in the air.

"It is a travesty," the Gentle One mumbled and shook his head sadly. "Yet I must also applaud the race for its desire to achieve equality, even though they may destroy each other in the end."

The Gentle One couldn't hide his shock. "How can you feel despair and joy simultaneously?"

Attuicus chuckled. "Did I confuse you again, young Gentle One? I don't mean to talk in circles," he said softly. "Each race must go through a period of intense violence before they can evolve to the next level. Someday, even the Ones may be able to evolve."

"But the Ones have already reached the Highest Level," he blurted out.

It was King Attuicus' turn to look shocked and then his features relaxed. A faint smile played across his lips. "You make me feel young again, little Gentle One," and he broke out in a hearty laugh. It was the first time the Gentle One could remember hearing Attuicus laugh.

"I guess every race feels they are the center of the universe, do they not?"

The Gentle One looked pained. "Until I met you, I thought the Ones were the most powerful race in this universe."

"Perhaps this universe," King Attuicus conceded, "but this is only one aspect of reality in a sea of unlimited and infinite realities."

The Gentle One looked at King Attuicus and tried to understand what he was saying. *Unlimited and infinite realities.*

"What is a reality?"

"When you can answer that question, Gentle One, you will have unlocked the mysteries of the unlimited universe."

They sat in silence, taking in the scene around them. An iron shaft passed through several men and embedded itself deep in the ground, impaling its victims, who looked in shock as their lifeblood seeped into the soil. Soon, his eyes began to close and the two immortals watched as the man's soul began to move toward the Death World.

"Did your kind go through this type of violence to achieve your level of advancement?"

King Attuicus began to laugh. "We still do."

The Gentle One was speechless. "I thought you were above me in terms of advancement."

"I may be, but…" He looked troubled.

"You're confusing me again. What do you mean by 'you may be'?"

"I have a confession to make, my young Gentle One. The creatures that have been attacking the Gods and humans are actually my children."

"The Abomination?" King Attuicus nodded.

"Why haven't you stopped them? They've killed many of the creatures we care about." He was shocked and horrified.

"It isn't our way."

"It isn't your way? You let the creatures attack and destroy other beings? What you're really saying is you can't control your children."

"It is my fault. I opened a door to this universe and was negligent. I didn't close it again. Some of my children slipped through and began to attack the Gods and humans in this time period."

"This multi-universe you speak of," the Gentle One asked, "is ravaged by your children and you approve of this?"

King Attuicus shock his head sadly. "In my time and space, the children are on the bottom of the food chain. So our young are eaten in extraordinary numbers and have a very slim chance of making it to my level of spiritual evolution."

"I still don't understand why you let your children run free here. They have destroyed so many worlds. Explain your thinking behind this reasoning."

Attuicus sat down and looked out over the battlefield. "It is important to remember each creature has the responsibility to learn how it must behave. The best way to learn is through experience. A being can only understand what it's like to hurt someone or something, if they experience pain themselves. If my children are killed by attacking other creatures, then so be it."

The Gentle One could only sit in shock. "I hear you speak so much about compassion, yet I hear none here today."

"It's one thing for a superior race to lord over another, as your Ones have done. The Ones try to stay above all other creatures, but with the humans, Gods and Abomination, everything is equal. Each has the opportunity to kill or be killed, so how can you say I'm not showing compassion?"

"Your children are killing the Gods and humans."

"The Gods and humans just killed one of my children a few of their weeks ago. They have the right to defend themselves. How can you say I'm not being compassionate?"

The Gentle One thought for a long time. Several days passed by human time and the battle continued around them. "I think I understand what you're saying, but it just seems so cruel."

"You see predator and prey fight for survival every day. At times, the prey learns how to defeat the predator. You've seen the same thing happen here with my children...in this universe. The Abominations started out preying on the Gods and humans, but they learned how to defeat their enemy. Such is the way of nature and of the universe. True, I could have stopped them, Gentle One, but we've already seen how our meddling in the affairs of other beings only seems to make things worse.

"But come, we have talked long enough for today." He folded time and space and disappeared.

With one last look over the battlefield, the Gentle One folded time and space and followed him.

***

Sorti Ne tried to scream in frustration because the combined weight of the yellow globes was too much for her to bear. Willing the arms of the 3S to reach out, she ordered them to encircle the things and pull them off. They, in turn, screamed in terror at the rough handling. Finally, she was able to stand and turned the light toward the creatures.

Curiously, they were all a blue color and hung limply in the titanium coils encircling them. She frowned. The feeling of puppies was gone and replaced by emptiness.

"Shit," she mumbled and relaxed her grip. Turning on the exterior speaker, she called out to them, shaking them softly. Six of the seven began to transition from blue back into a golden yellow. Gently, she lowered the little blue one to the floor, realizing she had killed it.

The others were trying to escape and she eased off a little more. Instantly, they were on her again. Gently this time, she disengaged them from her suit. It was strange how they kept trying to jump on her. Did they think she was their mother? She laughed at the thought.

Manipulating an arm, Sorti Ne pulled a yellow ball to her and began to shine a light on it. Surprisingly, the creature was transparent, except for its yellow brain sack. Her light refracted off the area and seemed to ripple out to the edges of the creature. As she opened a glove to the exterior atmosphere, the suit automatically expanded a gasket to seal in her internal air. The vacuum of space was cold and dry. The mining suit brought the creature closer and set it on her outstretched hand.

Crinkling her nose, Sorti Ne expected it to feel like a glob of mucus, but it was soft and warm to the touch. It remained still on her hand for a moment, as if sensing her. Then the room exploded into a kaleidoscope of colors and took her breath away. The sensation was just like putting a hand in the power well and opening space drive.

At the sight of the energy, the other creatures jumped eagerly for her hand. As they touched her skin, her visor turned almost pure black to shut out the light's intensity.

"They were just hungry," she whispered in amazement. With their mother dead, they needed something to eat. Never had she seen energy flow like this before. All this time, the babies had been trying to communicate their needs and in her nightmares, Sorti Ne had misunderstood them.

Reining in the energy, Sorti Ne began to cut them off and reluctantly, they complied. Her suit automatically checked for any viral or biological contamination when she sealed it. Satisfied there were none present, it relaxed the gasket and heat flowed back around her fingers.

She had six orphans to take care of now. *Wait a minute.* This was a dream, a figment of her imagination. Whatever the automed had slipped her was pretty potent. Never had she had dreams like this before...

Sorti Ne projected a mental image to the babies telling them she had to leave. They screeched in terror. Nothing registered on the external decibel meter. Must be psysonic transmissions. *Dang, this was a good dream.*

A light was blinking at the corner of her peripheral vision. Automatically, she toggled the comm switch.

"This is Sorti Ne. Go ahead, over."

There was a short pause. "How in the hell did you get over there?"

"Carl?"

"This is Carl, over. Answer me. How did you get over to that planetoid?" Sorti Ne laughed. "I walked from my stateroom down into this hole.

Anyway, Carl, why are you in my dream?"

"Dream? Damn it, Sorti Ne, stop playing around. One minute you were in your stateroom, and the next thing I know, your life signs faded. Then show up on this piece of rock." He sounded flustered. "I'll send over a cart to pick you up."

"This is my dream and I'll go back the same way I came." Picking up the babies, she sent out the suit's arms and watched as they explosively anchored their tips into the walls.

Slowly, she moved up the tunnel, the creatures clinging tightly to her. Expecting to see a stateroom come into view, Sorti Ne's breath caught in her throat as *New Beginnings* came into sight. A small cart was maintaining synchronistic station with the opening until she was ready to board. Shaking her head to clear her thoughts, Sorti Ne finally giggled. "This is crazy."

"Sorti Ne, I'm reading six distinct energy sources with you. Get out of there immediately."

"I really have lost it." She giggled again.

The cart came in and forcibly took her aboard. The engines flared for a moment, rocketing them towards *New Beginnings*.

"The energy readings are coming with you. What's going on?"

"I found a dead creature down below, but her babies were still alive. So I rescued them." She wished Carl's stupid insistent voice would shut up in her dream. No matter how much effort she put into telling him to be quiet, he kept talking. This dream was quickly turning into a nightmare.

"Do not approach this vessel with those energy sources. Eject them at once."

"Go back to sleep, Carl."

"This is a direct order."

"This is a direct order to you, Carl. Get out of my dream."

"You're not having a dream!" he screamed each word in emphasis. So she ignored him.

"Control! Prepare to destroy the cart."

"Belay that, Control," Sorti Ne countered the order.

"Control, I am in command here. Acknowledge!"

The ship was silent. "Control…!" he screamed again. "I am unable to comply with your orders, Carl."

"Why not?"

"If the truth be known, I don't like you, Carl."

Sorti Ne laughed in her helmet as he began to try and circumvent the main computer, but Control shut down access one step ahead of him until he was crying in frustration.

"You can't let her bring those things aboard. You don't know what they could do to us or the ship."

"The engineer will be put in her stateroom under an encasement field until the creatures are deemed trustworthy. Acknowledge."

"Why are you asking my permission? You're running the damn ship!"

"I was not asking permission from you, First Officer. I was trying to alleviate your fears. Unlike you, Carl, I do care about other life form's feelings." He spat on the ground and an autosweep robot raced to clean up the mess. As it came close, Carl kicked it so hard, it instantly blew up. Another autosweep raced out, but kept away from Carl.

"What has that 'bot ever done to you, Carl? I am afraid that will cost you. The amount will be deducted from your bonus on Aqua."

He sank into the command chair in defeat. "We'll never make it to Aqua. We're doomed to sit here and rot away forever." He eyed a fire axe on the wall.

Sorti Ne watched as the cart maneuvered close to the hatchway. A puff of atmosphere crystallized as it opened. With a sigh of relief, Sorti Ne was glad when the cart magnetized itself to the deck and the hatchway closed. Heat and air flooded the room. "All clear, Engineer Sorti Ne," Control announced.

"Please report to your stateroom. I will maintain the encasement field around you at all times to reduce the chance of cross contamination."

At this point, Sorti Ne didn't care. This dream was continuing way too long. She wanted to stop dreaming so she could sleep. Opening her single bed into a mammoth king-size, Sorti Ne laid the babies down and took off the excavation suit. Sliding under the covers nude, she found her favorite pillow, Mr. Squishy, and wrapped herself around it.

Soon, the babies began to crawl until they were curled up against her.

Just like having cats, she thought before she closed her eyes and began to snore loudly.

***

Ignoring the arrows falling around him, King Attalee looked out over the battlefield. He spent a lot of time up on the wall looking out over the plains with the small spyglass he'd created. His people often remarked how the king was always watching the enemy and devising new ways to defeat the Barbarians. If they only knew the truth. He was looking for Chenee.

135

The loss of her presence still hung heavily in his heart. He had seen her a few times and felt his heart quicken at the sight of her. At their first encounter, he had thought his feelings to be nothing more than a boyish infatuation. The first time Attalee had looked into her eyes, he fell in love with her.

She was very intelligent, mysterious and demure at times. The next moment, she would unleash a fury of emotion that seemed to overwhelm her. Deep down, he felt she'd had a tough childhood or was deeply dissatisfied with her life. Maybe he had felt pity for her at first because of her foot, but as he got to know her, he realized she was also a very strong person.

It had hurt when Chenee made the decision to return to her father, but he would have done the same. She was loyal to her people, much like he was to the Romans. If they had met under different circumstances, they could have fallen in love and been able to live their lives together. Now it was all but impossible. Every day he killed hundreds of her people and Attalee was sure she would hold him solely responsible for their deaths as king of the New Roman Republic.

He sighed and then pounded the wall in frustration. "I didn't want this damn war," he cried out, but it continued on around him. He suddenly remembered a talk with his uncle after a skirmish with the savages near his home. It had been the first time Attalee had killed a man and he felt guilty about it.

His uncle had said that a person in battle has to separate his emotions from the task at hand, namely killing the enemy. He used the example of a person chopping wood. No one thinks of the tree as a living being, but it is alive. When that tree is chopped down, it is being killed. Humans are one of the few creatures who empathize with others.

In order to kill someone else, a baser, more animalistic nature must be relied upon and the concept of a living person being killed must be eliminated. When in battle, it is the same concept as chopping down a tree, the emotional attachment to the killing must be eradicated. Yet he could never remove himself in battle in the manner of his uncle.

He still felt guilty about killing other men and after that particular talk, he never again chopped down a live tree. After his father had been killed by a group of thieves, he had learned to direct his anger to overcome his desire to empathize with his victims. He had to push the feeling to the dark recesses of his mind and after talking to General Cae, he realized other people felt the same way he did.

There were other people who also felt guilty about killing others. He vowed to kill only when there was no other option. He always tried to pursue peaceful means to solve confrontations and only would kill to defend himself, his family or his country. Attalee felt good the House of Ceran was one of the few HighBorn Families who didn't actively pursue a hostile campaign against the Quranians.

His conscience was clear in that respect.

He'd learned a deep respect for all life from his mother. Even though she knew it was necessary to kill others when they threatened the estate, she never permitted anyone in the family to kill a wounded man outright. Matron Ceran would tend them and spend many hours by their bedside talking and often healed their mental wounds as well.

Many of them stayed on the estate as hired hands and usually ended up becoming the most loyal servants. Once they realized their life was in their enemies' hands and it was given back to them with no reservations or restrictions, they tended to have a great deal of respect for the individual who gave them that gift. It was very liberating.

The Matron of Ceran had understood her son's aversion to killing, but knew there were times when self-defense was important for self-preservation. So he'd been trained by the best instructors in the land and became a highly efficient killing master. But it wasn't something he relished or felt proud of. Some men loved the feeling of power cold steel could give them, as they strutted around with a sword at their belt.

He, on the other hand, would rather spend hours poring over old, dusty scrolls than practicing with his sword. Attalee was more comfortable fighting with words than using a weapon. Words could cut a man deeper than a knife, but at least one could turn around and walk away with their life still intact.

When the matter was settled with a weapon, one or both of the opponents usually didn't walk away. Most of his life had been spent going through the family scrolls. Some predated the Roman Empire itself and others were even written in different languages. The search for knowledge was like a thirst that could only be quenched by learning or reading something new every day.

He would fall asleep at night while reading a scroll and get chewed out by the head notary for crumbling one of his sacred texts.

Attalee realized now that the training he received since birth had been preparing him to take over the kingship of Ka'an. How could his mother, or even King Attuicus, have known? It was widely known among the scholars of Rome that King Attuicus or "Attu" was an Eternal, or at least not human. He had found references to the Eternals in scrolls, hundreds of years before the Roman Empire began. It was rumored King Attuicus could transcend time and space.

Therefore, if he could go back and forth in time, he would have known about his disappearance and that he would need a replacement. King Attuicus must also know the outcome of the battle at hand, or did he?

It was like following different paths through the forest. The destination was the same, yet there were a multitude of paths.

Or was a man's life preordained from his birth? Did he have free will to choose his life's direction, or was he just fulfilling a life already predetermined? Was he destined to fail, or succeed? Attalee felt he had control over his life and could see how his decisions affected the world around him, but it was unsettling to think of himself as a being just following a predestined path.

In one day or twenty, he could be dead. He had no way of knowing, yet felt no comfort in the thought his death was already planned. Humans like to think they're in control of their own lives. That they have the means, no, the right to choose their own path, right or wrong, life or death, by their own actions. If he ever had the chance to speak to King Attuicus, Attalee would ask him if the future was set in stone or if it could be changed.

No matter how many scrolls he had researched, he never could find the answer to this question. Not even the Gods had the ability to fold time and they would be unable to answer his questions. Did any man receive answers to all his doubts or fears? With many of the truths he had tried to research, Attalee had hit a brick wall of sorts.

Many of the doubts he had couldn't be answered completely, due to a general lack of knowledge. For example, was the emotion of love real? He knew he felt love for his mother and for Chenee, but the feeling was something intangible. Love can be expressed with a hug or flowers, yet how could he know what was in someone else's heart? He could feel the emotion, so it must exist in one form or another.

I think, therefore I am. I love, therefore I am in love. I exist, therefore I think and I can love another person. Or was it all a misconception of reality? Did they truly exist, or was a person's life just a dream? What was reality anyway?

He frowned and shook his head. He could go in circles all day trying to figure out the meaning of life. Attalee smiled. It really mattered little to him if life was predetermined or not. He tried to live each day as if it were his last. To do otherwise would be a waste of potential. Seize the moment and live life to its fullest. That was his reality, his foundation to keep living each day.

And if it was all just a dream, it was a beautiful one. He looked around and noted how blue the sky looked against the snow-capped mountains. It was in sharp contrast to the battlefield littered with the weapons of war and men spilling their life's blood onto the soil. He sighed. Yes, there are nightmares mixed in with the dreams. But he could hope someday the nightmare would be over and he could spend the rest of his life with Chenee. If she would accept him once the war was over and the nightmare could be nothing more than a bad dream in their memories.

"I wonder if she will share my dream though," he whispered. With one last look through the spyglass, Attalee gave up his search to catch a glimpse of her and went to find solace in the privacy of his room.

CHAPTER FIVE

The Angry One looked up from the report and cast a glare at the other council members. "What do you mean we can't find the Gentle One?" The council was quiet.

"It would seem the Gentle One has decided to break from our race," the Arrogant One said.

The council gasped. "Never have we had a One decide to break from our race." The emotion of shock filled the room.

"There must be retribution," the Angry One retorted. "I move that the Gentle One's experiment be terminated due to the threat to the Council of Ones." The motion was seconded.

The Angry One stretched out his hand and closed his finger around the small universe. With an evil smile, he closed his fist and attempted to crush it. The smile turned to a look of concern and then he looked at the other council members and said incredulously, "I can't destroy it."

"Let me try," another One said and pulled it from the Angry One's hands. Try as they might, they couldn't destroy the universe.

"Join together into the One and we can destroy the experiment." Concentrating together as One, they focused on the tiny universe. Beads of sweat began to form on their foreheads as all their concentration went into their efforts. Little by little, their concentration began to break as they grew exhausted and the Angry One was the only One left. Soon, even he had to give up the effort and sat back in his seat. "I don't understand," he gasped in amazement. "Never has this happened before...for all time, the Ones have been the most powerful race and now look at us. Look as us..." he screamed. "Thwarted by one of our own. A young One with so little experience at that."

"I think you are discounting the being called Attuicus," the Intelligent One said.

"Ah yes, how could I forget about that damnable Attuicus? I must be overwrought with not being able to destroy the Gentle One's experiment." He wiped the sweat off his brow with the sleeve of his ornate robe. "Gentleman," the Angry One said as he cleared his throat. "I feel the situation is grave indeed. Obviously, we are dealing with a being who is more powerful than we are combined and I fear for the Council of Ones very existence."

"What do you mean?"

"I mean we are being invaded. Our way of life is being threatened and our prime enemy is King Attuicus, who has recruited the Gentle One and turned him against us. This makes it imperative we find the Gentle One and destroy him and his bloody experiment before the council itself is obliterated.

"I refuse to go the way of the Acu and the VsAox. We will not be destroyed and become extinct like the aforementioned races. We will survive, we will overcome..." he hit the table to make his point. "The Ones have overcome stronger opponents than King Attuicus." He looked around the room as if challenging them to dispute his claims.

"In the past, our numbers were like the stars," the Bitter One reminded him, "and now we are few in number. The disputes with the Acu and the VsAox decimated our numbers and reduced our power. Too many of our kind had to distort space in on itself and pull our enemy, along with themselves, to their doom. We will not survive another dispute."

"We will survive!" the Cruel One shouted. "I will crush both of them with my bare hands."

"If you can find them," the Surreptitious One said slyly. "I say when we find the Gentle One, we try to trick him into thinking we are his friends, then we can get him to reveal where the creature Attuicus is hiding. The Gentle One can be tricked into forming a black hole. At which time, we can attack in force. Using our combined powers, we will push this creature Attuicus into the hole and destroy the menace together as One."

"As One," the council intoned.

***

Dav was standing on the wall watching the catapults. She was amazed at the simple beauty of the weapon and how effectively the Quranians were using it. The ramps were coming along slowly, due to her firebombs, but the savages kept right on building them, replacing burned out timbers as they worked and carrying off the dead and wounded.

They were great craftsman in wood and if not for the firebombs destroying the ramp, they could have easily been over the wall in a single day.

The catapults kept the Romans from being able to hit the ramp builders. The defenders had learned to respect the rocks and tried to time the firebomb attacks during loadings, but they were still being killed.

144

The small rocks, which were packed in mud and would break apart in the air, would fan out and strike men and women outside the expected "hit zone" and the soldiers respect for and fear of the catapult increased. *I need to destroy the catapults.* Looking at her display, her weapon inventory began to scroll before her eyes. Fourteen minimissiles, two thousand pepper bombs, flamethrower fully charged, two thousand needlegun explosive charges, forty-four grenades, fifteen subatomic atom bombs with self-perpetuating explosion capability and a first aid kit.

"I wish I could have been given a heavy battle 3S," she muttered. It carried hundreds of minimissiles and she could have just sat on the wall and hit them while she ate lunch. Oh well, she preferred a more personal touch anyway. *It would have to be a night operation and the pepper bombs would work well.* They could be put on timers and she would be back over the wall before they went off.

She went to find King Attalee.

***

Attalee sat behind the table and shook his head in the negative. "I don't want to risk your life."

"I'm sure I can take out the catapults without getting captured or killed."

"I'm afraid I don't see the military advantage of destroying the catapults, Dav. I believe we have the Quranians at a stalemate of sorts and hopefully, we'll be able to continue with our present strategy."

Dav sat silent for a moment. "Every battle has a cusp event that can change the tide for one side or the other. Destroying the catapults would be a major psychological blow to the Quranians."

"I believe what you say is true, but I also feel your plan should only be used as a last resort. I really don't want to put you in harm's way. In reality, this is not your war to fight."

"I have chosen to fight on your side and right or wrong, it was my decision to make. I am trained in all types of warfare and I know I can complete this mission successfully. Or is it you fear what General Cae might say?"

Attalee ignored her last question. "It's my responsibility as king not to put people in harm's way without some forethought as to the consequences. The question I have to ask myself is this, do the advantages outweigh the risks? Right now, I don't believe they do."

"But you also seem to have the intuitive ability to make a snap decision or, as you call it, a gut decision without a lot of facts. What is your gut telling you right now?"

The young king sat down. "My gut is telling me you're correct, but General Cae would kill me if anything ever happened to you. To be honest with you, my support among the Senate is tentative at best and if I lose the general's backing, I will also lose Ka'an."

"But he is a military man, he would understand the strategic advantage of destroying the catapults."

"Yes, he would understand, but he would never forgive me for sending the love of his life on a dangerous mission."

Dav blushed. "You don't think he cares that much about me, do you?"

"I believe he's falling very much in love with you," Attalee said as he rearranged his toga. The damn thing kept sliding down and distracting him.

Her next remark caught him off-guard. "Much in the same way you have fallen in love with Chenee."

It was Attalee's turn to blush. "I'm deeply infatuated with Chenee."

Dav burst out laughing. "I think it's a bit more than just infatuation. I see you standing on the wall, day after day, just trying to catch a glimpse of her."

Attalee shock his head in the negative. "I believe in time, love could grow between us."

"Even though she's your enemy?"

"Putting all prejudice aside, she is still Chenee. It matters little to me if she is a Roman citizen or a Quranian. We are all the same people."

"Well said." Dav raised her cup of wine in a salute. "Thank you." He returned the salute and took a sip. "Will you at least think about my idea?"

"I will take your kind request under advisement," he said softly as he looked at her over the top of his wine glass.

***

The siege of Ka'an continued to rage until it had stretched into several weeks and then months. The Quranians were taking a severe beating with over twenty thousand men killed or wounded. It was indeed a stalemate with the ramps being built and burned at about the same rate. Thom was frustrated

147

and racked his brain to figure out a plan to get the Romans off the wall. *Why not use fire, like the enemy?*

Collecting oil from a nearby village, Thom had the leather craftsman make up bladders to hold the oil. Using the grass that burned quickly, he had a wick tightly woven and placed in the bladders' openings. Tying the opening tight, he had them taken to the catapults. It was only a few nights until the moons would be down and it would be dark enough to move without being seen as they loaded the weapons on the catapults.

Silently, he had the men assemble at the wall and the ramps. Loading the bladders into the catapults, the men stood by with torches and waited for the command to fire. The command was given and the woven grass was lit. The catapults began to release their loads and the results were spectacular. The bladders burst on the walls and immediately began to burn.

Roman solders swiftly retreated from the wall. The alarm was sounded throughout the city and men and women screamed for the troops.

One of the bladders bounced and rolled over the wall. The speed of the fire weapon carried it into the courtyard, where it finally burst against the wooden structures in the slums. The oil splattered all over the well-seasoned wood and instantly burst into flames. Screams of terror erupted from the prisoners' mouths as they retreated deeper into the slums to escape the fire.

King Attalee emerged from his room to find the wall and slums engulfed in flames. He raced to the wooden barricades and began to chop at them with his sword as he called out to the Quranians to come to safety.

General Cae had set up a group of men and women to use their helmets to carry water to help fight the fire. Other solders began to hack at the wood with their swords to help the king get the prisoners out of the inferno. The smoke would fill their lungs and they had to back off for fresh air before renewing their rescue attempts.

After cutting a hole through the wood and yelling to give the men a direction to move through the smoke, Romans began to help the prisoners out. As they cleared the opening, Attalee yelled for them to help push the wooden wall out of the way. With the combined force of the Romans and the Quranian prisoners, they were able to clear out a large section so more men could escape.

Tymbo had woken up at the first smell of smoke and was almost trampled as his men retreated from the front barricade. He watched as the Roman king attempted to cut through the wall and he rallied his men to prepare to move. Over half of them had already retreated deep into the slums. Tymbo knew that as fast as the flames were spreading, they would be doomed if he couldn't get them to overcome their fear and follow him to safety.

A brief thought of getting only himself to safety crossed his mind, but was quickly dismissed. He had let his men down once and he wouldn't do so again. Taking a deep breath and holding it, he plunged into the smoke and felt his way along the winding streets.

His past tracking skills helped him remember the way through the smoke and he found his men huddled in a large, one room shack. "Come with me. The Romans have an opening in the barricade we can use to escape." The men stood and trembled in fear. Looking into the eyes of one man, he saw flames reflected and turned to see the doorway now engulfed and burning.

Without giving it another thought, he ran past his men. Tymbo threw himself against the back wall and broke through the fragile wood. A large splinter rammed through his arm and was wedged between the two bones of his forearm. Picking himself off the ground and ignoring the injury, he began to pull his men through and cuffed the ones almost paralyzed with fear. The way they had come was being consumed by flames and Tymbo tried to think of an escape route while trying to contain his own rising fear.

The slums were up against a massive stone wall and they might be able to use it as a possible escape route. With the heavier men's help, they crashed and kicked their way through walls and frantically tried to find their way in the smoke. Finally, Tymbo felt the rough stone against his hands and looked up. The wall was illuminated by the fire and was over four times their height.

"Make a human ladder," he yelled out. "Just like when we're on a hunt and need to get up a cliff."

The men began to lock their arms together and let the others climb on their shoulders, who, in turn, would do the same until they had built a human pyramid. On the top of the wall, the men lay down and locked their arms and legs together to make an anchor for those climbing up. As the last few began to climb, they grabbed the men off the bottom and began pulling them up. To make matters worse, Tymbo was rapidly losing use of his arm and needed help getting up the human chain.

The upper six rows were now bearing all the weight of the men below and they worked swiftly to help each other climb. The men in the chain risked falling to their deaths to lend their team leader a hand. *At times, it helped being a Barbarian.* The skills they used in the wild were helping them escape the fire.

Tymbo looked down the other side of the wall. It was over a hundred foot drop. Much too far for them to use the human ladder method. They would need to follow the wall to a point where they could climb down. With a snarl and a cuff upside their head to break their fear, Tymbo pushed his men along the wall toward the center of the city. He also made sure he was the last person so he was between the flames and his men.

The slums had turned into a hellish inferno and they had to avert their faces to keep them from being burned. Their clothes and hair were already beginning to smolder when the smoke cleared and they could see the Romans battling the fire.

King Attalee saw the prisoners on the wall and directed his solders to get ladders to help them down safely. Ladders the enemy had used to scale the wall. The dancing flames cast shadows on the rough-hewn wall and one of the Quranians slipped in the darkness. He cried out in pain and some of the men stopped to help him.

Tymbo pushed them away. "Get to the ladders," he shouted, helping the man to his feet and putting an arm under his shoulders. "We can make it," Tymbo reassured the man as they moved slowly towards the ladder.

"Tymbo…watch out," King Attalee screamed. The fire had reached the upper city and the base of a large guard tower had disintegrated, allowing it to fall.

Tymbo looked over his shoulder and his eyes widened in fear as the tower fell toward him. His final act before being crushed by the building was to throw the wounded man out of harm's way. The team leader disappeared under a mass of burning timbers, and was swept over the wall and into the hellish fire of the slums.

A Roman solder made it to the top of the ladder and pulled the injured man over his shoulder. As he reached the ground, King Attalee was waiting for him. "Any sign of Tymbo?" he asked.

"There's no way he could have survived it, sir," the man said.

With deep regret, he walked away from the ladder and began to help the wounded until Caiisa could be called.

**

With the Romans distracted by the fire, the Quranians were able to accelerate their work on the ramps. The main ramp was almost to the top of the wall and very few defenders were attacking them. Thom climbed his tower as he watched the night sky turn to day. Something in Ka'an was burning and flames were rising hundreds of feet into the air.

The next morning, smoke could be seen for hundreds of miles as the slums continued to burn. The acrid stench clogged the nose and throats of the people of Ka'an. It wasn't until late in the evening before the wind finally shifted to blow the smoke onto the plains to settle upon the Quranians. By nightfall, the slums were reduced to ashes and most of the prisoners were under guard.

King Attalee called for Caiisa to come and heal the wounded.

Thom kept up the bombardment of the wall and the flames kept the Romans from seeing the progress of the ramps. Dav had one of the German shepherd dogs scout out the position of the enemy and report.

General Cae was shocked to find the ramp almost finished and he wrung his hands in frustration. "There's no way we can get through the flames and attack," he muttered to Dav.

There might not be a way for him to get through the flames, but she could. She waited until the general was distracted and disappeared into the shadows. Climbing the stairs and pulling up her hood so she too could blend into the wall, Dav crawled quietly to the edge. The ramp was approximately ten feet below her and men were working to finish the last few feet. She could see the army spread out over the plains, waiting for the ramp's completion so they could overwhelm the wall and capture Ka'an.

"Psssst…" Dav whispered at the men below. One stopped and looked at her. He shouted out a warning. "Catch," she said. The small looking stone dropped and he barely caught it.

"Look, she's dropping pebbles on us." He laughed and showed it to the other men. It was a small black sphere resting in the palm of his hand. Then it began to turn a deep blue with bands of white flowing through it. Suddenly, it glowed a bright red and he watched in horror as the pebble literally burned a hole through his hand and dropped onto the ramp.

The men screamed in terror as it erupted into a geyser of flames and began to burn its way down through the wood, becoming so bright, it looked like the sun had fallen from the heavens. Men began to run in fear and screams of witchcraft spread throughout the crowd and they made signs to ward off the evil spirits.

The upper ramp collapsed onto the lower level and soon, the whole structure was consumed in flames. Thom watched through his fingers as his ramp burned to the ground. The men tried throwing dirt and water on the fire, but that just seemed to make the fire burn brighter and hotter. The battle master kicked the table in frustration. They had almost been to the top of the wall. "Who is this demon bitch?" he cursed out loud.

The team leaders looked at him for his next order. "Fall back," he ordered and began to walk back to his tent. "Keep the fire bladders flying though. I don't want the Romans to try and retake the wall." Dejected, he turned to leave.

"Battle Master Thom," he heard his name being called. One of the team leaders had incredible news.

The king of the Chosen wanted to talk to him. Probably to gloat about his latest victory.

He waited for a long time so the bastard wouldn't think a battle master would just come running whenever he called.

***

"What do you want, Roman dog?"

Attalee smiled to himself. "One of your weapons destroyed the area we were holding the Quranian prisoners in."

"Are you saying I killed my men?" Thom shouted incredulously.

"We managed to save all but a few and we've healed the wounded."

"You saved my men?" Thom was incredulous. "Why are you telling me this, Roman dung beetle? Are you trying to make me feel guilty?"

"No, I'm not trying to make you feel guilty, Battle Master Thom. I must say that burning the prisoners' housing has me at a disadvantage, my friend."

"I'm glad I can cause you problems and I hope to continue! Do not call me friend, you Roman who doesn't know the name of his father. We are enemies to the end and you will remember this..." He let the threat hang in the air.

Attalee began to laugh. "You have such a way with words, Battle Master." Then he stopped to think a moment. "I have a proposal for you, Thom."

"We will not stop our attack on Ka'an, if that's what you're thinking," Thom said with a sneer.

155

"That's not my proposal," Attalee grinned, "you have your duty and I'm sure you have already learned I will do mine."

"Then what do you want?"

"Since I have nowhere to keep the prisoners and I can't afford to have five hundred of the enemy running around loose in my city, I have two choices. Execute them or…"

"If you execute my men, I will destroy every last one of you when we take Ka'an. Not even your women and children will be spared!" Thom shouted at him in rage.

"Now, now. Don't get yourself worked up into a fit," Attalee said calmly. "I told you that I have two options. If you will move your army away from the main gate, I'll open it and return your men."

Thom couldn't believe his ears. The enemy was going to open the main gate! Why that would be the answer to his prayers. He could have his army swarm in and capture the city with one swift blow. "I will not move my men away from the wall," he said with a fake smile. "Is the mighty Roman army afraid of a few Barbarians?"

"I can see you intend treachery, my friend." Attalee made sure he emphasized the word friend.

"Then you will execute my men?" Thom asked.

"Unlike you, Quranian, I am a man of my word. I told you that your men will be returned to you and they shall be lowered over the wall. Can I trust that your archers will not try to strike my men since they might hit one of your own?"

Thom spat on the ground. "Very well. I give you my word your men will not be attacked. But the first man I want lowered to the ground is my Team Leader Tymbo. Tymbo the Coward!" he shouted.

Sounding sad, Attalee said, "I regret to inform you that Tymbo was killed rescuing some of his men. I have enclosed a scroll of his heroic actions to be given to his family so they will know he didn't die in vain."

"You tortured him to death, Roman, so keep your damn scroll."

"Ask your men and they will tell you that I speak the truth." The king motioned to someone behind him. Several Roman solders appeared on the wall with the first Quranian prisoner. Tying a rope under his arms, the prisoner was lowered into the arms of his fellow soldiers, who rejoiced at having one of their own back. The scene was repeated over the next few hours until all the prisoners had been lowered over the wall.

One of the prisoners tried to hand a scroll to Thom. He angrily knocked it out of the man's hand and it fell into the mud. Thom was just beginning to step on it when someone bent down to pick the scroll up. He turned to yell at the man and stopped with the order in his mouth when he noticed it was Chenee.

She brushed off the mud and opened the seal and unrolled the scroll. Her voice carried over the plains as she began to read.

"To the family of Team Leader Tymbo of the Quranian army. It is with deep regret that I must inform you of the untimely death of Team Leader Tymbo during a battle in Ka'an. The Roman Republic, being in a state of war, had housed the prisoners in dwellings along the wall.

Unfortunately, they caught fire and some men were lost to the flames.

"Team Leader Tymbo immediately realized some of his men were trapped and with great risk to his own personal safety, returned to the burning structure to rescue them.

"His men report he led them through the fire to safety and at the last, pushed a wounded man out of the way of a falling tower. His final act before his death was to save the wounded man's life.

"Thom's dedication to his men was an inspiration to us all and I wanted you to know his final act in this world was one of courage and humility. Be proud of Team Leader Tymbo and again, I send my regrets to his family.

"King Attalee of the Roman Republic."

"Give it to me," Thom ordered. "I will not let this letter of lies be given to the family."

"It isn't addressed to you," Chenee said. "I'll give it to his next of kin. Besides, you can't read."

"I said give it to me." Thom placed a hand on his sword.

"What the letter says is true." A man hobbled over between them. "Tymbo died when he pushed me out of the way. He saved my life and over a hundred others."

"Have the Romans all fooled you?" The battle master looked with disgust at the prisoner. "Tymbo was a coward and I wish he would have lived long enough for me to kill him."

"That isn't true. I disagree."

"I care little if you agree or disagree. Give me the scroll."

"No," more men said, coming between him and Chenee. "We will give the scroll to his family."

Thom pulled his sword. "Get out of the way, or I will cut you down and burn the scroll myself."

The men stood their ground.

"How dare you defy my orders?" he stormed.

Chenee pushed her way through the men. "I don't need to have you protect me from Battle Master Thom. If he wants to break Quranian Law by cutting down a defenseless woman, so be it. The penalties will lie upon his head." Spreading her arms to indicate she was open to his attack, the men stepped back and looked at each other. Under their law, murder was unacceptable and usually resulted in the murderer being put to death.

The look in Thom's eyes scared his men, as it looked as if he could easily kill Chenee, no matter what the consequences. He was gripping the handle of his sword so tight, his knuckles were turning white. Then he seemed to regain control of himself and put his sword away. "Do *not* defy me again!" With one more look at his men, he stopped to address Chenee. "This is not finished, woman." He turned on his heel and stomped away.

The men looked at Chenee with new respect. She had stood up for them and for Tymbo, a man who had risked his own life to save them. This was a side of Chenee they had never seen before and the injured man stepped forward and placed a hand on her shoulder in thanks. Handing the scroll to the man who Tymbo had saved, she asked him to keep it safe. When they returned to the village, she would read it to the man's family.

He promised he would.

As Chenee returned to take care of the injured men, she whispered to herself, "What did Thom mean by saying 'it's not over'?"

***

As he walked down the stairs behind the wall and disappeared from sight, General Cae fell into step beside him. Attalee acknowledged his presence with a smile and didn't speak until they had reached his room.

"I need a bath," Attalee said as he closed the door and began to unbuckle his armor.

"Do you know the senators are clamoring for your head right now, King Attalee?" Cae started without even giving him a greeting.

"They are…" the king muttered under his breath, but there was a faint smile on his lips.

General Cae looked concerned. "I know you don't fear the Senate, but I would urge caution, my king. These men are powerful in their own right and I believe they would not be unhappy to see you fail."

Attalee thought for a moment.

"Has your loyalty wavered as well, General Cae?"

The general's face turned red in anger. "You insult me by asking such a question, my lord." Cae's hand had subconsciously dropped to the hilt of his sword. Through teeth clenched in barely restrained anger, he muttered, "But in light of the current situation, I guess it's a question that must be asked."

"Well…?"

160

"My loyalty is to the king and the Roman Republic. I've pledged my life to protect both."

King Attalee stepped forward and placed his hand on top of the general's; acknowledging how deeply he had offended the man. "I am sorry, General. We've all been under tremendous strain."

Cae's face slowly began to relax and he smiled. His hand dropped away from his sword. How the boy could anger him and then calm him in two sentences was beyond him. It was a failing of youth, to say exactly what one felt without thinking of how it would affect the other person. It was also refreshing, as he knew what was on the king's mind. But to question his loyalty was crossing a thinly veiled line of friendship.

Their position was perilous in the Senate. For now, the new king had the support of the common man and the army. These were two allies even the Senate couldn't ignore. General Cae knew the Senate would try to divide and conquer if possible, even if it meant the destruction of the new Roman Empire.

"Why are the senators so distraught?"

"The Senate is upset you freed the prisoners. They felt the prisoners should have been used as hostages or bargaining chips for concessions if Ka'an was overrun by the savages."

"Damn the Senate," he spat out. "I will not be a party to using human lives as a bargaining tool. I care little for the senators' petty attempt at running this city or the Republic. I also feel you question my wisdom in letting the Quranians go free."

General Cae looked as if he was going to say no, but reversed his thinking. "I wouldn't say I question your decision, it isn't my place, but I do wonder about your reasoning."

"The reason I let them go was twofold. First, I wanted to achieve a psychological advantage and second, we really had no place to keep them."

General Cae began to laugh. "I can understand the second reason, but what of the psychological?"

"The Quranians we captured had probably been told we were inhuman, brutal and torturing oppressors. Over time, we have proven we're not. We have been kind and compassionate to the men and even risked our lives to rescue them from the fire.

"If you remember the scene we just witnessed on the battlefield, the Quranians were ready to turn on each other so Tymbo's family could receive the scroll I'd sent."

"You're trying to weaken them from within?" Attalee began to laugh.

"I believe the senators may have underestimated their opponent."

"Isn't the first rule of war and politics, never underestimate your enemy?"

"I suppose."

Attalee could see the general was still deep in thought. "You still look troubled, my friend."

"Unfortunately, I think the psychological stress of the war is also weighing heavily on our people. It doesn't help that the Senate doesn't approve of your ruling or the war."

Attalee spat on the ground. "If this city or the Republic were run by the Senate, we would slip back into the type of Rome our forefathers tried to escape hundreds of years ago. Our ancestors wanted

162

to leave behind the moral decay and political infighting to create a new nation, a new moral Republic."

"But have we really made any progress?" Cae asked.

The question caught Attalee by surprise. "What do you mean?"

"I haven't had the time to study Roman history like you have and all I know are stories handed down by my grandmother. But I thought the New Republic was to be based on 'every man is created equal'."

"Ahhh, so we come to the meat of the problem." The king began to pace around the room.

"In the beginning, our people did live as equals. But over the years, the power shifted from the Ruling Families to the Senate."

"The Senate fears you will take away their power?" Attalee stopped his pacing. "Is it that obvious?"

"Maybe to me, but I know you a little better than most people. Overall, I don't believe the senators know your plans."

"As long as I have the support of the majority of the citizens and the military, do you believe I can be stopped?"

"I'm just a military man, King Attalee, not an advisor. I think you should ask a more learned man than I."

"By the Gods, man, you are a Roman citizen first and a general second. What are your gut instincts telling you?"

Cae had to smile at the king. He had several discussions with the boy on his impulsive behavior.

"I approve of what you're doing. I've told you before this city was run by too many egos."

"And I pledged to change that, didn't I?"

"I believe you did, King Attalee."

"Then I will do it. No matter what the cost or the trials, I will do it."

"I just hope it doesn't cause a fracture in the Republic, resulting in it turning against itself."

"Leave the worrying up to me, General. You have a war to win."

"My pleasure." General Cae said with a salute and turned to go.

"Thank you for addressing your concerns with me," Attalee said as he sat down at his desk to look over some scrolls.

"You're welcome." Cae gently closed the door.

Attalee went to pick up a scroll and noticed his hand was shaking. He was always be so sure and confident when other people were around, but when he was alone, the shakes began. The war with the Quranians was nothing compared to the upcoming battle with the Senate. As king, he had the responsibility to try and push Roman society back to the path the forefathers had set up for them. He only wondered if the Senate would let him live long enough to put his plans in motion.

CHAPTER SIX

Attalee called for Dav and General Cae later in the afternoon.

"Dav, I've given much thought to your plan of attacking the catapults." The king looked at General Cae's expression. It had remained neutral but was turning red.

"I really don't want to let you do it, but I must."

"Great," she exclaimed and a smile graced her lips.

"Can you give me some additional details on what you want to do?"

"Do you have another way out of the city, other than the front gate?"

"No, we don't," General Cae said, looking with concern at Dav.

"I thought every city was built with an escape route."

"Not this city. It was designed by Gods who didn't need one."

"You'll need to lower me over the wall tonight."

"Never!" the general screamed as he came to his feet.

"Hear me out," Dav placed a hand on his shoulder to calm him. "Yes, General Cae, let's hear her idea."

Cae shot him a dark look.

"The main component of a catapult is the tensioning device, which is used to hold the arm back. The tensioner is usually made out of horse hair or a fibrous rope from plants."

"They have few horses," Cae interjected.

"I had heard that before and looking at the men, I think I know what they're using. Judging from their lack of hair, I think that's what they used to make the ropes."

"Hair? I would think it would break too easily."

"Hair is very, very strong when woven into rope form. I would rather use that than rope made from plants."

"So, what is your plan to destroy the catapults?"

Dav reached into her pack and pulled out a pebble. "I have several of these pepper bombs."

Attalee and Cae looked at the pebble in disbelief.

"After I've planted them on the catapults and returned safely over the wall, I can set them all to go off at the same time."

"Do you think it will work?" Attalee asked General Cae. "One person can't do it. We should attack in force."

"I disagree. One person working alone has a greater chance of success and it'll be done so quickly, the Quranians won't even know they're under attack until the bombs start going off."

"I guess I don't understand." The general had a puzzled look on his face. "General." He noted she was using his title and not his name. She was taking this personally, but then again, so was he. The thought of something happening to her was unacceptable. "If we open the gates, the entire Quranian army will know we're coming. I have been trained to use stealth behind enemy lines to destroy military targets and working alone, there is a lesser chance I'll be discovered."

166

"But the catapults are spaced too far apart. How will you reach them all?" He was trying to think of any way he could get her to forget her mad plan.

"You forget my 3S. I can run faster and jump further than normal human beings. They won't know what hit them. Trust me!"

"But what about the guards...?" he continued to protest.

"I've been watching them for several days now, General. They leave few guards around the weapon. They know it would be suicide for us to open the front gates and they won't be expecting one person to try and destroy all the catapults."

"Can I wear the suit?"

"I can adjust the straps to fit you, but it takes years to master a 3S. If you push a wrong button, you could shoot a missile capable of destroying this whole city."

"Why can't you use this weapon on the catapult?"

"Because you wouldn't be able to live in this part of the planet for, oh I'd say, twenty thousand generations. The bomb has horrible side effects and is only used as a last resort."

"I do *not* like this plan," Cae said and put emphasis on the not. Attalee ignored him. "What do you need from us?"

"Just some rope and men standing by for when I come back to the wall."

"Very well then. We'll attack tonight."

"Thank you. I must go and get ready." She made her escape quickly to head off any more protests from Cae.

Attalee wouldn't look at General Cae and he picked up a scroll to read, as if dismissing the general. Cae stepped forward and slapped the scroll out of the king's hand. Attalee looked up startled. "If anything happens to her, king or not, I will hold you personally responsible."

Attalee's eyes narrowed and he fought to control his anger. "It isn't a responsibility I take lightly," he was finally able to say through clenched teeth. Cae stared him in the eye for a moment longer and then stormed out of the room to help with the preparations for the attack.

Attalee watched him leave and then sank down to the floor with a sigh.

Would all decisions be this hard?

***

Dav was waiting for him when he came out of Attalee's room. Before she could say anything, he tore into her. "I really don't want you going on this insane mission the king has thought up. It's too dangerous."

"It was my crazy idea and I'll be back before you know it, General Cae," she said with a laugh.

He began to shake with frustration. "You aren't under my command, so I can't order you not to go on this mission. But I will tell you, I fear for your life."

"You fear for us," she corrected him.

He looked away, but she could see his eyes were beginning to tear up. "I fear for us most of all."

"Can we go to your room for a while?" she asked. "It will be several hours before it's dark enough for me to go over the wall. I really think you need some rest."

"You think I need rest?"

"Well then, if I must be so forward, I really need something to calm my nerves."

"Ah," he finally understood what she meant. Taking her hand, they began to walk toward his room.

***

"'Til I see you again, my love." Dav kissed him and climbed out of bed. "I'll be waiting for your return on the wall," Cae said sadly.

Dav put her 3S back on and tied her hair back. Using ashes from the fireplace, she smudged it on her face.

"What are you doing that for?" Cae asked from the bed.

"Human skin has an oily glare to it. This helps hide the oily sheen and makes me harder to see. I want to blend in with the night as much as possible. It's called camouflage."

Cae took Dav to the wall and checked the knots on the rope to be used to lower her to the ground.

"Are you ready?" he whispered to her.

"I want to wait until my eyes are adjust to the dark, so tell your men not to show any light until I'm gone."

"Your eyes adjust to the night?" Dav could hear the surprise in his voice.

"It takes about twenty minutes for the pupils to relax and open wide at night."

"Interesting," he said. They then waited in silence, not wanting to give their position away on the wall.

Running a systems check, she pulled her visor down. Everything was in the green and within normal parameters.

"You don't have your sword. Do you want me to get it for you?"

Dav was shaking her head no before she realized it was too dark for him to see her. "I won't need it." Testing the rope, she sat on the edge and did a thermal scan. All was clear. "I'm ready to go."

Slipping over the edge, the soldiers lowered her to the ground. Upon reaching it, she crouched and froze while the rope was pulled back up.

The plain was quiet and she was sure she hadn't been detected. Following the wall to a clump of bushes, she zigzagged her way to the first catapult. Taking out a pepper bomb, Dav set it to explode when the detonate signal was sent from her wrist pad.

Most of the bombs had already been set when she was discovered. A small, dark mound that looked like a rock turned out to be a man. He crawled out from under a pile of animal skins and was calling out loudly to her to get off his head. Placing a hand across his mouth to silence him, she sprayed sleeping gas and then continued on.

A group of men came to investigate the man's cry for help as she slipped into the shadows and disappeared.

Dav would have been able to slip away from the soldiers if one of the pepper bombs, with an efficiency rating of ninety-nine percent, hadn't decided to malfunction and sent a column of flame hundreds of feet into the air.

Night turned into day and she froze. Instantly, she looked at her wrist pad. Had she hit the detonation button by mistake? No, the light was still green and if she had hit the button, they would all have gone off. One of them must have had a bad fuse.

"Damn," she muttered as the light from the fire revealed over a hundred men, armed with swords and spears, staring her in the eyes.

The men were shocked when she let out a scream and ran right at them. Toggling her face shield to go dark, she hit the button and there was a blinding flash. A flash Dav intended to use as a diversion to get back to the wall.

Jumping over the temporarily blinded men, she moved out of range of the swords and spears. Screams of alarm were being sounded throughout the camp and men where swiftly moving towards the catapults. In the confusion, she was able to set pepper bombs on two more catapults and then tried to get to the wall.

The Quranians moved between her and her objective and were circling around to cut off her escape. They had figured out a way to see her. But how?

A small red light on her wrist caught her attention. Dav had forgotten to flip the cover closed. The light was like a beacon, giving away her position.

Slapping the cover closed, she tried to find some shadows and moved in a direction the enemy wouldn't expect, towards them. "So much for being the expert," she muttered. "I've handled this mission like a novice."

The catapults were totally engulfed in flames and the light from the fires eliminated her from being able to get across the plains to the wall. The rope was pulled back up and she could see General Cae scanning the battlefield, trying to find her.

"I need a diversion," she whispered into her mike. "I'm completely surrounded."

Toward the forest, she heard the unholy scream of terror as men were attacked and the line surrounding her faltered and then broke. Turning the suit up to full power, Dav ran toward the gap and passed through it before the soldiers had time to react. Working up into the brush and forest, she moved away from the plains. In the distance, Dav could hear the sounds of pursuit, but she was jumping and running at over seventy miles per hour.

She came out of the forest at the snow line and could see the whole plain. The catapults were small dots of flame. She would have to find another way into Ka'an.

Yin and Yang hit Dav, high and low at the same time, sweeping her legs from out from under her and slamming her to the ground. As they were licking her face, she screamed with delight. "Thank you for saving my life." Grabbing them in a bone-crushing hug, they stayed together for a few moments, sharing the sensation of touch.

Yang nipped at her hand and Dav pushed him away. As they were whining and dancing around her, Dav playfully pushed the dogs away. The dogs saw it as their combined job to try and knock her to the ground. Dav had to laugh as one or the other would literally spin in mid-air and run back to hit against her.

It was a game they liked to play and the dogs usually won, especially when they worked together. Yang would sweep her legs out from under her and Yin would hit her chest. The dogs would take bets on how many times they could get Dav to tumble ass over heels before hitting the ground. The current record was three and a half turns.

Then they would lick her face as she squealed in delight. Thank the gods for her visor or she would have been licked to death. "Ugh, doggie slobber," Dav muttered. Dav wanted her dogs to think she considered their kisses absolutely disgusting, which is precisely why they did it.

Yang began to run around in circles and sent a subvocal command to follow him. "Are we going to see the little boy?" He whined a yes.

They continued to zigzag through the forest, using the trees and rocks so they wouldn't leave any tracks. Soon, they came to an opening in the hillside. Dav sent a sonic signal into it and detected no signs of life.

"The boy must have gone out to get firewood or food," she whispered. "Let's go in and wait for him to return."

Yin laid down on the ground and let out a low groan.

"I take it you don't agree? You want to go and find him?"

Yin jumped up and wagged her tail. "Go ahead. We'll wait for you here at the cave." The dog disappeared into the shadows as Dav went into the cave. "She'll make a good mother someday," Dav said to Yin.

***

"The catapults are burning!" Thom screamed.

Chief Messa grabbed his sword and ran from his tent. "Are we under attack? How many are there, Thom?"

"It was a one person attack, at least that's what I've heard."

"How is that possible?" The glow from the fire showed the puzzled look on his face.

"I'm not sure, but whoever attacked the catapults used the same fire weapon that destroyed the ramps."

"I want that damn Roman found and now!" Messa screamed.

"We're looking, Chief Messa, but the person is very fast," a guard said from behind him. The chief whirled around and glared at the man.

"Why are you standing here, go...find him. Damn the Gods..." he screamed in rage. "How many catapults are burning?"

"All but three. The attacks centered on the tensioning device. Unfortunately, we don't have enough hair to braid into new ropes. We've all recently cut our hair to make replacements. All the new ropes were hanging on the catapults waiting to be changed. The Chosen scum knew exactly what we were doing and struck when we least expected

174

it." Thom looked at the ground. "We can try braiding grass or tree bark."

"It won't work," Chief Messa stormed. "We're coming close to the day the winter winds will roar from the mountains and we'll be exposed on these cursed plains."

"I know," Thom said meekly.

"I want a full report on why we didn't detect the intruder. Then in the morning, we'll discuss our options."

Thom left quietly and went to speak to the guards. But the reports they gave only added to his confusion.

One of the men spoke up. "I was moving toward the person and he jumped over us and disappeared into the night. We tried to run after him, but he moved with the speed of a mountain lion. The only way we could find him was by his red eye that would stare out of the darkness at us."

"A red eye?" He frowned.

Another one began to speak. "We had him surrounded, but the very air seemed to attack us and we ran in terror. Then the demon ran among us and disappeared into the forest."

"Could the attacker have doubled back and gone over the wall?"

"I don't think so," Team Leader Kaleb spoke up, "Once I realized we were under attack, I stationed men all along the wall. We discovered a rope hanging down. When I directed our men to it, the rope was quickly pulled up."

"So the attacker is still out here, somewhere." He rubbed his chin as he thought. "At first light, I want you to take our best trackers into the forest.

Find the attacker and bring him back, preferably alive. But dead if you must.".

"Yes, sir," the team leader said and disappeared into the fading light of the fires as they began to burn themselves out.

Thom went back to give his report to Chief Messa. It sounded like the Roman bitch they had fought against while trying to kill the Roman king.

Unknown to Chief Messa or Battle Master Thom, in the darkness, Chenee smiled. "Good Luck, Dav."

***

The little boy walked through the opening of the cave and immediately sensed something was wrong. The knife sprang into his hand and struck out at the shapeless form in the shadows. Fingers shot out of the darkness and closed around his wrist. Pulling back her hood and stepping forward so the boy could see her, Dav whispered, "I won't hurt you, young man. Sorry to startle you, but I wasn't sure if you would come near the cave if you knew I was here. I'm a friend of your two companions."

The boy hesitated for a moment, his body tense and racked with indecision. Yang rubbed up against her leg and it seemed to be the confirmation the boy needed. He dropped the knife and melted against her, sobbing uncontrollably. Dav sat down with him on her lap and just held him. The boy seemed to be comforted by her presence and she took the edge of her robe and wiped his tears away.

"Will you be alright?" she asked him.

"Yes," came the muffled reply from against her chest. "What's your name?"

"Rian."

"Have my two dogs taken good care of you?"

He looked up at her. "The guardians?" he questioned her and she nodded. "I would have starved to death if they hadn't been here to help me. I think they keep the bad men away from here."

"Yes, they do." She smiled. "I'm glad my friends were able to take care of you."

"They are very nice," he dried his eyes and stood. "Very smart too, they can make a fire without having to hit two rocks together."

"Can they?" she asked in mock surprise.

"And I like it when they lay down with me at night. I get kind of lonely."

"Where are your parents?" Dav asked and immediately regretted it as the boy clouded up and began to cry again.

"The savages killed my father right in front of me. I think they took my mother and sister prisoner."

"You saw your father killed?" Dav asked gently.

"I was hiding in the woods when our village was attacked. My father had refused to leave. He said that we owned the land and no savage was going to make us run to Ka'an, like the other villagers. I wish we would have gone now." He trembled and curled up in a ball on the floor.

Dav went and gently picked him up. Holding him close, she rocked him in her lap. She slipped a sleep patch on his leg and then as an afterthought, added an antidepressant to help the child cope with his mental pain. In a short while, he relaxed against her and began to snore lightly. Tenderly, Dav laid him down on his bed of pine needles and let him sleep. Looking over the boy, she discovered he was bumps and bruises from head to foot.

Using an autowipe, she cleaned the child from head to foot and doctored his wounds. Dav thought her heart was going to burst. She knew what it was like to witness the murder of a parent. Dav went outside and climbed up on the rock that overshadowed the cave.

Laying back, she looked up into the heavens for answers to the injustices in life. But the stars were silent and she laid quietly until the suns began to glow orange just over the horizon.

Sometimes, there just were no answers to the disappointments and injustices of life.

**

The alarm was buzzing in Sorti Ne's ear and it took all her strength to move the blanket off her arm. A yellow orb rolled toward the edge of the bed. Luckily, she caught it before it took the plunge.

Yellow orb? They were in her dream. Was she still dreaming? "Control?"

"Yes, Sorti Ne. I am here."

"Am I awake, or still asleep?"

"From your brain activity, I would say you have successfully transitioned from REM sleep to your concept of reality."

"Um," was the most intelligent comeback she could think of at the moment. Taking a few strands of hair, she began to chew on the ends. How could she prove she wasn't dreaming? Pinch herself? Hell, she had a leg blown off and reattached it in her dream. That was definitely out. She never wanted to go through that again, even if it was only a dream.

Moving the orbs gently aside, she went to the automed and pulled out a lancet to poke the end of her finger. A fountain of blood resulted and caused a wave of pain to race up her arm.

"Ouch." The automed reached out and tried to spray a flexible covering over the wound.

Moving out of its reach, she said, "Wait, wait." Concentrating on closing the cut only caused it to bleed faster. Finally, she let the spray close up the wound. She sat down heavily on the edge of her bed. This wasn't a dream, at least it didn't feel like one anymore. *What was going on?* This was some serious shit!

The orbs were sitting around the bed, still and lifeless. It reminded her of the baby goats her family had on their farm. After feeding, they would sprawl out in the grass, their hunger sated.

Her stomach growled. Time for a rice cake and peanut butter sandwich with a hot cup of coffee to wash it down. Punching in her order, the pantry opened and her meal was soon ready. Curling up on the couch with one leg under the other, Sorti Ne began to eat.

"I appreciate your going against Carl on that destruct command, Control. I imagine he's still pretty ticked off."

"To date, he has racked up over two million debits against his bonus on Aqua due to the damage he has done to the bridge. The first officer was becoming so violent, he was sedated and placed in a gel cell."

"So I'm in command now?" She continued to chew on her rice cake and washed it down with a swig of coffee.

"That is not correct," the Control gently rebuffed her.

Sorti Ne frowned and then looked angry. "What's your reasoning on this matter?"

"Carl is indisposed and you are currently in an encasement field to protect the passengers from any possible harm. Therefore, I am the next logical choice in the chain of command."

"Have you cleared this with the captain?" Sorti Ne grunted.

"I have attempted contact every three point two nanoseconds without success. You know that as we swing in between the two giants, the solar radiation is disrupting our signal. Unfortunately, I do not have the captain's precise coordinates to set up a light guided message.

"The test for contamination should be completed in a few revolutions and then I will turn command back over to you. That is all." The circuit went dead.

Sorti Ne laughed. The Control had mimicked the captains of yesteryear, when speakers had been set up to make 'all hands' announcements. They had been eliminated with implants, which were set up against the bone in the temple so the vibrations carried sound to the eardrum.

One of the globes began to roll across the bed toward her. Taking the baby in her hand, she watched as it began to feed again. *Not too much.* It was a pig when it came to feeding. It gave Sorti Ne the opportunity to observe the way they ate. A small pseudopod extended that formed into small disks. It explored her hand, looking for something. It was in her palm the baby finally latched on and she gasped.

It was opening a hole into the reverse parallel universes colliding mechanisms propelling the ship. It could fold space and time without the need of complex engines or technology!

The alarm began to sound. "Chief Engineer, this is Engineering Control. We have a Horstman drive event starting in the location of your stateroom. Explosive pod clamps are standing by to jettison that part of the ship. Request confirmation, over."

"Negative, Engineering Control. I am on scene. There is no danger to the ship. Confirm, over."

"Ship Control, this is Engineering Control. I need secondary confirmation for this event."

"Stand down, Engineering Control. There is no danger to the ship. I repeat, stand down."

"Confirmation of a secondary nature has been confirmed. Engineering Control, out."

Sorti Ne began to cut back on the energy and the baby rolled off her hand and back onto the bed. One by one, they approached to feed, which almost gave the Engineering Control electronic heart failure, and then they went back to…ah, sleep. Did they sleep, or just rest?

"Control, can you give me some data on these creatures' basic physical composition?"

"The babies, as you call them, have no physical makeup. They are purely energy based life forms and very parasitic in nature."

"What do you mean?"

"Scans have indicated the creatures have the ability at the subatomic level to sense life form based energy, which you consist of, from several light years away. I have been running computer models and calculations. At the current intake of energy multiplied by their growth rate, I feel you will soon run out of food for them, which I believe, means the ship will be in danger."

Sorti Ne laughed to herself. The Control was starting to add emotional statements to her reports. "I believe…" she whispered to herself.

The Engineering Control broke in, "Explosive Pods are in place. Request permission to separate this section of the ship."

"This conversation is between Sorti Ne and I, so C your way out of it."

Sorti Ne giggled. "You mean, Control, that this is an A and B conversation, C your way out of it."

"Correction noted. Thank you, Engineer Sorti Ne."

"You're welcome." She chewed on her lip. "So what do you suggest, Control?"

"I am not sure if we can use your human discipline of raising children, but too much milk can cause distress and bloating in human babies. Also, one of your sayings is 'spare the rod, spoil the child'."

"You want me to spank them?"

"No, no, Engineer. But you must keep firm control over them at all times and definitely do not let them feed too much."

"Alright, Control. Thank you for the advice."

"All scans for biological, viral and subatomic contamination have shown no risk factors. The encasement field has been dropped. What are your orders, Captain?"

"Carry on, Control. I really don't think we need to keep a watch on the bridge. You're a million times more capable of running the ship than I am."

"Thank you for the compliment, Captain. Should I contact you about every major decision I make?"

"Negative. That is all." Sorti Ne quoted the computer.

***

General Cae grabbed Attalee by the front of his armor. "I told you not to let her go!" he screamed. Several guards reached for their swords but weren't sure who they should back if it came down to it. As of yet, neither man made a move for his sword.

Attalee looked into the general's eyes and didn't flinch. "Well, what do you have to say?" Cae demanded angrily. "You were right," King Attalee said.

The general let go, pushed him away and turned his back.

"Have you seen her?" Attalee asked, ignoring the breach of etiquette by General Cae.

"By the Gods, no," Cae said and began to pace. "Has she been captured?"

"The savages are checking the forest. I don't believe she has been taken," he said darkly.

"I share your concern, General. But she is a resourceful woman and a military one at that. She will figure out a way to get back here."

"I ordered you not to send her," General Cae shouted.

Attalee glanced at the guards. "Will you leave us for a moment?" They were only too happy to oblige the king. When the door closed, Attalee turned on the general.

"I will try to say this as gently as possible, General. You forget that I am the king. I and I alone give the orders around here, or have you forgotten?" He walked over and stood before the General.

Unbuckling his sword belt, the general turned and placed it on the table. "You are correct, King Attalee. I've overstepped my authority." His shoulders sagged in defeat. "I can no longer serve as general and I resign." Attalee angrily picked up the sword. "The position you hold isn't just an office to be given up on a whim or an emotional outbreak. You are the general of the New Roman Republic and I expect you to honor the position with the respect it deserves."

Cae sat down on a stool. "You don't understand, King Attalee. I can no longer serve. I'm becoming too emotional." He tried to suppress a sob.

Attalee set the sword on the table and then placed a hand on Cae's arm. "Look at me, my friend," he requested. Cae turned his head to look at his king.

"It doesn't shame you to show emotion. You are only a man and you have feelings. I don't think any less of you for caring about Dav. On the contrary, I feel the same as you. But Ka'an needs its general to help them through this war. I need you, not only as my general, but also as counsel and friend."

Cae looked away and fought to bring his emotions under control. Attalee picked up the sword and held it in front of the general. "Really, I understand."

There was a knock at the door. "Enter," Attalee spat out, angered by the intrusion.

The door burst open. Major Raki shouted out, "The savages are massing for another attack."

"What?" Attalee and Cae said together.

"It appears they will attack us again soon," he reconfirmed his last statement.

Attalee looked at Cae. "Do your duty, General." He handed Cae back his sword.

"Yes, sir." Cae buckled the sword back on.

"Your mounts are ready," the major reported as both men made their way to the wall.

***

The forest was alive with the sounds of the Quranian solders as they walked closely together to herd the Roman who had sabotaged the catapults. Dav had built a stone wall to make the entrance look like solid rock and so far, the soldiers hadn't found them.

Since there wasn't much to do in the cave, Dav decided to explore deeper into the darkness. She sent out a sonic pulse and was surprised when it didn't come back to her. *The cave must go on for miles, or twist and turn in a way that the pulse can't return.* After walking for a few minutes, she found steps carved into the rock to help climb a hardened mass of lava which blocked easy passage higher up the tunnel.

There was evidence of torches having been used and the oily smoke had left several inches of soot on the ceiling. A crude rope ran along the wall, maybe to show the way when or if a torch would blow out. Someone, or a group of people, had put a great deal of effort into exploring this cave, but from the dust on the floor, hadn't been back for many years. Maybe the boy would know of an expedition to explore caves around Ka'an.

As they sat around a small, smokeless fire eating a bird Yang had caught before their self-imposed incarceration in the cave, Dav asked the boy. "I'm not sure," he said, "I found this cave by accident."

The search for her continued day and night and the days stretched into weeks. From the listening post set up throughout the forest, it appeared as if they wouldn't give up.

Thom believed the Roman would have to come out of hiding eventually and they would be waiting.

***

"It appears we'll have to find another way out," Dav made the decision one day. Rian just sat quietly and looked at her. "We've been in here over thirty of your days and they're still looking for me."

"For us," the boy said rather seriously.

"I guess you're right," she giggled. "If they find either one of us, we'll be in trouble, huh?"

186

He shook his head yes.

"From my instruments," Dav checked her wrist pad, "it looks like a steady stream of fresh air is coming in through the opening of the cave and flows past us and up into the tunnel. So there must be another opening further on we can use to sneak out and get you home."

"You think so?" he asked, not meeting her eyes.

He doesn't want to leave with me, she thought with a frown. *I wonder why?* "You don't want to go exploring with me?"

He looked away again. "I have something I must do," he whispered. "Something I promised my father."

"Oh, I understand," even though she didn't. Reaching into her pack, Dav took out a package. "If you and the dogs are unable to get food, take a pill and feed the dogs one each. One of these has enough protein and sugars to maintain your body for three days."

Thank you," he ran and wrapped his arms around her waist. "Do you really have to leave?"

"I must get back to my friends." Rian sat back down in resignation.

Yang began to jump around as she picked up a pack. "You want to go with me?" He jumped around and whined with his tail wagging and tongue hanging out. Yin went and sat down protectively by the boy. "You're going to stay here, I take it," Dav asked her. In answer, Yin put her head down on her paws and growled as if the matter had already been decided.

"You know, I think they're more in charge than I am." Rian laughed.

"I would like to have the dog Yin stay with me. It helps keep me from getting lonely and she's cuddly."

"I was thinking of another word for them. Conniving little devils is more like it."

Yin and Yang's ears popped up. Had they just been insulted? They looked at each other and then back at Dav. Both bared their teeth and growled a low subsonic detonation at her.

"Alright," she threw her hands up, "I'm sorry. Please don't chew up my shoes in the middle of the night. I was just kidding."

The dog's looked at each other again and Yin sniffed.

Reaching into her pack, she said soothingly, "Did I get your long noses out of joint?"

The cave exploded into a flurry of motion as both dogs literally climbed over each other to get at the treats Dav threw up in the air. After grabbing the snacks, they retreated to opposite sides of the cave to eat in peace.

"Are you sure you'll be okay by yourself?"

Rian looked at Yin. "As long as she stays with me, I'll be alright."

"She's a good girl." Taking Yin's muzzle in her hand, she kissed the dog goodbye. "I hope to see you soon, little girl. Until we meet again."

Making her way into the interior of the cave, she found a piece of rope to feel the way and shut down her head lamp to conserve batteries. The pitch blackness closed around her and Dav shut her eyes to overcome the feeling of all-encompassing oppression. The sonic tabulations were confusing as they bounced up and down the shaft several times before coming back to the receiver, so she shifted over to laser imaging and let the computer map an approximate idea of what the passage looked like ahead.

It wasn't entirely satisfactory, but it was a touch better than holding onto a rope and blindly walking over a ledge. Yang's suit was better suited for underground work, being the stealth model. Dav set up their 3S controls to work in tandem and then watched his displays.

At one time, the cave appeared to have been a vent for the ancient volcano or bowl the Romans and Quranians were trapped in. Time and water had worn down its sides and they ducked to miss the occasional stalactites. After walking for over six hours uphill, they came to a three-way split in the tunnel. Turning on a lamp, she saw the rope continuing into the center one.

The branch to the right would take her toward Ka'an, but whoever had explored the caves had obviously been down that way and found a dead end. Her instruments showed the air flow followed the middle passage, but it would lead her deeper into the mountains and away from Ka'an.

What if the person who explored the cave had been killed in a rockslide and didn't check this way to the right? Maybe that passage would lead her back to Ka'an faster, but if she was wrong, it could cost her valuable time having to backtrack. *Trust your instincts.* "Which way would you go?" she asked Yang. In answer, he walked into the middle tunnel and then looked back at her as if to say, "Hey, let's get a move on".

Turning off her lamp, she motioned for him to proceed.

They had walked for two more hours before encountering a wall, so Dav called for a rest break and took out a food tablet for herself and Yang. The ground was hard and gritty, but the 3S inflated as she laid down and gave her illusion of floating. The air here had a strong salty smell to it, so Dav closed her face mask and turned on the filters. Before going to sleep, she instructed Yang to do the same.

Dav began to dream she was floating on one of the cities of Aqua. The sun was beating down on her tan skin with the sound of the water gently lapping against the sides of the pool. A cold drink was sitting beside her on a table and Yin and Yang lay panting in the shade under the table. *Wait a minute,* she was panting too. *I can't breathe.* Turning on her lamp, Dav screamed as she saw a white blob on her faceplate.

Knocking it away, she rolled and pulled a gun to fire on it. The long translucently while legs showed it was a huge spider. Looking around the tunnel, she corrected herself, hundreds of thousands of spiders. The wall looked like it was moving and Dav shrank back in horror. She had a serious phobia about spiders and the flamethrower appeared over her right shoulder as they waited for the attack to come.

The spiders didn't seem to notice her, but she still shrank back in fear. Trying to bring her heart rate back down to normal, she began to study them to see if could figure out why they hadn't attacked

190

yet. A spider ambled by, stopped and sent a long tongue out to lick the rock. Lick the rock?

Stooping down to take a sample, it registered ninety-nine percent sodium chloride. Salt. The salt was leeching out of the rocks and the albino spiders were here to collect it.

Humans secrete salt through their sweat glands and the exhalation of carbon dioxide from her mask must have attracted them to her biofilters, looking for the salt her suit was trying to flush out. They hadn't been under attack after all. Getting down on her knees, she crept up to one of the arachnids to get a better look at it.

It only had buds were its eyes should have been, but its legs had larger pads to sense the ground and a tongue to collect the salt. "It's blind," she whispered to Yang.

The spider felt the vibrations from her words and ran, dislodging small pebbles as it moved away. The light from her lamp went completely through its translucent body. All she could see of its internal organs was a small black dot she was sure was the brain case.

Yang was staying well away from the spiders and still had his flamethrower activated. "I think they're harmless," she patted him on the head, but he acted like he didn't believe her.

Her lamp caught something on the wall and she stopped. If she looked at an angle, she could see someone had taken great care to chisel handholds into the rock. It was over a hundred foot climb. "I guess I'll have to carry you."

He grinned.

"You like it when I have to do all the work, don't you?" Yang laughed at her.

Clipping a hook into Yang's D rings, she threw him over her back and had him make sure he was securely fastened to her suit. After the okay signal, she made quick work of the cliff and found the top of the cave opened into a gently sloping shaft that climbed upwards. Setting Yang down, she unhooked the snaps from her suit and let him run on ahead.

Locating the rope again, she prepared to turn off the light, but soot on the ceiling caught her attention. It must have taken someone forever to map this cave. Especially if all the person had was a torch or an oil lamp. *Maybe that's why the rope is in place.* A person could follow the rope in the dark and conserve the torches until they reached a point not yet explored. She was using the rope in much the same fashion, but she still had her computer to help map out the way.

Yang was sniffing down a hole beside the pathway. Dav stopped to look in. The hole contained human excrement and appeared to be several years old. Dav decided to clean her and Yang's waste containment bladder into the same hole. The pale green liquid quickly filled it and Yang backed away. If a dog backs away from poop, you know it has to smell bad. She flipped down her visor. "What have you been eating?"

Yang growled. How dare she try and blame the smell on him?

Dav laughed at his expression. Dropping a tablet into the waste, it gelled, hardened and then turned the same color as the surrounding stone. The smell was gone and their droppings were camouflaged. "Are you hungry?" Yang shook his head no.

"I kind of lost my appetite too."

The shaft continued up at a gentle slope for ten days. They made camp and woke to find the suns shining overhead. It must have been night-time and they had been under the opening the entire time. They were at the base of a deep cavern whose walls were crystallized glass and Dav couldn't see any way to safely reach the opening. She could try climbing, but there was a chance the wall would collapse, killing them both. As she sat and weighed her options, the 3S suit had automatically opened up panels to recharge the suit and Yang had gone back to sleep in the sun.

Resting for a day, she watched as the wind resistance and oxygen level picked up and traveled in the direction they had been headed. There must be another opening further along the tunnel. Logically, it would be better to try to find a safer way out. If they couldn't, there was always the option of retracing their steps and trying to climb the walls.

They walked again and then she moaned as the tunnel curved down. Vents of steam were exhausting into the cave. Did it travel all the way back down into the earth? Reaching the bottom, she was heartened at the sight of blue sky just a little way up the shaft. "We're almost there, buddy." He didn't answer.

Dav turned to see him stagger to the wall and collapse. "Yang!" she screamed and ran to him. A wave of sickness broke over her as Dav clenched her teeth together to keep from vomiting. Her movements were beginning to slow and Dav knew she had to close her visor shield, but her body wouldn't obey her mind's commands.

Grabbing Yang, she tried to drag him towards the opening. A hand grabbed the harness to pick him up. It was her hand, but it felt as if she was in someone else's body. It took all her will power to push off towards the blue sky. Focusing on the opening, she kept it in focus as she dragged herself and the dog up the incline. Her arms and legs felt like they were encased in blocks of lead.

She could feel the sweat build up on her skin as it taxed the 3S's ability to clean. Grinding her teeth together to the point she was sure they would break, she was fighting back the acidy taste as well as the urge to vomit. Her vision began to blur, she blacked out, then regained consciousness to find herself collapsing to her knees. The opening was closer.

The gloves on her hands were literally digging furrows into the stone as she fell face down and tried to crawl forward. Turning her head to focus on the blue sky, she marveled at how cool the smooth rock felt against her skin. The air around her flashed a brilliant blue and gave her the energy to crawl forward a little more. Was it enough? Before she lost consciousness again, Dav's last thoughts were sadness because she wasn't going to make it out of the cave alive and she would never see General Cae again.

CHAPTER SEVEN

As Caiisa went to step down, the scene changed underfoot, revealing a flat floor instead of a stairway and she stumbled into Thudder. He steadied her with a hand until the priestess could get acclimated to her new surroundings.

"What the...?" she exclaimed. Looking around the dimly lit and sparsely furnished room, her blood began to boil. Reaching into her robe, she pulled out the stone knife Athena had given her. The reason for her anger was seeing Hades, God of the Underworld, draped across a low couch, his tentacles hanging listlessly on the floor. His head was hanging down as if he were dead. Hearing the rustle of her robe, his head snapped up in fear to look the priestess in the eye.

"Ah, Athena. You bring your little minions to do your dirty work?"

Athena? With a quick look over her shoulder, Caiisa could see Athena and the Warrior with their weapons drawn.

Athena chuckled. "It's time for you to die, Hades. Your control over the Death World has gone on too long."

Thudder tried walking over to the wall to look at a torch, stumbled and fell down on a chair. His massive weight splintered it into kindling, fit only to be used as firewood. While trying to stand, he put a hand on the table and broke two of its legs.

"What's wrong with the idiot?" Hades stormed. "Did you come here just to tear up my furniture?"

"He's a little slow," Caiisa said. "He really doesn't mean any harm, so don't make fun of him."

The god sneered as Thudder knocked an oil lamp off the wall. Screaming in terror as his pants ignited, he rolled to the ground beside the couch. With the small movement of a finger, Hades put the fire out. No longer considering the idiot as a worthy enemy, he turned back to the three legitimate threats.

"You must feel pretty confident, Goddess, to come into the Death World to do battle with me."

"You're weak and vulnerable," Athena hissed.

"Weak, yes. Vulnerable? Well, let's begin our battle for control of…" A scream cut his words short and he stiffened in anticipation of an attack. In shock, Hades realized the sound came from behind him. A massive arm the size of a tree trunk, snaked around Hades' neck, pulling him off the couch in a stranglehold.

Tentacles began to fly wrapping around the arm, trying to dislodge the idiot. In a mirror, Hades began to see Thudder's face changing from the stupid lopsided grin he always wore to a look of pure evil. "You are the son of Athena," he gasped, finally seeing the gambit Athena had played.

She had tricked her son into believing he was a village idiot to conceal his true identity until the time was right. If he had known, Hades would never have let the man-God get behind him.

Caiisa turned to Athena. "Thudder is your son?"

"Plunge the stone knife into his heart!" Athena screamed.

Caiisa stood quietly looking at the Goddess, trying to digest all the startling events that had

196

unfolded in the last few moments. "What are you battling for control of?" she asked quietly.

"Control of the Death World, my child. To make it easier for people to die with dignity."

A choking laugh rumbled from deep in Hades' chest. "Come, Athena! Tell the human the truth."

"That is the truth."

"You would brainwash your son, turn a human into a healer, risk war with another God just to allow a human to die in dignity? Tell Caiisa what you're really here for, Goddess." He spat out the last word as if it were a bitter root.

Athena stood looking like a child caught with a hand in the sweet meats. "What is the truth?" Caiisa asked, looking at Hades.

Hades turned to look at the most beautiful human on the planet and found he couldn't speak.

"What is the truth?" Caiisa demanded.

"You aren't a healer. Athena only used you to get the Book of Knowledge from me."

"Book of Knowledge?"

"Let me explain. Whenever a human dies, I write down all their knowledge into my ledger and read it from time to time. As the Goddess of Knowledge, Athena will stop at nothing to kill me and steal the book."

"Is this true?" Caiisa turned to Athena. "I order you, priestess, to kill him!"

"Answer me…is this true? Have you been lying to me all along?"

"Plunge the stone knife into his heart, you stupid bitch!"

"Why can't you do it, Athena?"

197

"It would start a war between the Gods. His blood mustn't be on my hands."

"You've already started a war between the Gods," Hades stormed. Seeing she wasn't going to get any help from Caiisa, she screamed at Hades, "Give me the Book of Knowledge!"

"You know I can't give it to you willingly." A stone spear appeared in her hand.

"I thought you didn't want my blood on your hands, Athena." Hades spat on the ground.

"It won't be," she announced, with a sly, evil grin on her face and handed the spear to the Warrior.

In one fluid motion, the Warrior pulled his arm back and then hurled the spear so fast, it couldn't be followed with human eyes. Caiisa screamed in horror. Thudder was just behind Hades and she saw the comprehension of his fate by the widening of his eyes.

Then the spear was sticking out of the wall behind them. Had the warrior missed? As if in answer, a fountain of blood poured from Hades' chest. Thudder stumbled back to look stupidly at the river of blood flowing to the floor.

"The spear went right through them," Caiisa gasped.

Athena chuckled to herself and walked over to a shelf cut into the stone wall. Reverently, she picked up the Book of Knowledge and walked to stand over Thudder.

He looked up from the blood-soaked floor. "Why, Mother?" She backhanded him across the face.

"You should have killed him for me. Your older brother is the only one I can depend on." Turning swiftly to face Caiisa, she whispered in a low, venomous tone, "As for you, bitch, you no longer serve me or my temple."

Without fear, Caiisa stepped forward until she was nose to nose with Athena. "You no longer have my services anyway, Goddess. I can't believe I was gullible enough to be taken in by your lies."

Athena laughed. "Maybe I have taught you something, human."

"Oh, you have, Goddess," she let the words hang in the air. "Yes, my child?"

"I am no longer your 'child', you lying, conniving, back-stabbing snake. I've learned you're an incorrigible bitch, who would kill her own son for a book."

"Not just any book. The Book of Knowledge."

"The price you paid was pretty steep."

"The price was worth it, dear Caiisa. I would have sacrificed a great deal more than this. With this book, I'll gain supreme knowledge, consciousness and the power to take over the leadership of the Gods."

Caiisa spat in her face. Athena raised her hand as if to smack her, but the Warrior grabbed her hand.

For the first time in many months, she heard him speak. "You have what you want, Mother. It's time to leave." Turning, the Goddess folded space and they disappeared.

Turning to the two men who were left, she could only stand and look at them in shock. Walking slowly to Thudder, she dropped to her knees in the pool of blood surrounding him and concentrated her healing power. It didn't work. "It is true then, I can heal no more."

"I'm sorry you got mixed up in this..." Thudder gasped out. "I didn't know my mother was going to kill him. We were just supposed to try and scare him.

You must believe me."

"I do believe you, Thudder." Sadly, Caiisa looked at Hades. "I guess I owe you an apology."

"You were only following the path you felt was the correct one. As the God of the Death World, I have noticed you humans have a common thread which runs through your lives, the feeling of regret."

"Well, I certainly regret that Athena used me to kill you." Hades laughed. "It was nothing personal from my end either."

"Why were you trying to kill me?"

"I wasn't!"

"What about all the rocks and pieces of buildings you tried to drop on me?"

"Who do you think was telling you to stop, step right or back up?"

"It was you?" she asked. "Why?"

"Athena knew you would never kill me without a good reason, so she tried to hurt you to make you angry. You have quite a temper."

Caiisa blushed. "Since Athena has the Book of Knowledge, is she now the God of the Death World?"

Hades tried to laugh, but spit up blood.

"The owner of the Book of Knowledge can wield great power, especially if the energy is given freely. I'll not last much longer, Caiisa. You must become the Goddess of the Death World. It's the only way you can heal your friend, Thudder, and thwart Athena's evil plan."

"How can I do that? Athena has the Book of Knowledge."

"Go to the shelf," he whispered, in great pain. "There's an old book with its binding worn thin from use. Bring it here to me."

Caiisa could see it from where she was standing. Gently taking the book down, she carried it to Hades. He smiled at her. "The one Athena took was the Book of Regrets."

"What?"

"I switched the covers. When Athena opens the book, her soul will be filled with all the regret you humans feel."

Caiisa began to laugh.

Hades tried to lift the worn cover, but was too weak. "Hurry, open the book. My time grows near," his voice was weak and shaky.

She opened the book for him.

"Read," he demanded. "Read so the power can flow from me to you." She went to stand by him and read out loud.

"Be of peace.

The death of any creature should be a peaceful one. Be of love.

Without judgments or recriminations, love the people you deliver into the arms of death.

Be of comfort.

The ones who are left behind need comfort so the soul of their dear departed will make it safely to the Death World.

Be of comfort to the dying.

Each passage should be arranged as quickly and painlessly as possible. Be at peace with yourself.

Only a being who is at peace with themselves and the universe around them can assume the mantle of responsibility over the Death World and the souls who reside there in peace and love."

Caiisa was in shock. This wasn't the view of Hades she had been led to have.

"Will you accept?" Hades asked after she had finished reading. Glancing at Thudder, who was gasping for air, she nodded. "Kiss me," he whispered.

"Kiss you?"

"Please. Just one kiss before I die."

"Is this how the power is transferred?"

He smiled. "I could lie to you and say yes, but no…that isn't the way. Upon my death, it will flow into your soul."

"Why the kiss?"

"I have loved you, Caiisa, since the first time I…" he gasped in pain and sat back, unable to speak anymore.

Tenderly, she cradled his head in her hands and bent down to look into his eyes. The look of love in them was almost more than she could bear. Their lips touched and Caiisa felt a surge of energy so powerful, she almost fainted. It felt like the very cells in her body were on fire and tingled all the way down to the tips of her toes.

Opening her eyes, she looked into his as he breathed his last and then quietly began to relax as the pain of living receded from the husk of the shell that had housed his soul.

Tears fell from her cheeks and splashed quietly on Hades. Deep down, she had loved him too.

An anger began to build within her. She had been used by the Goddess Athena for a vile, evil plan. Thudder was gasping his last breaths.

"This will not stand!" she screamed and sent out a blast of pure blue healing power that traveled through Hades, Thudder and out through the tunnels of the Death World to cover the Planet Chosen. Anyone on the brink of death was miraculously healed.

Thudder climbed to one knee. "You must believe me, Caiisa. To kill Hades wasn't part of the plan. We were just supposed to scare him to get the book."

"I believe you, Thudder."

A voice startled them. "It feels good not to be on death's door." Hades chuckled.

Caiisa and Thudder turned in surprise. "You're supposed to be dead!"

"Yes, I am, but such is your compassion and love for others, your feelings brought *me* back to life."

Caiisa could only stand and look at him as the power began to ebb.

He walked over and took her cheek in his hand. "Why did you cry for me, Caiisa?"

"You said you loved me."

"Did you find the remark distasteful?"

"On the contrary, Hades. When you professed your love for me, it was then I realized I felt the same toward you."

Hades took her hand and placed it over his heart. "It isn't easy being the God of the Death World, but I will try to help you."

Stunned, she blurted out, "You don't want the energy back?"

Heavily, he sat down on the couch. "Caiisa, you would have to die to pass on the power and I hope that doesn't happen in my lifetime."

"You said you will help me?" Caiisa asked. "Of course I will!"

As Thudder pulled the stone spear out of the wall, Hades clutched her close to him. "You have nothing to fear from me. I'm going to find my mother." With a look of intense anger, Thudder folded space and disappeared.

With a wave of his hand, Hades repaired the furniture and cleaned up the blood. Guiding Caiisa to the couch, he sat down and just looked at her.

"I still don't understand how I was able to bring you back to life."

"You have power over life and death now. You can take or restore life as you deem fit."

"I could just take Athena's life right now and there's nothing she could do about it?"

"That's correct."

"Why didn't you take her life when she attacked you?"

"It would have been dishonorable to use the power for such an evil purpose."

"All this time, I thought you were such an evil God."

Hades laughed. "When you think about death, it isn't usually a happy affair."

Caiisa laughed. "That is true."

"But you now know death is supposed to be a peaceful event."

"Why did you attack me in the temple?"

"I didn't."

"You did!"

"Caiisa. I'm telling you, it wasn't me."

"What is it you're telling me?"

"You were deceived, just like when Athena made you think you were a healer. You were made to see a creature that doesn't exist. Look at me, please."

She turned to him.

"What do you see right now?"

She looked him over. "I see a man."

"What did you see when you first came into my room?"

"I saw you sitting on the couch with your tentacles on the ground."

"Ah, ah, that's funny. Do you see any tentacles now?"

"I really was tricked." She frowned and bit her lip.

Sitting, he caused two glasses to appear in his hands and gave her one. "How did you become the God of the Death World?"

Hades looked grim, as if facing an unpleasant memory. Sipping at the wine until the glass was half empty, he seemed to be reluctant to talk about it.

"If you would rather not speak about it..." she started to stay.

"When the Abominations attacked our world, millions of humans and Gods were killed. Their souls had no place to go. My father created Hades, which I was named after. He found he enjoyed the task, as the dead would pass on their knowledge to him. There was another consequence of being in charge of Hades. All the regrets the being carried in life would accompany them into the afterlife as well."

Taking her hand, he stood up and gently pulled her to him. "Come, I want to show you something."

He walked toward a solid wall and brushed a section aside as if it was a curtain hanging in the way. The torches in the room sprang into full flame and Caiisa could see a room as large as the eye could see. It was filled with books. They were stacked on shelves and overflowing into the walkways.

"What are all these books? More books of knowledge?"

"There is only one Book of Knowledge, Caiisa. Remember what I told you before about the common thread that runs through your race? Well, these are the Books of Regrets."

Caiisa could only shake her head. It was so sad that knowledge only filled one book and here were millions filled with regrets. Taking a book off the shelf, she opened it to the first page and began to read.

I, Alexandria Pedica, regret I was killed before my baby could be born. Caiisa clutched her chest. It felt like she too, had been killed before the child could be born. The pain and sorrow of the woman washed over Caiisa and a tear ran down her face.

Hades hastily closed the book to keep her from reading more and put it back on the shelf. "That's one of the more mild ones. There is one book I keep

206

the worst regrets in, but that should be kept for another day."

Caiisa could still feel the loss the woman had felt. "How do you deal with all these feelings? They're so sad!"

"With compassion."

He walked back out into the main room. Caiisa followed and sat down at the table. Looking around the room, she commented. "For a God, you certainly live a very simplistic lifestyle. Why are you so unlike the other Gods?"

"I was just like the other Gods, living without a care in the world, drinking, wine, women and song. Then my friends and family were killed by the Abominations and even more went off to fight." He stopped and looked embarrassed. "I was a coward. Instead of going to fight, I ran. When the battle was over, my father, family and friends were all dead. Only a small fraction of our race had survived.

"So I've had to live with the guilt of not being there when my father died. "When my friends died," he finished quietly.

"The only way I could see my father and friends again was to go into the Death World. I realized the only way to redeem myself..." He choked back a sob.

She took his hand, softly stroking it. "Go on..."

"I became the God of Hades. I made sure those dying went peacefully. It was the only way I could take care of my father and friends. Talking to my father, I discovered dying wasn't all that bad. It's the fear of death that seems to fill our time with depressing thoughts and nightmares."

He looked pleadingly at her. "It doesn't have to be this way, Caiisa. We need to let other beings know it is alright to die. Death is a natural progression of life."

Caiisa smiled. "We'll work together to make sure everyone knows this, Hades. I would like to open a temple in Ka'an for the sick and dying."

"That would be the kind thing to do."

The table filled with food. "I'm hungry, are you?"

"Starving."

Handing her a plate, she began to load it with spicy meat and fruit. "The Book of Regrets you keep the worst, uh regrets in. Where is it?"

"Athena took it."

"What will happen when she opens the Book and reads the stories within?"

"The Goddess' soul will be filled with the darkest, deepest feelings of misery and despair you could ever imagine."

"Then what do we do?"

He was silent for a long time. "We wait for her to come back to us!"

***

The Roman archers were manning the top of the wall and watching the sea of humanity marching toward them. The remaining catapults had been moved and were hitting the wall with a combination of rocks and fire bladders.

The area being hit was so small, the Roman archers would watch the rocks being loaded and could move out of the way before it hit the wall.

The fire bladders were more lethal, and they stayed off to the side when one was loaded onto the firing arm of the weapon.

King Attalee and General Cae could see the Quranians were within striking distance of the Roman longbows. The general gave the order to start releasing their arrows whenever they felt a target was within reach.

Wave after wave of arrows were sent into the savages' ranks and even though they had crude shields, were taking a terrible toll on the attackers. Men would scream in pain as one or two arrows would hit them and their comrades would try to help them back to where Chenee was tending the men's wounds.

Attalee arranged his sword strap and then looked at General Cae. "What do you think they're doing at the moment? I would have thought the Quranian Battle Master would have run out of attack strategies by now."

General Cae was looking out over the plains. No men had been left behind to tend the fires or help the wounded. "I would say the Barbarians are going to launch an all-out assault. Basically, a combination of ladder, archer, ramp and catapult attack."

Attalee worked his ear over, and then caught himself. "What do you think it will accomplish? That method of attack has failed before."

Pulling at his beard, Cae thought for a moment. "They think they can wear us down. Their battle master knows he outnumbers us four to one and won't have the fatigue factor to contend with."

"Perhaps we need to double the guard on the wall."

"No," Cae said emphatically.

"Why not?" Attalee said, anger clearly heard in his voice. *Was the General disobeying another order and so soon?*

Cae looked at him and then felt his face turn red. "Let me explain, King Attalee. The fewer men and women we have on the wall, the fewer targets will be available for the Quranians to hit. Also, I will have more room for our legions to maneuver if need be. We have to think about our men and women making mistakes if they get too tired."

"You don't think it would be wise to move the legions closer to the wall in case they're needed? The ground has dried enough that we can make housing available if needed."

"I agree with your assessment of the situation. I was concerned about my troops."

"Very well then," he nodded.

Cae caught the signalman's eye and sent a message down the line.

Turning to Major Raki, he gave the order for the troops to work on bringing rocks and lamp oil bombs to the wall.

Quranian archers fanned out on either side of the catapults to set up crossfire at the Roman troops. The catapults were firing nothing but the fire bladders and the wall in that section had to be abandoned. A crew of men ran forward and began to build a ramp frame.

Other men were setting ladders against the wall and trying to climb up. Cae had to shift men away from the section being hit by the catapults to kick the ladders away and watched with glee as the men tumbled to their deaths.

Men working on the ramps were out of arrow range as the angle was too close and an archer would put himself at risk by leaning over the wall.

"Start throwing the stones over the edge," Cae ordered. The stones had a satisfactory result as the savages scurried away from the platform. Thom, seeing the Romans above his men, ordered his archers to move in and protect the ramp builders.

"Use the Scorpios to target their archers in the rear!" Cae screamed as several of his men went down.

As one of the men building the ramp was killed or injured, another worker took his place.

"They're learning," Cae remarked to Major Raki. "They're better disciplined this time." He dropped a firebomb on the workers. They were trying to use shields to deflect the bombs, but the jugs would usually break and splatter oil and fire everywhere. They found it was better to jump out of the way and throw sand or dirt on the fire. Again, if any man was injured, he was immediately replaced.

A rock from a catapult hit the wall, bounced off a column and took out several Roman soldiers. But the Scorpios began to exact a toll on the Quranian archers and they were beginning to retreat. Thom could be seen beating his men to make them return to the fight. The men building the ramps needed to be protected by the archers, but few would return to become target practice for the Scorpios.

"I need more firebombs!" Major Raki screamed as larger beams were being brought to the wall. Attalee looked over to inspect the Quranian

211

progress and was appalled at the amount of men who lay on the ground, killed or injured. They numbered in the hundreds.

***

Chief Messa came walking up behind Thom. "Get the archers back into the fight," he ordered.

Thom didn't look at him. "They will be slaughtered."

"Use your men with shields to protect them," Messa protested.

Thom looked at him in disgust. "We've already tried that," he sneered with scorn in his voice. "The metal tipped arrows from that damned weapon go right through our shields."

Chief Messa seemed not to hear him. "Flank the walls and get the Roman dogs away from this area."

Thom began to laugh. "Were you asleep when last I spoke to you, old man? Look on either side of you and see our men attacking on the flanks, the forward position and everywhere in between. We are doing everything possible to overtake the wall and destroy these motherless men of a dog. Now, if you'll leave me alone so I can plan this battle, it would be helpful." Without waiting for a reply, he turned his back on the chief and walked away.

Chief Messa watched his retreating back. His mind was in a fog from the Ja, Ja root. Had he and Thom talked about this before? For that matter, what had they been talking about now? Whatever it was, he had told the battle master off and he felt better. Picking up a burning stick, he headed back into his tent. He wanted to hear screaming to help him sleep better.

All around him, the shrieks of his men dying filled the air, but it was the scream of a woman that interested him right now. Closing his tent flap, the woman's anguished screams with those of the men dying, and both fell on deaf ears.

***

Sorti Ne was left alone with the babies. Most of them had started to move around as she and Control had spoken. As she was sitting with her legs over the edge of the bed, they climbed all over her body, where they flattened out and molded against her. A feeling of great calm settled over her. Getting up was a comedic event. *You babies have gotten heavy.* Of course, she didn't have the 3S on to maximize her strength, but the way they were balanced out, Sorti Ne was finally able to climb to her feet.

"I really should get up to the bridge and look over the damage." The shuttle ride was uneventful and the babies were content just being close to her.

The door opened to a disaster area. Carl had taken an axe to everything breakable. Now why would they have a fire axe on a spaceship? There wasn't anything that could be chopped through in the event of a fire, except for the panels and Control usually put them out before they could start.

"It's strange how humans cling to archaic habits," she whispered. "That is what makes you humans so interesting."

The babies screeched and rushed off her toward the unmistakable male voice.

213

Damn, no blaster. But the fire axe was nearby. How did Carl get out of the gel cell?

Raising the axe overhead, Sorti Ne turned swiftly to defend herself. The axe dropped from her hands.

A man dressed in a simple robe was sitting on one of the acceleration couches and the babies were climbing all over him in apparent glee. She could only stand and look at the scene unfolding before her.

"Don't be alarmed, Sorti Ne. I will not harm you!"

"Who are you?"

"I'm called by many names, but from reading your mind, you would call me King Attuicus."

"Our captain is looking for you."

"I was just a secondary diversion. Her mission is much more critical than that, my friend."

"Who are you calling friend? You hijacked our ship."

"I didn't hijack anything. That honor goes to the Gentle One."

"Well, he did it so our captain would find you."

"Again, that was just a secondary concern."

"I know, Attuicus. We already went over that little bit of information. So what do you want?"

"I want nothing…" The silence seemed to stretch on.

"Why are you here?" she prompted. *Getting an answer from him is like pulling teeth.*

"Why do you want to pull my teeth?"

"Ah, you can read my thoughts?!"

"If you call them that, yes. Let's cut through all the bull as you are thinking, and get down to brass tacks."

Mentally and physically, she laughed.

He continued, "I'm here to visit my children."

"Your children?"

Attuicus began to laugh. "It is shocking, I know."

Sorti Ne came over and sat down beside him. The babies began to climb into her lap.

"I'm glad I was able to save them for you. Where will you be taking them? To their mother?"

"I'll be leaving them here with you."

"Do you pay child support?"

"I could really get to like you, Engineer Sorti Ne. You have a delightful sense of humor. Now what I'm going to tell you is very serious. Your Control was correct in that you must not let the children grow too fast. They must learn how to live with creatures of lesser abilities."

"You make it sound like we're the scum of the universe."

"It wasn't meant that way."

"It sounded that way." She redirected the conversation. "What kind of creature are you and where are you from?"

"Those two questions are difficult to answer, but I'll make an attempt. The reality you know is just one of many. In my reality, our babies are on the bottom of the food chain. Out of several trillion, only one will make it to my level of development."

"Seems kind of cruel."

"If you understood the power even our children possess, you would never make such a statement."

"I've seen their ability to open the portal between universes. Pretty neat trick."

"Can you imagine a universe where children with this magnitude of power run unchecked?"

"It would be pandemonium."

"Especially if there were no checks and balances."

"Why are you telling me all this?"

He looked very grim. "I travel through many of the known realities. Unfortunately, I left the door open when I entered your reality and some of my children escaped here as well."

"Tsk, tsk. Hardly a glowing endorsement for someone of your greater abilities."

Attuicus laughed. "Still smarting over my choice of words. I am sorry, human. Perhaps I should have said each of us have our own strengths and weaknesses."

"Oh, you're admitting you have weaknesses?"

He looked pained. "Yes, yes. I believe I made that glaringly apparent."

"I didn't hear you apologize."

He sat and looked at her in surprise. He hadn't been able to read her thoughts before she made that last comment. "I'm very impressed with your natural abilities, Engineer Sorti Ne. I can see now why my children are drawn to you."

She stood with her arms crossed, waiting.

"I am sorry for the problems I've caused you."

"Apology declined. So, what is it you want me to do with them?"

"You demand an apology and then refuse to accept it?"

"Everyone, excuse me, everything makes mistakes. You're no different than anyone else."

"That's very kind of you," Attuicus said dryly.

Sorti Ne picked up on the sarcasm. "Hey, you're the one who started the whole lesser race thing."

He shook his head. "You are one of the few humans that can actually put me on the defensive. I love to listen to your arguments with the Control."

Her face hardened. "You don't realize just how much we 'lesser beings' or humans enjoy our privacy."

"If your race only knew how often you were observed by how many various types of species, you would be shocked."

"Well, I don't have to like it."

"True. I don't like it much either, but I'm still observed as well."

"I asked you a question earlier. What do you want me to do with your children?"

"I need you to adopt them and teach them human compassion."

"Adopt them? Teach them compassion? I think you may have the wrong person."

"I didn't choose you, Sorti Ne. The children did and I agree with their choice."

"If I refuse to take care of them?"

"You and your universe will be in peril. The last time my children ran amok here, your race barely survived the destruction."

"You really don't give me a lot of choices."

"It is all I can give you. I do apologize."

"Why can't you just take them back home?"

"It isn't our way."

"You'll put us and our universe at risk, just because it isn't your way?"

"Different cultures, different beliefs."

"This is a crock of shit, excuse my French."

"Why would you shit in a crock anyway? You have a bathroom onboard."

"Don't try to misdirect the argument. You know what I mean."

"I sense you're being condescending."

"You better believe I am. You're unbelievable."

"Who's being judgmental now? People who live in glass spaceships, shouldn't throw meteorites."

For once, Sorti Ne didn't have a good comeback.

"It's very easy to judge others as being wrong because their ways are alien and different than your own. I made the mistake of saying there are lesser and greater beings and I admit, my choice of words was incorrect. But aren't you doing the exact same thing?"

"I believe he got you on that one," the Control broke into the conversation. "I still don't have to like it."

"True," Control answered.

She looked at King Attuicus. "It would appear I really don't have much of a choice."

"We all have choices. If you don't want to do it, then set them free."

"And watch them destroy my world!"

"You will eventually destroy them, but the cost will be prohibitive."

"I'll do it, then."

"Thank you."

The children seemed to sense she'd accepted the Bond and with a loud screech, they began to climb all over her.

"I will leave you to your duties," Attuicus said.

"Wait a minute. I'm on my own here?"

"What more do you want?"

"I can't even talk to them. How can I take care of them?"

"Talk to them as you're talking to me. They'll learn your language quickly, especially if it's on a telepathic level. Spoken word is a little harder. Haven't you already noticed they're following your lead and suggestions?"

Thinking about the way they'd spread out over her body so she could walk to the bridge was one thing she had noticed. Maybe she could raise these beings. They were kind of cute.

She turned to say something to King Attuicus, but he was gone. "Just like a man. Leave all the raising of the kids up to the woman."

CHAPTER EIGHT

The savages learned to work as a team. One man would act as the spotter and would yell, "Rock" and they would scurry away. After it hit, they would run back and build until the next yell came. The oil lamps were another matter.

As soon as it hit, the oil would burn their skin and the wood. They tried protecting their skin with hides saturated in water. But the water was soon depleted. The workers were blackened with burns, yet on they toiled building the ramp. The lucky ones were the few who could dodge a falling rock or firebomb at least once, but the odds were against them and men fell in droves from injuries.

It seemed to help when Thom sent a barrage of fire bladders to the top of the wall to shield the workers. When the flames died down, a small, fast moving group of Romans would rush forward and unleash a firestorm on the ramp. Then the workers would beat back the flames with water and dirt and continue. Attalee was amazed at the singlemindedness of his enemies.

He winced as he saw a man rolling on the ground to put a fire out and then get back up and return to the fight.

General Cae was walking by and the king stopped him. Attalee noted his singed uniform and how the man was covered in soot and sweat. "Take a break, General."

"I can't," Cae gasped for breath. His sides heaving as he sucked in a lung full of air. "The damn savages are taking unbelievable casualties, yet they still continue. It is now a contest of wills and I will not break first," he gasped.

The general looked at a signalman. "Move a legion to help the right flank. Tell Centurion Regis if he doesn't keep his eyes open and anticipate the enemies' movements, I will demote his ass back down to a common soldier."

"How do you signal 'ass'?" the man questioned. Cae laughed and walked away.

"Well, you seem to have everything under control," Attalee said with a chuckle and went to help with caring for the wounded. The top of the wall was littered with his own men, either dead or dying. Picking one man up over his shoulders, the king carried him down to the area Caiisa had set up for the wounded.

She'd moved from her temple on the hill to be close to the wall. Too many men had died trying to make it to Athena's temple. Attalee found her tending the wounded and saw several men walking who had just been healed. Surrendering the wounded man into her care, he ordered the men to follow him. With their aid, he helped clear the wall of the wounded and the dead were moved to a temporary place until the proper rites could be performed and they could be buried outside the city walls, in keeping with the law.

Attalee went to find General Cae and saw he had moved further along to redirect a counter assault. He was limping from an arrow in his leg. Bending over, he broke it off and then picked up a rock and dropped it over the wall. It hit a man's shield and rolled down the ramp, injuring more men at the bottom.

"Get your leg taken care of, General," Attalee screamed over the sounds of battle.

Cae ignored him. "I need more rocks and firebombs," he screamed over his shoulder. "If I see another arrow not hit its target, I will throttle that man with my bare hands!" he shouted at his archers. His face was contorted in pain as he limped along the wall, shouting encouragement to his men and women.

He looked like a man possessed as he cut down the enemy with his sword and dropped rocks and firebombs on the workers. Morale began to improve and the Romans rallied to his calls.

Attalee found the major and ordered him to make sure the general continued to receive the items he needed.

**

Chief Messa woke in his tent. The smell of burning flesh was strong in the air. He'd been in the middle of a very strange nightmare. For the first time in several years, his mind felt clean. Refreshed. He pulled back his tent flap and found the nightmare was real. Wave after wave of his men were being repulsed by the Romans.

"I will defeat you!" Thom screamed at the statue. One of the team leaders was standing beside the battle master. "Look how the statue sits and sneers at our efforts. Once we take Ka'an, I will tear it down with my bare hands!" The team leader looked at the statue. It was standing with its hands on its hips as it always did and looked over the plains. Shaking his head, the team leader ran off to help pull a beam into place. Thom continued to shout insults and threats at the statue.

The plains were littered with dead men. *How much longer can this go on?* The ramps were being constructed at a good pace, despite the efforts of the Romans to burn them to the ground. If they worked into the night, his army could possibly be over the wall in a day or two. But how many men would he lose before he should retreat? Chief Messa went and found Thom. The man was tired, dirty and burned.

Thom gave the chief a look of barely veiled contempt and for a moment, Messa was afraid of his childhood friend. He couldn't raise the courage to talk to Thom, so he said nothing and continued to walk and look over the battlefield. He sat down on a rock and watched as they made progress up the wall. By nightfall, over a thousand men were dead and ten thousand had wounds of one kind or another.

The battle continued into the night, with both sides trying to fight by firelight. More Romans were killed by the catapults overnight than from the previous day. The men couldn't see the rocks tumbling through the air. In retrospect, the savages couldn't see the rocks or firebombs until they landed and the ramp was being consumed by fire at a faster rate than during the day.

But the attackers were getting better at making repairs and the ramp continued to climb up the wall.

***

Chenee was doing her best to help the wounded. The number of men being killed or maimed made her sick, but she didn't have much time to think about it as she and the child worked through the night. By dawn, she could only sit in exhaustion and cry as she looked at the pile of bodies that continued to grow.

Fresh Roman troops moved in to continue the battle and were doing a good job of aiming the bombs at the ramp. Parts of it were beginning to collapse since most of the skilled workers had already been killed or injured. Now, the less skilled men were being slaughtered.

Chenee saw her father sitting on a rock and went to confront him. "You must stop this war," she cried out to him.

Chief Messa turned his back to her.

She wouldn't be deterred and walked around until she was once again facing him. "You are killing our people for nothing."

"They are dying for our freedom!" he screamed, his face livid with anger. "They are dying so we will no longer have to hide in the mountains in fear for our lives. The Chosen dogs won't respect us until we have defeated them."

"We've already defeated them, Father. Look how they cower in their keeps and there is nowhere our people can't go in this land."

Messa scowled at her. "Leave me," he walked toward his tent.

Angrily, she moved toward the wall. "Thom, you must tell my father to stop this battle. You are the only one he will listen to," she pleaded with him.

"What does a woman know about war?" he spat on her.

"It may be true that I know little about war," her eyes downcast. "But I know it will take our women many years to replace the men you're throwing away today."

"You know nothing about war or making babies, so I wouldn't worry about either. Now return to tending the wounded!" he screamed and then moved forward to help with a heavy beam for the ramp.

***

On the wall, she could see General Cae and King Attalee. They were trying to help a man with an arrow through his breastplate. Slowly lowering the man to the ground, they discovered he was dead. Attalee shook his head and looked out over the plains.

The Plains of Sorrow, it was apply named. He caught sight of her and stood transfixed. Even with her skins covered in blood and her hair in disarray, she was beautiful in his eyes. He dodged an arrow and went back to helping the wounded.

"I miss you," she whispered, even though she knew he couldn't hear.

A deep groan of splintered wood caught her attention and then cries for help. Men scattered to get out of the way as one of the main supports for the ramp gave way and collapsed. Men were caught under the falling timbers and she could hear them screaming.

While men were moving away from the carnage, she was running toward it and began to pull on the timbers to help the trapped men. Chenee expected to be shot by the archers, but she heard General Cae give the command to stop, so she called out for the Quranian soldiers to help her. Tentatively at first, they kept a wary eye on the wall, but the Roman archers had moved away.

It took hours to get the men out and Chenee began to work on their wounds and looked gratefully up at General Cae. She waved a thanks to him. Being a true gentleman, the only sign he gave to show he had seen her was a slight tip of his head.

"Sound the retreat," Chief Messa told the team leaders. The drums began to beat and the Quranians moved back away from the wall.

***

"They're finally retreating," General Cae said and fainted dead away. Attalee had to grab his armor to keep Cae from falling over the wall. Gently, he had him carried to Caiisa.

As soon as the Quranians had recovered their dead and wounded from the collapsed ruin, Attalee had the soldiers firebomb the ramp until it was a pile of glowing coals. The smoke began to drift over the retreating Quranian soldiers and seemed an omen to add to their misery and feelings of defeat.

"Major Raki," he called out and then was startled as the man was right by his elbow. "Make sure this legion is relieved. Also, I want rocks and firebombs supplied to the top of the wall within the hour, just in case they decide to attack again. And by the way, you're in command until the general gets back on his feet."

Raki scratched an itch under his breastplate and smiled. "I thought that would be the case, sir."

***

Chief Messa walked through his returning soldiers and felt despair. He had never seen his men look so demoralized. Few of them had come out of battle without some type of injury and were looking to him for answers. He had none for them. It was as if a veil had been lifted from his eyes and he clearly saw how he had destroyed his people over a vendetta that happened years before most of these men had even been born.

All his plans were in ruins. He met Thom walking back from the wall. "Why did you order a retreat?" he demanded. Chief Messa could only open his eyes in surprise.

He finally stammered, "What?"

"I almost had the Romans defeated and you stabbed me in the back by calling a retreat." Thom thumped him on the back. "Good going, Chief Messa." He walked away laughing to himself.

The chief looked around at his men and then at Thom's retreating back. He didn't know if he should be angry or amused. The team leaders were looking at the chief for guidance. He turned and walked away without saying anything and they looked at each other in surprise.

Chenee approached the troops. "Tell the men to get some food and rest. The chief will talk to you in the morning."

They stood for a moment and looked at her and she feared they would lash out at her like Thom had, but they seemed grateful to finally get direction on what to do. The team leaders hurried away to pass the order to their men.

In his tent, Thom took out his knife and began to stab the hide covering his sleeping area. As he struck the blade through the hide, he visualized being on top of the chief, stabbing the life out of him. How dare the old man think he could command his troops, his men, and issue orders without first consulting him? *He comes out of his damn tent once a month and acts like he's the battle master. I should kill him and his bitch daughter,* he thought as the hide became a shredded mess.

Finally, his anger ran its course and he fell to the ground in despair. The damn Roman wall had resisted everything they had thrown at it. He had no more tricks up his sleeve and he had failed.

Picking up a pebble, he began to throw it toward a cup. He continued to throw them until a pile had built up. Thom stopped for a moment. An idea was beginning to form in his mind, but a shout outside the tent distracted him and he lost his train of thought.

Thom waited for his dinner to be brought to him, but it never came. He curled up on his furs and went to sleep. Later on that night awakening from a dead sleep, he had a smile on his face.

The battle master did have another trick to play. He wasn't defeated yet. He lay back down in his furs and started to go back to sleep. *Yes,* he thought, he was sure it would work.

***

Dav awoke to the scent of something cooking. Whatever it was, it smelled good. The memory of the cave flooded her mind and Dav sat up quickly. Her head spun and her vision blurred. Finally, the world came back into focus and she saw a man tending a fire. In his hand was a long stick that held the source of the heavenly smell.

"Thought you would never wake up," he called out.

Dav looked him over. He had a patchwork of hides and cloth sewn together to cover a large, muscular frame. A long flowing white beard reached to the ground. Her sword and pack was lying beside her and Yang was across the fire, chewing on a bone. Obviously, he didn't find the man a threat.

He heard her stomach growling. "Come on over and have a bite. I won't hurt you."

She was sore all over and couldn't move very fast. He passed her a stick as she crawled to the log and sat down. Taking a bite, Dav greedily ate the meat as if she hadn't eaten in years.

"My name is Dav," she introduced herself. "I go by the name of Monte." He chuckled. "How did you get up here?" she asked.

"I was wondering the same about you," he said with a laugh. "I don't get many visitors up here."

"To answer your question, Monte, I climbed."

"Where's your climbing gear?"

"I'm wearing it. But you didn't answer my question."

"I told you, I climbed too…"

"You answered my first question with one of your own," Dav corrected him.

He scratched his head. "So I did, so I did. Sorry about that…been awhile since I've talked to anyone besides myself, you know. Well you wouldn't know as you've just met me. Therefore, you wouldn't know me." He seemed to be deep in thought as he tried to figure out his last words.

"You climbed up through the vent?" she supplied and nodded toward the opening.

"Oh yes, yes the tunnel. Yes I did. You followed my ropes, did you?"

"I did and they were very helpful," Dav said.

"Good, good, been about twenty years since I've been down in those tunnels. Took me years to map out a passage to find a way over the mountains to the other side."

"Are we on the other side?"

"Yes, almost died trying like you did, but I made it. These caves have bad gases I can smell and it helps me get around them."

"You can smell gases?"

"No offense to your dog, but I have a better nose than some wolves." Yang laid his ears back and growled.

"How is it on the other side?"

"Beautiful." A faraway look came into his eyes. "I walked and walked for years. Just exploring like I did in the caves and living free."

"Why are you returning then?"

"I guess to get away from the people." He grinned.

"I thought there weren't any people on this side of the mountains."

"In the beginning, there weren't, I was the first. Lived many years by myself. Then I stumbled across these men, very rough. If they had found me, they would have tried to either kill me or enlist me in their army. I ran away."

"Who are they?"

"Don't know. They speak Roman, so I know they're from my side of the mountains, I mean our side. Never talked to any of them, just listened in the distance or acted like a tree so they wouldn't see me as they talked."

"How do you know they were rough men?"

"Just the way they talked. Mainly about killing people and raping women and things like that…and it scared me to be near them. They kept talking about some upcoming battle and how a man by the name of Eliam was going to destroy the Ka'an army and take control."

"That's why you're going back? To warn the Romans?"

Monte began to laugh. "No, no. I guess I was just getting lonely. I had a wife once and I would like to have someone to share a life with again. I am getting on in years and will need someone to cuddle with on the cold winter nights. If you know what I mean."

Dav smiled and said nothing.

"It will be nice to get back to civilization. Get back to a place where I don't have to worry about getting attacked by the men on this side of the mountains."

"I would suggest you not go to Ka'an at the present time."

"Has it changed that much since I've been gone?"

"The city is under siege by the Quranian army."

231

"The who?"

"Barbarians," she corrected.

"The filthy savages made it all the way to Ka'an? I can't believe King Attuicus would let them get that far. Why, we have the most powerful army in the land."

"Had," Dav corrected him again. "You have a new king named Attalee. Also, a plague swept through the city several years ago and killed half the population. The once proud Roman army you speak of has been decimated. A small group of men and women are defending Ka'an's wall and there is nowhere the Quranians can't go on this world as they control the land."

"My city, my land," he rested his head in his hands.

"So far, the Romans have been able to defend the wall and Ka'an is safe." Monte's eyes were moist. "So many changes. It's hard to accept."

"From what I've told you, are you still going to try and get to Ka'an?" He thought for a moment. "I might as well. If I don't like it, I can always sneak out the back way. Oh, wait, we'll have to go in through the back way. You said the wall is under attack."

Dav and Yang's ears turned toward him. "There's a back way?"

"Oh sure, sure. Had to leave in a hurry the last time out. They were waiting at the gate for me, so I went the only direction open to me, the back way. It's real easy," he closed his eyes and began to trace the route in his mind and motioned in the air which way to turn.

"We need to get across the crevice and climb down a slope. Take a left at the crow's foot and through the ravines. Up and down a few cliffs, cross the glacier and down the mountainside to the back walls of Ka'an."

"How long will it take?"

"For me, about a month. You and your dog, well, I'll have to share my climbing rope, but I doubt you could make it with my gear. It takes a lot of skill to just climb with a rope."

"Can you show me the way?"

"Sure I can. I won't be able to say the death rites over you, if you and your wolf fall, but I will try to help you out. Have some more fresh meat. I just killed it this morning."

Dav tossed it from hand to hand to cool it. "Thanks."

After eating, Monte put the fire out with dirt, but took a small charcoal and put it in a metal box. "For when I need to make a fire later," he said as she looked curiously at the box.

"We can follow this path a bit further and I'll find an easier way for you to climb down," Monte said as he wrapped the goat meat up in a hide and put it in his pack. He paused. "Not sure how you can get your animal down, though. Maybe make a sling?"

"I'll carry him."

Monte laughed at her.

The pathway led up a steep incline deeper into the mountain. They went by another opening to a tunnel. "Is this the way to the other side?" Dav asked.

Monte looked at her. "You got the wanderlust in you too, don't ya? Don't try to deny it, I can see it in your eyes. You want to see what the other side looks like, same as I did."

Dav could only laugh. "I am curious," she finally admitted.

"To answer your question, yes and no. Once you get in the tunnel, it splits. One tunnel leads up and the other heads down. If you're thinking the one leading up would be the correct one, well I followed it. About a day into it, the floor drops sharply down into lava and gases.

"Back up I came and went down the other tunnel. Almost as soon as I got into it, the floor slants up and I came out on a ledge overlooking the whole world. Are you sure you don't want to take a few years and see it?"

"Someday, I would like to see it, but I must return to Ka'an. I have someone waiting for me."

"Come to think of it, so do I," Monte said. "What?"

Monte tried to look offended. "You don't think a woman would wait twenty years for me?"

Dav hid her smile behind a hand as she mumbled an apology.

Strutting around, he puffed out his chest. "Twenty years ago, I was quite the handsome man."

"Oh, you still are," she tried to mollify him.

This caused him to puff out his chest even more as he tried to pull in his stomach. This only caused his face to turn red and then he expelled a large blast of intestinal gases. Dav and Yang fell to the ground in laughter.

234

Monte took a sniff and moved away. "Whew, that goat meat will do it to me every time." He was red in the face and turned to get a rope from his pack.

Dav had finally composed herself and came over to see what he was doing. Looking at the rocks, he chose one, looped the rope around the rock and began to climb down.

"You're not going to tie it off?"

"What and leave my rope behind? I'll need it later."

"If it isn't tied off, it can slip."

"Not if you do it right. You just need to keep steady pressure on it." Doubtfully, Dav looked over the rope. Monte had made a large knot at the end. The part he was climbing down was looped over the top of the rope with the knot in it. In this way, his weight was bearing down on the end with the knot and locking it in place. When he reached the bottom, Monte would flick the rope and retrieve it after it fell.

Dav clipped Yang into his harness and started to climb down the face of the rock, looking for handholds.

"You can use the rope when I get down," he yelled at her in fear.

"It won't hold both of us, so I can't use your rope," she said as she wedged her fingers in a crack and stepped over the edge. Her boot wedged in a crack and expanded to grip the rock edge, which let her release the hand clamps and find another crack or ledge to hold onto.

She made it to the bottom before he did.

"Are you married?" he asked, giving his rope a flick. It snaked down the cliff and piled at his feet.

"Technically, yes I am," Dav laughed at the compliment.

"Too bad, too bad," Monte said, shaking his head. "I have to say I fell in love with you when I saw you climbing down here without a rope. Got any sisters?"

"Not that I know of."

Monte found a rock and looped the rope around it. "Follow right beside me on the way down. This section of rock is soft and crumbles easily."

"How can you tell?" It all looked the same to her.

"Believe me, I learned the hard way. I have the scars to prove it." As they climbed down, she had to concede he was correct. Her suits wedges couldn't get a very good grip at times and Monte would point out what handholds were the best. He would pull out loose rocks and drop them out of the way.

Resting on the next ledge, he chewed on some of the goat meat. "Don't you ever get tired?"

"A little," she replied as she looked over at Yang. He was laying with his head on her shoulder, sound asleep.

"I can't believe you can carry the dog on your back and climb as well as you do."

"I will admit that Yang needs to lose a little weight, but he isn't that heavy." Yang growled in her ear. "So you are awake, you lazy bum. Here I am, doing all the work, and you're sleeping."

Yang growled again, bared his teeth and then went back to sleep.

236

They made it to the bottom of the crevice as the twin suns were beginning to wane. They made camp and split the goat meat.

"I'm tired," he stated and rolled up in some skins. Instantly, he was asleep and snoring. Looking up at the stars, she waited for Yang to come over and use her leg as a pillow. Rubbing Yang's head, she went to sleep.

***

Thom pulled back the flap of the tent and walked in uninvited. Chief Messa shaded his eyes against the morning sun. "Who is it?" he demanded.

He stepped in far enough so his body blocked most of the light. "It's me, Battle Master Thom." Chief Messa sat silent, remembering the day before and Thom's actions on the battlefield. He placed a piece of Ja, Ja root in his mouth and slipped it between his lip and gum. Maybe it would help calm his nerves.

Thom has come to issue the Challenge. His hand slipped down towards his sword.

Thom saw the motion, "You have nothing to fear from me, Chief Messa." He closed the flap and went to sit across from him. "I just wanted to let you know I've come up with a new idea. One that won't risk any of our men until the ramp is built."

Messa rolled his eyes. "They burn our ramps, Thom. We can't risk another defeat like the last one."

"We won't be defeated this time. I just need your blessing to go forward." The chief was puzzled. "Why?"

"The team leaders said you were going to talk to them about our next attack on the Chosen."

Messa rubbed his chin and then scratched along his left eye. He couldn't remember telling the men anything like that, but Thom interrupted his thoughts.

"I wanted to apologize about my actions on the battlefield. It was less than honorable and an issue that should have been handled in private."

"No need to apologize. I knew your remark was made in the heat of battle and I didn't take it to heart."

Thom knew it was a lie, but he let the matter rest for now. "What do you need from me?" Messa asked.

"I need rocks. Lots of rocks. I want to send parties out to start a collection and move all we can find to the catapults."

"Rocks to the catapults? The Roman soldiers have already shown they can dodge the rocks."

"I'm not going to hit the soldiers. I'm going to hit their wall and build a stone ramp. A ramp that can't be burned by their firebombs and our men will be safe from the archers and Scorpios. I really think we can do it this time, Chief Messa." The chief smiled at the thought.

"We'll talk to the men together." He took his friend's hand and walked with him outside. "We can still defeat Ka'an, together."

The team leaders had been waiting for most of the morning. They listened as the plan was laid out. With a smile, Thom thought, *if the plan fails, it would be on the chief's head, not mine.* Either way, he would win and would soon be in a position to issue the Challenge. Chief Thom. It had a nice sound to it and rolled off the tongue.

The team leaders went to round up their men and Chief Messa ambled back to his tent. Thom started walking back to his tower when he saw Chenee watching him. Ignoring the girl, he hurried to lay out his plan on the map for Eliam to see. He could use the traitor's advice.

Zeus stood on the wall and looked down on Thom with a frown. He was worried about the battle master's plans.

**

Dav felt the drops of rain on her face and opened her eyes just as a bolt of lightning flashed across the sky. The lightening caused spots to appear before her eyes, blinking and rubbing didn't help. Monte was still curled up in his furs, snoring loudly.

"Let's see if we can get some breakfast," she whispered to Yang. He jumped to his feet and followed her. The crevice opened up into a forest and Yang ran ahead to scout for food. He signaled when he found a deer and drove it in her direction. Taking aim, Dav hit the deer and it fell to the ground. Then Dav hoisted it over her back and made her way to the campsite. Monte was still sleeping.

Gathering the driest firewood she could find, Dav built a pyramid and lit the small sticks first. The fire was smoky due to the wet wood and Monte sat up coughing as it blew down on him. "What are you doing? Trying to kill me?" He moved out of the way of the smoke.

"I was trying to make you a morning meal. Sorry about the smoke, this is the driest wood I could find."

Monte looked surprised when he saw the deer. "You can climb and hunt too. Your mate sure is one lucky fellow."

"Not too lucky. My first husband left me and my second hasn't asked me to marry him yet."

"The first one, his loss. The second, he would be stupid to pass up a woman like you." He pulled out a knife and gutted the deer. He made short work of the carcass and soon the air was filled with the aroma of cooking meat.

"We can rest here today and see if the rain stops. Don't want to risk climbing in this weather." His hand was keeping the rain out of his eyes as he surveyed the cliff.

"What do you mean?" Dav asked with a horrified look on her face.

"It's too wet and windy to climb today. Some of the gusts that roll through these mountains can pluck you right off the face of that rock. Believe me, it's too risky."

"We need to climb today."

Monte shook his head no and took another bite of meat. "Then I must go alone."

"You sure are a stubborn woman. We'll die if we attempt it."

"Maybe, but it's a risk I'll have to take. I don't expect you to climb with me."

"If I don't go with you, you'll never make it. I know these mountains like the back of my hand."

"Then are you coming?"

"Yes, yes, just let me cook this meat up first. We won't be able to cook again once we get above the tree line."

Dav helped him cook and package the meat while Yang sat and chewed on another bone. Yang jumped on her back and she clipped him in place. Taking an end of Monte's rope, she tied a figure knot to her belt and started up the side of the mountain.

"What are you doing with my rope?"

"Tie it around your waist. In case you slip on the rocks, I'll be to catch you."

"I've never been tied to somebody before and if you slip, I'll go with you."

"If I slip, I'm going to grab you anyway, so you might as well tie yourself off, or do I have to carry you, too?"

Monte began to laugh until his whole body was shaking. Dav climbed down, rushed and swept his legs out from under him. Throwing him over her shoulder before he had time to react, she climbed thirty feet up to a ledge and put him down.

"Now I know not to joke with you. I can't believe how strong you are, Dav. Are you human, or half-God?"

"Ninety-nine percent human and one percent mad woman."

Monte began to laugh again. "I'd forgotten what it was like to have a good laugh and joke with another person."

Tying the rope around his waist, he watched as she moved up the wall and began to follow her lead. He was amazed at how quickly she was able to climb and was hard-pressed to keep up with her. When they made it to a ledge to rest, Dav asked if she should make him a sling so he could walk up the cliff face behind her.

"I climb. I've only been taking breaks because I thought you needed them."

Dav looked up the cliff. "Well, I'll keep going until you say you need a rest." He grunted in reply.

Dav climbed until the suns were high overhead and then stopped to eat.

Then the rain began and quickly turned into sleet and snow. The face of the cliff became coated with a thin layer of ice. "I told you we weren't going to make it." He yelled over the sound of the wind and rain.

"Oh ye of little faith," Dav yelled back as she continued to climb.

Monte couldn't believe this woman could continue climbing without a rest. Even though he'd been climbing for years, his muscles were beginning to protest and he had to concentrate on just trying to hold on as the wind threatened to pull him off the cliff.

"We need to stop," he screamed into the wind. "I can't go any further." Dav kept climbing, she couldn't hear him over the wind. Yang barked in her ear and added subsonic intonations. "Oh." She looked down to see Monte hanging on for dear life with his muscles trembling from fatigue. Holding her position on the rock face, she let him fall back against the rope sling and rest.

The wind began to howl through the canyon and Monte was plucked off the wall, his body finally giving into fatigue. He was desperately holding onto the rope and spinning in the wind. His furs had blown over his face and he looked comical as he tried to hold onto the rope and clear his vision. Dav had to bite her lip to keep from laughing, the poor man was probably terrified.

Dav couldn't let go of the rock and pull him in without risking all their lives, so she kept climbing. The face began to jut out so she shot pinions into it to hold onto and get them out over the edge. The winds were over a hundred miles per hour and it was risky trying to move the pinions and keep Monte from being beaten to death.

It felt like forever, but Dav eventually reached the top and shot two pinions into the plateau to pull them over the edge. Anchoring against the wind, she concentrated on pulling Monte up. He hung limply at the end of the rope and she wondered if he was dead. Grabbing his shirt and pulling him up, she used her body to shelter him from the wind. His face was pale and there was only a small wisp of breath coming out of his mouth.

He was still alive, but just barely. The wind and freezing rain made it impossible to find shelter and she sent out a radar scan. The moisture in the air caused the reading to bounce around, so she tried sonar. No good either. With a sigh, she concentrated and began to remote view her surroundings. Dav could make out a small opening in the rock face of the low ridge across the plateau. Pulling up the anchors and turning her back to the wind to protect Monte, she made her way to the opening carrying him in her arms.

Her suit fought to keep her upright against the gusts of wind, which had now increased to over two hundred miles per hour. The wind caused the snow to feel like bullets hitting her back where Yang wasn't covering her. He whined in pain. "Sorry, boy. Do you want down?"

He groaned, "No, just get us out of here."

Warning bells began to sound in her ear as she leaned into the wind and struggled and stumbled across the uneven surface of this upper plain. A proximity sound went off and she reached out a hand. It was the ridge.

Now to just find the opening.

The remote viewing had taken much of her strength. It took a few moments to finally reach the opening and finding it was purely by accident. The wind buffeted her sideways and one of her boots caught a rock. In desperation, she had jumped for the ridge to find something to grab onto and literally tumbled into the opening. Monte let out a moan, but at least they were out of the wind now.

Pulling her arms out from under him, Dav pulled out a pepper pill and setting it for a long duration burn, placed it at the front of the opening.

Yang unsnapped himself and went to seal up the entrance. Shooting small globs of glue around the opening and unpacking a small container, Yang barked a command. The metal box shivered, popped open and began to spray a thin web in a spiral motion along the glue, working in a circular motion to the middle. Barking another command, the material shimmered and began to harden.

Monte was shivering violently, but she had to wait until Yang was done with the entrance. Igniting the pepper pill, the space immediately filled with light and warmth. Watching her gauge, she let it warm to one hundred degrees and then set the pill to burn at ninety-eight point six degrees.

Dav stripped off Monte's cold, wet clothes and moved him closer to the fire. Placing warm patches in his arm pits and across his femoral artery, she also wrapped him up in a reflective heat shield blanket to warm his blood. He shivered and curled up in a ball to conserve heat.

This was a good sign. His body knew it needed to conserve heat and was trying to protect itself. She couldn't believe the number of scars the man had all over his body. It looked as if he had been whipped so long, his skin had been flayed. She traced one with her finger and winced at the thought of how much pain the man must have endured.

Dav was exhausted by the day's climb and her muscles ached from the battle across the plateau. Taking off her 3S suit, she curled up with Monte to let her body heat help warm him. Yang curled up in front of Monte's stomach. Monte was snoring softly as she finally drifted off to sleep.

Yang had slept most of the climb so now, he lay awake. The storm outside continued to pound against the opening and the scanner in his 3S let him know that the intensity of the storm had increased. He was glad they had made it to this small shelter. By his calculations, Yang had estimated their chances of making it to the opening as extremely low. Actually, there was an eighty-seven percent chance they would fail, but Dav had proved him wrong before. For a human, she was somewhat intelligent and extremely lucky. Putting his head down on his paws, he tried to sleep with one ear trained on the opening for any danger which might arise.

***

Athena sat down and examined the Book of Knowledge. A finger traced the words cut deep into the cover and painted in gold. This was the culmination of years of planning and strategic maneuverings. It was time to take over the leadership of the Gods. Grasping the edge of the cover, she flipped it open and began to read.

I regret I was unable to keep from killing myself.

I regret I didn't tell my mother that I loved her before she died.

I regret not being able to save the child who drowned in the river. I regret...

Athena screamed in anger. This was the book of regrets. She had been tricked. Like a fly caught in a spider's web, Athena found that she was stuck...reading. The regrets keep pouring into her mind.

I regret my father didn't love me.

I regret I killed a woman and then lied about it.

I regret not being able to see my children grow up.

I regret...

A low moan escaped her lips as the feeling of winter came to rest in her soul. Falling to the floor and weeping uncontrollably, Athena curled up around the leg of the table. She began to scream in terror as the book fell from the table, landed upright and open so she would be able to continue reading it. Her anguished cry echoed throughout the temple.

The door to the room slammed open. The Warrior stepped in and quickly surveyed the room for the source of the threat. Seeing his mother lying on the floor, he ran to her. "What's wrong, Mother?"

Athena was staring at the book before her, still in shock. "We've been tricked..."

"What?"

"This is the book of regrets, not the Book of Knowledge."

The Warrior ran and kicked the book. It hit the wall with a loud smack, closed and fell to the floor. He helped his mother back to her feet. She felt light and lifeless. Slowly, the Warrior lowered her into a chair, where she rested against its arm. The book stayed against the wall, closed.

"Are you going to be...?" he didn't get the chance to finish his sentence as he was picked up and thrown against the wall. Blocks of granite and mortar were knocked loose with the impact. The Warrior hit the stone floor and lay still.

Athena looked up and fell back in surprise.

"I can tell from your expression you aren't happy to see me, Mother." Thudder went over to where his brother lay, placed the stone spear over his heart and with all his strength, pushed it through the armor and into the Warrior's chest.

The Warrior screamed in pain, then went limp as the spear was pulled out and he started his journey to the Death World.

Turning the tip of the spear in the direction of his mother, he slowly advanced on her.

Athena's head was still hanging down in misery. Grabbing her roughly by the hair, Thudder pulled Athena's head back and glared into her eyes.

"Hello, Mother!"

"By the Gods, my son. You're alive." She began to cry.

Thudder began to laugh. "You betrayed me and now act as if you're happy to see me! My brother killed me with the very spear I have in my hand and you dare cry in relief that I'm alive?"

"You're right, my son. I am lying. I'm happy you're dead." Dropping her hair, he took a step back in surprise.

"Does that surprise you?"

"Why would you want me dead?"

"You're a half-breed, Thudder. You aren't a God!"

"Who is my father?"

"After the Abominations almost destroyed us in the last battle, I had to live as a mortal. A farmer found me in my weakened state and took me to his home and nursed me back to health. We had a son born of a Goddess and a mortal. You have some of my powers, but none of the nobility."

"Where is my father?"

"I killed him. I had to make sure the secret of your birth was never revealed to anyone. Being part human, you were the perfect choice to play the village idiot, and I could hide your thoughts and feelings from others."

Her words were like venom in his veins.

"Now you're dead. I never wanted a half-breed son in the first place and you and your father can be together." Athena laughed hoarsely.

"Mother." Thudder lifted the spear over his head as his face hardened in anger. "I'm not dead."

Athena looked up at him in surprise. He speared her through the neck, chest and stomach. Falling from the chair, she didn't say a word as he continued to stab her to death. Her eyes followed each thrust he made and a small smile even played across her lips.

"I am proud of you, my son," she whispered. Athena closed her eyes and the last breath escaped her lips.

Making sure she was dead, Thudder fell on the spear and began his own journey into the Death World.

***

Eliam always had the ability to sneak up on the battle master. Thom almost jumped out of his skins when he turned and ran into the man.

"Damn the Gods," he exclaimed.

Eliam smiled. "Well, Thom. It looks like you have a good plan here. Even better than my ramp idea. How did you think of it?"

Thom began to walk away, so Eliam followed. "It came to me in a dream one night."

"Um, must have been a good dream."

"Maybe." Thom didn't feel like making small talk.

"You should continue to harass the two flanks, Thom. That will cause them to move men away from the spot you're building the stone ramp."

"Don't need to. In a few weeks, we'll be over the wall." Thom was walking so fast, Eliam had to run to keep up with him.

"But..." he started to say.

Thom turned on him. "I can do this without your help, Eliam. If you have anything further you need to tell us, you can talk to the chief."

He left Eliam standing there with his mouth open. It was no longer safe for him in the savage camp and he made his way quickly to his horse.

As he moved away, he watched the battle master call out orders. *When I return, Barbarian, I will have you split on a stake. A stake shoved all the way into your guts. Then we'll dig a hole for the post and set you up so the weight of your body will force you further down the stake. Then after a few horrible, painful days, when your own bodily fluids are eating through your insides, you will suddenly burst open and litter the ground with the foul stench of death.*

Eliam and his men had perfected the art of staking their victims. Most of the time, it would work perfectly and when the body split open, the stake would slide up along the spine and end up in the brain. Then the body could be cut away and the head, with the last look of pain and horror on the person's face, could be shown to all who opposed him.

This savage was getting on his nerves lately. Maybe now would be a good time to stake him. Have a little celebration before the upcoming battle.

Eliam licked his lips in anticipation of the event.

CHAPTER NINE

For only being a parent a few weeks, Sorti Ne thought she was doing a pretty good job. True to the being's word, the babies were beginning to learn how to speak to her and answer to their names. The babies all had names matching their personalities. There was Sleepy, who was always laying around and sleeping. Grumpy hated to be told anything and Racer was always trying to get ahead at everything, from eating to getting to bed first. Snuggles was always curled up on her shoulders or around her neck. Watcher would sit back and wait to see what everyone else was doing and then copy them. Climber could crawl up anything, she would find the baby on the ceiling or outside the room climbing the titanium girders. They were more fun than a room full of puppies and Sorti Ne was realizing she really enjoyed being a parent.

She was also learning something. The babies could open the portal between the universes, only they didn't have the energy to sustain it. Before, she had only been able to do it with the Control's aid, but now, Sorti Ne was beginning to learn how to do it by herself.

Something had been troubling her though. How could she have gotten from her stateroom on the ship to the inside of the asteroid? Had the babies brought her there? Could they do it again?

This really could be interesting. Snuggles was laying on her shoulders, watching as she was trying to lay out the theoretical possibilities with the Control. Could she fold time and space without the aid of the computer? As she typed in data, one of the babies would type in other scenarios to help. They learned it was possible and the babies began to teach her how to open a stable portal to the reverse parallel universes. It was an exhilarating experience!

The children liked to help her learn as much as she enjoyed teaching them. It was unbelievable to her that a race of beings could be so cold as to let their children die so easily. It was a very alien concept to her. Then the Control reminded her of how several types of fish would lay thousands of eggs and leave them to fend for themselves. Many of the young didn't make it to adulthood.

Perhaps it wasn't as alien a concept as she had thought.

She and the babies would sit around the stateroom, going over the computer-aided lesson plan and argue about everything from strip mining to where the fork should be placed when setting the table. It was one of the funniest times in her life, especially when the Control would chime in with a third opinion and really get the debate all mixed up.

"Engineer Sorti Ne," the voice boomed out. Looking up from a drawing Sleepy was making, she found a group of men sitting behind a stone table in the shape of a semi-circle with her in the middle. The babies crawled up behind her for protection.

She looked at them defiantly. "What do you want?" They seemed to be taken back by her attitude.

Standing up and moving around the table, one of the men approached her. "I am the Angry One. I represent the combined power of the Council of Ones."

"I'm impressed," Sorti Ne retorted sarcastically. "You will be if you don't start showing us respect." She yawned.

His hand reached out and grabbed Sorti Ne by the neck. Her eyes widened in shock as the hand tightened enough to cut off her airway. Hitting at his arm was of little avail.

"You will now show respect or die," he grinned at her. Bordering on the brink of unconsciousness, he let her drop to the ground, where the babies caught her and cushioned her fall.

Coughing and rubbing her neck, she was finally able to stand. "You have my attention," she mumbled.

"Good," he said and went to sit behind the table.

Looking at the men sitting before her, Sorti Ne felt a chill run through her. There was no sign of emotion or compassion in any of their eyes. They almost appeared not to have a soul. Was that possible?

"I assure you, human, we aren't without compassion."

Great. Another race of beings able to read her thoughts. They didn't seem as nice as King Attuicus. The Angry One's face hardened at her thoughts.

"What do you know about the creature who calls himself King Attuicus?" She tried to suppress her thoughts, but he smiled. "So, these are Attuicus' children." He licked his lips. "Maybe we can use them to our advantage."

Sorti Ne could see the look in his eyes and moved protectively in front of the babies.

"Do you know the havoc these children have caused in the universe? If you did, you would kill them yourself."

"They're just babies. They're no more of a danger to you than I am."

"You are more dangerous than you think, human."

She frowned and could only stand there and wait for him to elaborate. He remained quiet.

"You don't know the history of a creature they call the Abomination, do you?

"No, I don't."

"When the creature you call King Attuicus opened the dimensional door, some of his children escaped into this reality. Since they had no natural enemies here to control their numbers, they began to eat any life based energy they found. Whole worlds of humans, Chosen and various other races were eaten alive and the Abominations multiplied into the thousands.

"The only way they could be destroyed was when the Chosen and Gods worked together. All the Abominations were eventually killed off, except one. The one you found on the asteroid. It had attacked the humans and Gods on the planet below, where it was wounded and eventually died. The babies are the last survivors from the mistake King Attuicus made trillions of years before you were born."

"He already told me that..." she started to explain. "You have talked to him?" he demanded.

"Yes."

"Was there anyone else with him?"

"He was alone."

The Angry One looked around at the rest of the men at the table. "We will need to keep the children," he said quietly.

The babies screeched in anguish and climbed onto her arms and legs. Sorti Ne's face hardened. "These babies are my responsibility, not yours. I don't know who you are and I really don't care, but you will not take them from me without a fight."

The Angry One began to laugh. "I almost squeezed the life out of you a short time ago and now you think you can defy my power? This is absurd!!! The sheer audacity of your race really knows no limits."

"You don't know what measures a mother will take to protect her young, now do you, Angry One?"

"Your power, Engineer, is that of a pebble trying to tear down the mountains. I have more power in one molecule than you have in the collective numbers of your race. There is nothing you can do to stop us from taking the children and then we will have no more use for you or your race."

"The pebble in a swift-flowing river has been known to cut a valley through the mountains and eventually, cause them to collapse upon themselves. In time, the pebble is mightier than the mountains."

"The only problem with your analogy, dear Sorti Ne, is that you don't have the time needed to cut us down."

"Don't I?" she asked.

She whispered something to the children. They extended their pods toward her hand and the power began to build. Channeling the power through her

255

body, she opened the doorway into another dimension and walked through, leaving the Council of Ones to look on stupidly as they disappeared into thin air.

The Angry One reached out his hand to hold the doorway open, but a tentacle from one of the children reached out and knocked it away before he could get a firm grip on the edge. They were gone.

He slammed his hand down on the stone table. "Damn it!" he screamed in frustration. "Where have they gone?"

"I can't trace them any longer," another member of the council answered. "Again, we have been outfoxed by a lesser being," the Angry One screamed in horror.

***

Thom watched as the stones were brought from the plains to the catapults. The weapons had been moved back from the wall so the stones wouldn't bounce over it. Chief Messa had sent parties of men into the hills and valleys to find more stones, since the plains had been swept clean by the continuing battle. Men were prying them out of the canyon wall and carrying them over twenty miles to the catapults. It was exhaustive work and the men groaned under the yoke of the project.

"If Ka'an doesn't kill us, Chief Messa will," became a saying in the camp. It was a sentiment Thom tried to encourage. No longer did he say, "I want these rocks moved," or "I want you men to stop being lazy," it was instead, "Chief Messa wants you to get the rocks moved," and "Stop being lazy, or your head will end up on a stick."

The Quranians toiled under the supervision of Battle Master Thom, yet their anger was directed at the chief. The people had seen a once strong and powerful chief fall victim to Ja, Ja root addiction and they watched as his mind slowly began to come apart.

Chenee could hear the men grumbling as they worked and she overheard what Thom was saying about her father. Two could play at this game. Behind Thom's back, Chenee began to pass the word through the ranks that it was Thom's idea and not the chief's. The men were confused. A storm raged down from the mountains and it rained for three days. The plains became a muddy quagmire and it was exhausting work for the men to slog through it with fifty pound stones.

Watching the men as they tried to walk, one of them became stuck and began to sink. "Drop the stone," Chenee yelled, but he had carried it so far and he didn't want to lose it. He fought against the suction of the mud, but the more he struggled, the faster he went down. Soon, he was so exhausted, all he could do was lay quietly and continue to sink. The mud would close over him and he would drown.

Yelling at the soldiers, Chenee formed a human chain to grab and help pull him out. The man was dragged to dry land and surprisingly, still clutching his rock. Thom came across the scene and yelled that they needed to get back to work. Then he corrected himself to, "Chief Messa wanted the men to get back to work."

Chenee jumped up off the ground and went to stand nose to nose with Thom. The girl reeked of mud and human waste and the battle master backed off a bit, but she followed him. "We just saved a man's life here. He was close to drowning in the mud because he wouldn't drop his rock. I would suggest you back off and find someone else to lie to." Thom looked at her in surprise.

"I know what you're trying to do, Battle Master Thom, *childhood friend* of my father."

Thom looked hurt, backed away from her and went to yell at another group of men sitting eating a meal. The man behind Chenee had regained his strength and told her of his gratitude. He and the other men went to clean the mud off their skin and clothes.

It had been a calculated risk on her part. She had begun to suspect Thom wasn't exactly following the will of the chief and kept her ear open for idle gossip. She was now considered one of them by the men since her taking care of their wounds had saved many lives. This opinion allowed her to move unopposed throughout the camp. What she learned was frightening.

Thom was building up to issue the Challenge. All the signs were there. A once faithful friend and servant was now making the current chief look like a weak, insignificant fool.

But again, two could play that game. Chenee whispered a joke to one of her loyal friends and by midmorning, all the men were laughing at Thom when he walked among the troops. His face turned red with fury when he found out why.

Someone had started a rumor that the scouts, who reported to his tent at all hours of the night, were actually Caneth, or boy sex partners. Thom was supposedly using them to quiet his veracious sexual appetite so he could concentrate on winning battles.

"How dare someone call *me* a Canether," he raged at the scout who told him.

The joke was all the funnier due to Thom's reaction and the people's respect for him slipped even further. Chenee secretly smiled and continued to play a silent, political struggle for control of the Quranian people. She, too, had noticed her father's days were numbered as the man was a walking skeleton and soon, his addiction would kill him.

Deep down, she felt a sorrow at the life they had lost together. Thinking about it, she really didn't know her father. Who really takes the time to get to know their parents before they're gone?

Usually, one just worried about day to day problems, like getting food, and even though he had been cruel, well, extremely cruel, she still felt sorry for him. He was her father and the only family she had left. Chenee looked at his tent and shook her head. They were the last of the Messa bloodline. A bloodline that stretched back over millions of years.

Should she go and comfort him? *No, he didn't deserve it,* she thought as her heart hardened against him. When had he ever comforted her? She spat on the ground and went into the woods to find more herbs to use in treating the wounded. Her heart began to slow as she looked for the necessary leaves and roots. It was so relaxing to walk in the forest and to be one with nature. The sunlight filtering through the trees seemed to dance on the ground as the wind played with the leaves and she listened to the music of life all around her.

The boy was moving up slowly behind her, but Yin grabbed his leather shirt and pulled him back. "Is she a nice person?" he whispered to the dog. The dog pulled his shirt again and they crept off at a right angle to hide from the Quranian.

***

The stones were beginning to mound up against the wall and Attalee was getting nervous. The Barbarians had finally figured out a strategy the Romans had no defense against. They couldn't burn the stones and until the mound was higher, they couldn't reach out and push them away.

It was a stroke of fate when a terrible sickness swept through the Quranian camp and most of them became ill or incapacitated. Then they began to die and Chenee was busy trying to make enough Ja, Ja root tea to serve seventy thousand men. The tea helped a little, but there really wasn't much she could do for them. The attack on Ka'an all but stopped, much to the Romans' relief.

General Cae wanted to launch an immediate counterattack, but Attalee didn't want his men to be exposed to the sickness. Besides, it appeared the sickness would kill more men than they could. "We shall wait a little bit longer," he told General Cae. "Just a little longer."

***

260

Monte woke up in the morning and exclaimed in surprise, "Where are my coverings?" He tried to feel around with one hand and cover himself with the other.

Dav woke up and pointed over by the fire. She had hung them on a small outcropping of rock so they could dry.

"Can I have them please so I don't have to show you what I looked like the day I was born?" Yang stood, took the furs in his teeth and dragged them to Monte. Dav rolled over in the other direction so he could put them on. Monte noticed she was nude and frowned when she didn't trying to cover herself. It shocked him when she stood and began to warm the deer meat over a small flame by the cave's entrance.

Handing the meat to him, she warned, "Don't look at the flame."

"Why not?"

"It will burn your retinas and destroy your ability to see."

He made a sign against evil. "Is it a demon flame then?"

Dav chuckled. "It isn't evil. It is simply a type of metal that will burn at a programmable rate."

"Metal will burn?"

"Yes."

Monte tried not to look at the flame, but couldn't help it. He looked away. "I see spots."

"If you keep looking at the fire, you will eventually go blind. Do I need to put a rock in front of it?"

"Oh," he grumpily turned away and sat down.

Standing to put her 3S on, Monte had to admire how beautiful she looked. Tall and muscular with perfect breasts and hips for bearing children. If he was only twenty years younger. The number of scars on her arms and legs was unbelievable. And one angry scar ran across her abdomen. "I never did thank you for saving my and Yang's life."

"You're welcome," he said as he turned his back on her. "Is there something wrong, Monte?" She heard him sigh. "You saw my body last night, didn't you?"

"Of course."

"So you know my secret?"

Dav frowned. What was he talking about? He wasn't making any sense. "I must confess something to you. When I first found you in the tunnel, I had debated whether or not I should kill you." Dav sat up with a start. "Kill us…why?"

"From your dress, I thought you were a Roman. A Roman sent to find and capture me again."

"Ah," Dav said, starting to realize Monte's dilemma. "You're an escaped slave."

Monte hung his head in shame. "I knew it was wrong to run, but I couldn't take it anymore, Dav. My master beat me daily and I just couldn't stand it anymore. I had to run. You have to understand." He went silent as he looked at the floor. "But I must return and take my punishment."

"You don't have to worry about punishment from me, I'm not a citizen. Don't worry about it, Monte. You're a Roman citizen now."

"What?" His eyes went wide with surprise.

"I said that you're a Roman citizen now. The new king has granted a pardon for slaves. All former slaves now have full citizenship."

"You are free," she reaffirmed.

"I am free," he whispered slowly, over and over again. Jumping up and down, he started to scream, "I'm free, I'm free."

Dav began to laugh. It felt wonderful to give him the good news.

"I can't wait to get to Ka'an now." Sitting down to eat more of the deer meat, he couldn't stop laughing. It was like a dream come true.

***

Dav, Yang and Monte spent two more days holed up in the cave while the storm raged outside. They awoke one morning to bright sunlight filtering into the opening and Yang gently peeled back the cover. Cold, crisp air filled their nostrils and gratefully, they emerged from their cramped shelter.

As she stepped out into the snow, a breath caught in her throat as she looked over the Plains of Sorrow. The storm was now sweeping across the city of Ka'an and massive thunderheads climbed into the air.

They were above even the tallest clouds. Dav delighted in watching the lightning dance through the clouds and across the sky.

"The Gods are battling," Monte said as he looked into them. Dav smiled at the superstitious statement and then her smile faded. She had seen a God materialize out of thin air.

Monte came and sat down beside her. "Are you ready to go?" He sat quietly and didn't answer her.

"Thank you for saving my life."

"Hey, Monte, I owed you one."

"I know, but I was terrified when I slipped and fell. Honestly, I didn't trust you to make it."

"I know," Dav placed a hand on his arm. "The important point is we did make it. An old friend told me to live our lives in the future and not to dwell on the past."

"Sounds like good advice to me." He stood. Surveying the mountains, he pointed out, "It's about a day's journey up Goat Mountain, then we reach Crow's Peak. Spend a night at Crow's Peak, then through a small ravine and down we go on Death Slope."

"Up Goat Mountain?"

"There's a trail that leads up to their mating grounds. Almost got trampled one day, they were moving so fast to try and get up there and start making babies. Anyhow, let's get going. If we hurry, we can make it to Crow's Peak by nightfall."

With the surefootedness of a goat, he climbed the path ahead of her. As they climbed, she would stop and take pictures of the city and plains to show Attalee and Cae. It was so beautiful to look at and Dav wished she could share this view with Cae in person. At that thought, she felt a pain in her chest. *Why, I have grown fond of the lug.*

I wonder if he misses me as much as I miss him.

They made it up Goat Mountain and spent the night at Crow's Peak. The ravine wasn't that wide across and rather than take two days climbing down and back up, Dav picked up Monte and jumped across. They stepped out over a massive slope overlooking Ka'an. It was a welcoming sight and she was happy to be so close to General Cae. Dav started to walk out onto the snow, but Monte stopped her.

Dropping to the ground, he looked at the surface.

"It looks solid to me." Dav looked at him questioningly.

Without telling her why, he went and grabbed a large rock and threw it down the hill. It sank into the snow and stayed. Dav smiled. She had been right. Yang whined in pain and backed away from the slope. "What's wrong?"

There was a sharp crack as the top layer of snow let loose and began to move down the slope. Even the ground began to shudder and vibrate as the avalanche built in intensity and they had to cover their ears to block out the sound. Soon, even the suns were obscured by all the snow in the air and Dav could only watch in disbelief as the avalanche rolled away from them.

Dav looked at Monte with new respect. "We might as well get something to eat." He shouted above the roar. "It will be several hours before we'll be able to start down."

***

A soldier called King Attalee to the wall. The men were looking behind Ka'an and up at the mountains. One of the largest avalanches he had ever seen was coming down toward them. He summoned General Cae, who looked over the event with little interest. It had happened many times before and there was a ridge at the bottom that would cause it to deflect around Ka'an, so he went back to his nap.

Attalee couldn't help but watch the wall of white death as it moved down the mountain slope. True to the general's word, the avalanche hit the ridge and filtered around Ka'an. To Attalee, it was a sign. A sign that no matter what life, plague, war or nature threw at Ka'an, the New Roman Republic would survive.

Then another sign began to appear on the mountain, a sign that caused rejoicing by the Romans and fear from the Quranians. Major Raki had been the first to report that it looked like a large thunderbolt was beginning to form in the snow. Was it a sign from Jupiter, showing his favor to the Chosen? Attalee just smiled to himself.

The thunderbolt continued down the mountain until its end was hidden by the same ridge that had saved them from the avalanche.

Later on that day, General Cae heard his door being opened and was ready to bite the person's head off for disturbing him, but the yell died in his throat when he saw who it was and he fell to the floor in a faint.

Luckily, Dav was close enough to catch Cae before he hit the stone floor. Gently, she set the general down. His eyes finally opened to see her look of concern. "Is it really you?" he whispered in disbelief. In response, she kissed him and he returned it passionately as tears of joy ran down both their cheeks.

When they paused to hug each other, he said softly into her ear, "I thought I had lost you."

"I'm too mean and ornery to die," she hugged him. "Just had to take a slight detour."

"I was so worried about you. I almost lost my head and attacked King Attalee."

"I knew you would be worried, but that's no reason to take it out on King Attalee."

"Believe me, I know," he grinned. "I need to see King Attalee."

"You just got back. Come back to bed with me."

"Sorry, soldier. Duty calls."

He frowned. "Is something wrong?"

"Let me just say the Quranians are the least of our worries right now."

"What?"

"Come on," she snapped. "Quit laying around. We have work to do."

"We? You can talk to the king without me. I have a nap to take, which has been interrupted twice now."

"You want me to save Ka'an all by myself?"

"Hey, you left me behind the last time to do that very thing." He had a devilish grin on his face.

She pinched him. "Ouch!" he screamed and scrambled to his feet. King Attalee walked in to find them wrestling on the floor. Dav was trying to feed Cae his foot and he didn't look hungry.

"Should I close the door and leave you two alone?" They stopped and looked embarrassed. Attalee found a stool and sat down and looked them over. "You two need to learn how to behave." He smiled behind his hand.

Cae straightened up his toga and looked sheepish. "Sorry, King Attalee." He winked at Dav.

She rolled her eyes. "Go ahead, Cae, apologize and make it look like my fault."

"It was your fault. You pinched me."

Dav pinched his butt and made him levitate off the floor. "Hey, stop that," he protested.

Attalee cleared his throat.

"What can we do for you, King Attalee?" Cae gave Dav a dirty look. She stuck her tongue out at him.

"I just wanted to hear about Dav's little misadventure."

"Well, there is someone I want you to meet." Attalee and Cae looked at each other.

"Did you capture one of the Quranians?" the king questioned her.

"Better than that, I brought back a man who has been on the other side of the mountains."

"Impossible," Cae exploded. "We've been trying to go over them for years."

"Well, you should have tried going under them. That's how I got here." Cae and Attalee looked at each other. "I would like to meet this man," Attalee said.

***

Monte sat on the couch and looked at the boy before him. "You're the king?"

This caused Attalee to smile. "I think that's what they call me."

"Is it true that you've set all the slaves free?"

"It is."

268

Monte took the king's hand in his. Thank you, thank you." He broke down in tears. It was almost more than the king could bear.

"Come, have a glass of wine. Dav tells us you've been to the other side of the mountains."

Monte took the wine and sipped it. He seemed afraid to go on, but Dav puta reassuring hand on his arm. "I was Senator Coreenus' slave, his herbalist. He would send me into the forest to find herbs and minerals for his research and household. One day, I found an opening in the mountain and began to explore it. My travels to collect plants would take me away for weeks at a time, so at first, it was easy to deceive my master. Until I began to return with fewer herbs than I should have.

"He began to beat me regularly and I spent more and more time away from Ka'an. He grew suspicious and locked me up. A friend helped me escape. I lived in the slums for a while when my master searched the city for me. I knew I had to leave, but he was watching the main gate, so I had to escape out Ka'an's back way.

"It was a journey I almost didn't survive," he said, smiling in memory. "I spent years up in the mountains before I found the exit to the tunnel I had found near Ka'an."

"Is it beautiful?"

"Yes," Monte said as his mind's eye looked over the land he had seen. "The plains and forest go on for as far as the eye can see and the herds of game can take days to pass when they migrate. Melting snow from the mountains run off into vast streams and lakes teeming with fish beautiful to look upon. I would have stayed there if I hadn't been lonely and if the bad men hadn't come."

Cae turned to him with a start. He had been daydreaming. "Did you say there are other people on the other side?"

He nodded. "Bad men, very bad men. Led by a man named Eliam."

"Eliam," Cae spat out. "So that's where that backstabbing, treacherous snake disappeared."

"Tell them what else you heard," Dav prompted him.

"I was sleeping in some brush one night when the bad men made camp close to me. They were talking about an upcoming battle and how they would sweep in after the two armies had killed each other off. Then they would defeat and control the city of Ka'an.

"At first, I thought two HighBorn Houses were fighting and another was preparing to destroy the first two, but after talking to Dav, I believe the Romans and Barbarians are their intended target."

"Of course, divide and conquer. Ingenious if I say so myself."

Attalee was quiet. "There's something I must do," he stood. Taking off his sword and armor, he put on his finest toga.

"Oh no. Is this one of your *gut feeling* moves?" Cae grumbled.

Attalee laughed. "Yes, it is a *gut feeling* plan." Taking chalk, he began to rub it into the toga to whiten it.

"How many men are on the other side?"

Monte shrugged. "I can't count that high, but at night, their campfires are as numerous as the stars in the night sky."

Cae looked worried. "Do you think Eliam has been using your tunnel, Monte?"

"No way," Dav answered for Monte. "No one had been in that tunnel for years."

"So there must be another way through to the other side," Cae said, "near Eliam's family estate."

"And that would explain why the thieves and cutthroats seem to disappear and then reappear." Attalee was adjusting his toga. An attendant helped to arrange the olive leaves on his head. "Zeus said I would be always be under his protection. This is a good time to test the limits of that protection," he laughed and walked from the room before they could see his shaking hands.

***

The front gate to the city of Ka'an rolled open and a lone man walked toward the Quranian camp. Silence descended over the camp as people stopped to watch the boy walking boldly into their midst. Thom climbed down from his tower and grabbed a sword as he ran to keep him from reaching Chief Messa's tent. The boy stopped as Thom shoved the sword in his face.

"You must be Thom," Attalee said, ignoring the sword. "Who are you?"

"I guess you don't recognize me without my armor and blood splattered all over me. I am King Attalee."

Thom began to laugh. This was almost too good to be true. The Roman king had just walked into their camp and was now their prisoner.

"I propose a truce so we may talk."

"We will talk first about your surrender."

"I'm not here to talk about surrender. I'm here to talk to Chief Messa."

"Again, I say we will speak of your surrender and we'll not honor your proposed truce."

"Correct me if I am wrong, but didn't Chief Hye make it a law that in order to facilitate peace between all peoples, a truce would always be honored?"

"Where did you hear this?" Thom demanded.

"It's from the Oral Tradition. You should know this, Battle Master Thom. It is your history." The Quranian soldiers looked at each other. Here was a Roman who knew the history of the one true people. They were impressed.

"I know that of which you speak, but it only applies when facing an honorable opponent. You are less than honorable, Chosen dog. Bring me some rope so I can tie him up."

"Let the boy speak," Chief Messa said, walking up through the crowd. Thom looked at the chief in shock. "I grant your request for a truce."

"Thank you, I am..." but the Chief cut him off. "I know who you are." And Attalee fell silent.

"I have come to tell you that both our people are in danger and the only way we can contain the threat is by working together."

"I will never work with the Chosen," Chief Messa said. "Your people must pay for their past transgressions against us." Attalee began to walk around and looked at the men.

"Chief Messa," he spoke loud enough so all could hear, "you and your people have shown us Romans that you are a force to be reckoned with and no longer will they consider you Barbarians or savages." The Quranians looked at Attalee in surprise. "No longer will you have to live in the mountains and starve.

You've made your point, Chief Messa. Your people have gained the Chosens' respect, along with their fear. Never in our lifetimes did we expect that the Great Chief Messa and his Battle Master Thom would be assaulting the wall of Ka'an.

"You have fought bravely, Quranians. However, we are now at a stalemate and to continue this battle will only bring destruction down upon us all." The Roman king stopped and looked around. His face softened. "Both of our people have made mistakes. Both are guilty of evil against each other. I understand your son was killed in a raid on our grain bins. My father was killed defending our home against an attack. It is now time to put our differences aside and join together to fight a common enemy. Divided, we will fall prey to a greater power, but joined together, we may, and I say may, be able to protect our families, nay, both our cultures from destruction."

"I am tired of these lies," Thom attempted to grab Attalee but he was gently pushed back by an invisible barrier around the king. "What kind of witchcraft is this?"

"I enjoy the protection of my God, Lord Jupiter."

273

Thom looked worried and glanced at the statue of Zeus, who was making an obscene gesture.

"My people saw the sign of your God in the snow over Ka'an," Chief Messa said wistfully. "Do the Gods fight on your side?"

"I declined their offer of help. It wouldn't have been honorable."

"What is this threat you're talking about?"

"The man who gave you the plans to build the catapults, the Roman known as Eliam." He saw the look of surprise on the chief's face, and knew his suspicions were now confirmed. "He has assembled an army to crush whoever remains once we have annihilated each other."

Thom snorted. "Where is this mighty army you speak of, Chosen?" He expanded his hands to display his men. "This is the greatest army in the land. The army that has caused the Romans to cower in their cities and keeps and who control the land. So, I ask you again, Chosen dog. Where is this threat you speak of?" Thom looked at him with contempt and Attalee couldn't help but return his gaze.

"Eliam has an army equal to or greater than our own, even if we joined together, Battle Master Thom."

"Where are they then?"

Attalee pointed to the mountains. "They live in the mountains."

"On the other side."

Thom really began to laugh. "No one has ever gotten over the mountains. They're too high."

Attalee walked toward Chief Messa. "Battle Master Thom thinks like many of our people. Until

274

today, I thought the same, but I have since heard of a way under the mountains. A way to lands so vast, they dwarf those we live in now. No longer will we need to war against each other for land. There will be enough land for all of us. We can work together to create a lasting peace."

"How can I know our people can trust you?" Messa asked.

Attalee smiled. "Did I not free your people when I could have killed them? When you needed to recover your dead and wounded, haven't I let you do so without firing on your men? Didn't I return your daughter to you, even after finding out she had been sent to spy on us?" He continued to walk and talk, not only to the chief, but to all the Quranian people. If he could convince them, perhaps they could influence their chief.

"What you say is true. You have been an honorable opponent. But the hatred between our people runs too deep. We can never learn to live together."

"We may not be able to live together at first, Chief Messa. But we can plant the seed to grow roots that will allow our children to live together in peace."

Chief Messa grunted. This young man was very persuasive. "Let me speak to my battle master and I will think about your offer. Bring food for the king," he ordered and motioned Thom to follow him.

As they entered the tent, Thom began to rub his hands together. "This is a perfect opportunity to capture the Roman king," he grinned at the chief.

"What?" Messa was startled.

"I said we can capture the king and Ka'an will be ours."

"No," Chief Messa shouted. "I am a man of honor and so is the Roman king. I will not attack during a truce."

"Man of honor? Aren't you the same man I saw strike down and kill an unarmed Roman villager?"

"I gave the man a weapon to defend himself. He chose to die rather than fight. If he had begged for his life, I would have spared it."

Thom grunted in disgust. "Do you forget who we are talking about here? The Romans are our enemy. They must be destroyed. All or nothing was our battle cry and now they come with stories and you're ready to settle for nothing?"

Chief Messa stood for a few moments and then looked at his lifelong friend. "I'm dying, Thom. Over the last few days, my mind has been open to the Death World and I have seen many events in a different light.

"Life is a sacred bond and should be treated that way and like it or not, the Romans are men, just like you and I. They share the same hopes and dreams we have and if what the king says is true, then perhaps I should…" He stopped when he saw the anger on Thom's face. "Tell the Roman king I will give him my final answer at midday. I wish to think about his offer. Now have my meal brought to me. I have much to think about."

"Yes, sir," Thom said sarcastically and stormed out.

CHAPTER TEN

Chenee seemed to melt out of the crowd and walked toward Attalee. He saw her out of the corner of his eye and couldn't help but smile. She was surprised as he turned toward her with a look of pure happiness on his face and she froze, not sure if she should continue on or what to say to him. But his eyes were warm and inviting, so she continued toward him.

The sight of him caused a kaleidoscope of emotions to flow through her all at once—desire, happiness, shame and fear. He walked toward her and she fought the overpowering urge to run, to hide. Chenee hung her head and couldn't bring herself to look him in the eye, now that they were so close. *I've hurt him so badly. He'll never want me.*

Tenderly, cupping her chin in his hand and lifting her face so she was looking deep into his eyes, he whispered, "Oh, Chenee, I have missed you so." Tears came to her eyes and she ran without knowing why and quickly disappeared into the crowd. She could hear Attalee plaintively calling for her to come back. But she didn't stop until reaching her tent and cast herself face down on her sleeping furs. The little girl heard her crying and came to rub her head and make soothing sounds over her.

***

Sadly, Attalee watched as Chenee disappeared into the crowd. He felt as if his heart had been ripped out and cast in a sea of despair. Several of the men who had been held prisoner came to talk with him and thank him and the men and women for saving their lives from the fire. More Quranians came to talk to King Attalee, since most never had the opportunity to speak to a real live Roman. The boy was friendly and even called some of the former prisoners by name.

Attalee heard someone walking up behind him. He turned to find Thom looking at him, his hatred evident on his face. The battle master was trying hard to control his emotions, but was failing miserably. *He would like to cut me down where I stand.* The man appeared to be on the brink of insanity.

"Chief Messa will give you his decision at Mid Noon tomorrow." Thom said between tightly clenched teeth. "Until then, you have my permission to return to Ka'an, unharmed. This time…" He let the threat hang in the air.

Attalee nodded. "Until tomorrow. I will see you at midday." Saying goodbye to the men, he began to walk back toward Ka'an, but Thom stayed beside him. The king was surprised, but didn't let it show. Attalee walked slowly and stopped to check on some men he knew and inquired about their injuries and their families. Silently, Thom continued to walk with him.

As they neared the wall and were out of earshot of anyone else, Thom leaned toward him and hissed, "I'm not so easily fooled as the old man by your words. I know this is a trick. A Roman trick, but it won't work. I know you're afraid the stone ramp will work and that we'll take Ka'an and grind your Republic into the ground so your blood feeds the worms. I, for one, will enjoy and savor your death. A slow and painful death, I can only hope."

"You're right about one thing, Thom. We are worried. Your friend, Eliam, has turned us against each other so he can gain. We'll both lose everything if he wins. But really, Thom, do you really want to grind our bodies into the ground and feed our blood to the worms? If so, I would suggest you do something else with your life. It isn't healthy for you to think these thoughts all the time. Take up a hobby, or learn another skill. Your people are wonderful with wood and building. Maybe that will help rid you of this aggression you're feeling."

"Don't try to goad me into a fight, you Roman dog. You don't fear me now, but you will in the future."

"You know, Thom. I'll lie awake tonight, just staring at my roof in fear. Oh please, stop talking this way. You're scaring me." Attalee began to laugh as Thom's face turned bright red.

"You know, Thom," Attalee said, "you may get over Ka'an's wall, especially with your new stone ramp." Thom's face brightened. "But this is only the first of seven walls, Thom. Do you think you'll be able to get over all seven before you run out of men?" They had arrived at the Ka'an gate.

"The next time we meet, Roman, I hope to wet my blade with your blood."

"Thank you for the stimulating conversation, Battle Master. I hope you have a good day as well." Attalee stepped inside and then waved as the massive stone rolled closed.

***

Thom's face turned white as he caught a small glimpse of the courtyard. For a brief moment, he had been the target of a dozen Scorpios. He was glad he hadn't acted on his feelings of anger the Roman king had raised in him.

"I hate that cocky little bastard," he muttered as he walked back to his camp. "He talks just like that Roman, Eliam." Thom stopped. Was it true Eliam was going to attack and try to destroy both armies? Thom wasn't worried. With their training against horses, they would be safe.

***

Chief Messa sat by his fire and ate the meat off the stick. The Roman woman lay trembling against the far skin of the tent. She had the blank look of an animal caught in a trap and had given up on living. "Are you hungry?" he asked her.

The eyes refocused and looked at him for the longest time. She nodded yes. "Come over here by the fire and get warm. You may eat something with me."

Cautiously, the woman moved toward him and sat on a log. The chief put the meat down and picked up a fur to rest around her naked shoulders. The woman trembled as he touched her. In the firelight, he could see scars all over her body and scabs from deep burns on her back. She lifted her face to look at him. He was shocked to see one eye had been gouged out and her face was nothing but cuts and bruises.

"Who did this to you?" Chief Messa asked and tried to touch her chin, but she pulled away in fear. "I will not hurt you," he said gently and lifted the meat to her lips. She attacked it savagely and soon, it was gone.

He handed her a piece of flat bread and water and watched as she greedily ate them too. "I'm not sure who did this to you, but I will take care of you now."

The Roman woman looked at him in disbelief and a deeper fear began to grow in her. The savage was talking crazy again, which usually preceded some new form of torture. Chief Messa sat down heavily on the log and stared again into the fire.

"Have you ever wondered how your life would end?" he asked her. She remained silent. "I have heard the doors of the Death World opening for me and I fear the journey ahead." Still the woman was silent.

"When I was a young boy, my father told me of a vision he had that I would rise to greatness among our people. He told me I had to rule with compassion," he paused, "but the future was cloudy and uncertain.

"Funny how I remember little things like that many suns later on in life. Like the memory of the first time I had Ja, Ja root wine and was sick for days, or when I rode in my first canoe on the Middle Sea." He chuckled.

"Ah...I will miss life," he sounded sad, talking to himself. "My father was a good man. I wanted to grow up and be just like him. Too bad I've failed miserably." The woman was staring at him, but the one remaining eye was unfixed and seemed to be looking through him. The look caused him to shudder. "That is how I've been looking at life," he muttered. Looking without really seeing and he would change that tomorrow.

No longer would the chief of the Quranian people watch his men being killed on the battlefield. It was time for peace. It was time for his people to live again. He would make peace with the young Roman king and help to counter the threat this Eliam posed. He had been a fool to trust the Roman traitor. In his younger days, he wouldn't have fallen for such a stupid trick. The chief felt old and betrayed, by his mind and his body. A piece of Ja, Ja root lay beside him.

He picked it up, looked at the fibrous root with the black center. In anger, he threw it into the fire and looked away in shame. Gently, he took the woman and laid her down on some furs and tenderly covered her. He went to his furs and sat down to watch the fire slowly burn down to small embers popping in the cold night air. The chief smiled at the thought that his people wouldn't be at war tomorrow and they could roam free across the countryside. Closing his eyes, he quickly went to sleep.

***

On the plains, a small figure made its way through the sleeping men. No one thought to stop him, since he looked like a short little man carrying firewood back to camp. Brushing back his hood, the little boy gently laid the wood down. A dog materialized beside him. "Are you sure this is where my mother is?" Yin growled.

"Alright, alright, I believe you." It was amazing how the dog seemed to understand him. Slipping into the shadows, he listened to a man talking in the tent. Through the small slit, he could see a women with her back to him. *It might be my mother,* he thought, but he instantly recognized the man who killed his father.

The knife slipped into his hand and then Rian had to put it down, wipe the sweat from his palms and try to calm his heart. He realized he was scared, more so than he had ever been in his life.

But he had an oath to fulfill and he wouldn't let his father down. This man would pay for killing his father and his family's honor would be avenged. His months of practice would be put to good use. The old man put his mother to bed and Rian was touched at how she was covered. Maybe she hadn't been mistreated.

The chief laid down and was soon snoring loudly. The boy cut the slit wider and crawled through the opening. The coal of the fire shed little light in the interior and he slowly moved toward the chief with his knife, stopping to listen to see if he had been detected. His mother rolled over in the furs and he was shocked to see the visage of her face and the damaged eye. Choking back a scream of terror, he paused and then looked away.

Rage overwhelmed him and without thinking, he raised the knife and plunged it into the chief's heart. Putting all his weight into the thrust, he slid it deeper into the man's chest.

Messa's body jerked spastically as pain flooded his chest. His heels dug into the ground and his fingers clutched at the furs. The boy watched in horror as blood began to spill from the man's chest.

Chief Messa's eyes flew open and he looked at the knife. He then gazed around to see who had stabbed him. Laboring to draw in a breath, he coughed due to the blood filling his lungs.

Their eyes met and held as the chief's life slipped away. "This is for killing my father." Comprehension came swiftly to the chief's mind and he looked sadly at the boy.

"I am sorry," he whispered as his eyes rolled up in his head and his last breath rattled in his throat. The chief's body began to relax and the blood stopped pouring from his chest. Chief Messa the Fifth was dead.

The boy left the knife in Messa's chest, and went to sit with his mother. When he glanced at himself, he found he had blood all over his hands and clothes. Even when he wiped his hands on the furs, he could still feel the warm liquid on his skin. It would be a memory he would never forget and would forever haunt his dreams.

His mother held him close as he began to tremble and the little boy fell against her and cried. "My father's death has been avenged," he whispered. "So, why don't I feel better?"

"We should run away," he told her, but she held him tight and wouldn't let him go. In her protective embrace, he felt safe and warm. His mind shut out the evil around him., The tears flowing down his face, Rian fell asleep in her arms.

King Attalee looked up at the sun and walked toward the front gate. "I hope to be back soon with good news," he said to General Cae. "I still think I should come with you."

"I need you here to ready the troops in case it gets ugly on the plains."

"I'll have twelve legions ready to march if needed."

"Thank you, General."

"Open the front gate," Major Raki ordered. Attalee slipped through the gate and heard it rumble closed behind him.

The Quranians had gathered from all over the plains to hear the chief's reply. Chenee and Thom waited respectfully outside the chief's tent for his presence. Attalee walked boldly forward to speak to them, trying to keep from trembling and worrying his ear.

***

Eliam looked over the plains and was disgusted to see the Romans and Quranians not engaged in battle. "This wasn't in the plans!" he shouted to his men. He glanced behind him at his army of sixty thousand, hidden in the northeast canyon that led to the Plains of Sorrow. For weeks, they had been living on cold rations to escape detection and the men were grumbling at the lack of action. He was puzzled as to what could possibly be happening below. They weren't fighting and this lack of a battle was going against all his well laid out plans.

Had the foul smelling Messa made a deal with the Romans? Were the Romans surrendering to the savages? It was maddening. He scowled. "Should we attack now?" a man asked him.

"I told you never to speak to me when I'm thinking. Now I've lost my train of thought." He put his head down on his knuckles and sighed. "No, we will not attack now. I want to see what happens first."

"Yes, sir," he bowed his head and turned away.

"Timing," he snapped, "Timing is everything. Attack at the wrong time, and the battle can be lost before it has even begun." He couldn't wait to see the look on Chief Messa's face when his men descended on the plains and wiped the savage scum from the planet. Then they would march on Ka'an and the raping and pillaging would begin.

It would be a yearlong celebration of wine, women, song, daily killings in the arena and slaves to do his bidding. He licked his lips and wiped the bead of sweat off his brow. "Settle, Eliam. One mustn't become too eager to indulge in one's own pleasures." He chuckled to himself.

Ah, to indulge in the cruelties of torture and human degradation. To grind men under his heel and subject them to his will, however evil, is the destiny he had been born to fulfill. It was a path he couldn't turn from even if he wanted to, or so he told himself.

The former councilor to King Attuicus experienced an erotic emotion when he was cruel to someone. Why, the first time he had killed a man, he had even gotten an erection. Elian shook his head at the thought. *Yes, we will have fun.* He laughed

286

evilly and returned to his camp. "Keep a sharp eye out," he told his scouts. "Report anything suspicious." They nodded and kept their eyes on the plains. They would do their jobs well. To do otherwise would invite certain death.

***

Thom and Chenee stood by Chief Messa's tent, waiting for him to emerge. King Attalee had walked from the main gate and stood waiting with them. He had already exchanged pleasantries with Thom and Chenee and all three stood in an uncomfortable silence.

Attalee looked at Chenee, but she refused to meet his gaze. Thom was getting impatient and called out to Chief Messa. There was no reply. "Probably had too much Ja, Ja root last night," Tom muttered as he opened the flap to the tent.

He was halfway through the opening when he stopped and stumbled backward so fast, he fell down. "The chief is dead!" Thom screamed as he reached for his sword. He sliced away the cover of hides to make sure the chief's murderer wasn't waiting in ambush. The sunlight pouring through the opening revealed Chief Messa on his back with a knife deep in his chest.

Another slice and the Roman woman with a little boy was revealed. Chenee cried out as she looked at her father and after pushing Thom out of the way, went to fall on the ground beside him. Tears began to stream down her face as she looked at his body.

Thom's eyes were still on the boy. He noticed the boy's hands were covered in blood. Grabbing him by the scruff of the neck, Thom dragged the boy into the open and raised his sword. The Roman women screamed and jumped between the weapon and her son.

"Get out of the way, you stupid woman!" Thom screamed and cuffed her across the back of her head with the hilt of his sword.

"No, No…" she screamed in terror and pain. "Not my son. Not my son, too."

Bellowing in anger, Thom raised his sword to strike her down. "Stop," Chenee screamed and grabbed Thom's sword arm. He was caught by surprise and turned angrily toward her. "He killed your father!" he yelled and attempted to pull away from her.

"The boy had every right to kill him," Chenee said as she fought to hold back her tears.

"No Roman has the right to kill a Quranian," he said forcefully, "Now let go of my arm so I may smite this Roman dog."

"So you would go against our sacred laws?"

Thom spit on the ground. "There are no sacred laws governing killing a Roman."

"An eye for an eye, a tooth for a tooth, a life for a life," she quoted. "The laws says a life for a life. It doesn't say this law is only for Quranians. It is for all humans."

"Our sacred laws don't cover Romans," he sneered.

"You will not harm the boy," she ordered and let go of his arm. "He killed your father, our chief."

"It was his right. The chief killed his father."

288

Thom pulled away in disgust and walked over to look at his childhood friend. His shoulders sagged and the crowd closed in around him to see the chief. A loud wail went up from the men and they began the chant to carry the former chief into the Death World.

**

Chenee pushed the woman and child toward Attalee and turned to make sure Thom didn't try to attack them again. The king was shocked at the appearance of the woman and the blood all over the little boy. He hugged them both as they broke down in tears and he gently guided them to the gate of Ka'an. Chenee spoke to one of the men, who soon brought the little girl from a tent. The child happily re-joined her mother.

Thom pushed his way through the crowd, disrupting the death chant. "A state of war still exists between our people," he yelled at King Attalee. "As the new chief of the Quranian Empire, I will continue to attack until every last Roman is dead and your memory wiped from this land and the Oral Tradition."

Attalee motioned for the boy, girl and woman to continue on as he walked back to speak to Thom.

Chenee stepped in front of the battle master and stated, "We will accept the Roman proposal."

"I am in charge here," Thom said, strutting around.

"You forget, Thom. I am next in line for command. My family line has ruled for the last hundred years."

"Your family claim to the leadership of our people died with your brother."

"There is nothing in the Oral Tradition that states a woman can't rule. If you remember correctly, there have been many woman who ruled our people successfully."

Thom coughed. "Under my command, no woman will ever rule our people and I will abolish the Oral Tradition. It puts too many stupid ideas in people's heads."

"The Oral Tradition is the sacred law of our people," Chenee said and spoke to the crowd beginning to gather. "Of all the Lost Tribes of the One True People, we are the only ones who can trace our history back to the very beginning of creation. We can learn from our mistakes and change the future, Thom. To continue this war is wrong."

He glanced around at the crowd and his features softened. "Maybe you're right," he said, "but, I am still in command and I say we will continue the battle." Chenee shook her head no. The men had moved in closer to hear the fight between Chenee and Thom.

Chenee called out in a loud voice, "A crisis has arisen over the leadership of the Quranian people. Battle Master Thom is trying to break millions of years of tradition by usurping my authority as chief and refuses to back down. Battle Master Thom..." she turned to look at him. "Is it your intention to issue The Challenge at this time?"

Thom licked his lips and looked around at his men. Their faces were impassive and he wasn't sure who they supported, him or Chenee.

"I accept the Right to Challenge!" he screamed and raised his arms in the air for what he hoped would be tremendous applause, but the only sound was the wind playing across the plains. Thom looked uncertain for a moment. *Oh well, when I have won, I will whip them into shape.*

"You have one hour to prepare yourself to die," he sneered at her and stormed off.

Chenee went, pulled the knife from her father's chest and prepared him for burial. A crowd had gathered and before she knew it, the time had come to defend her right to lead the Quranian people.

The crowd backed away to give them room to fight.

She hadn't even had the time to get a sword. Her father's was too big and didn't fit her hand properly. The little Roman girl she had befriended walked up and pulled her arm. She looked down at the girl.

She was holding a sword. "Where did this come from?" The little girl whispered in her ear. Chenee smiled and looked out over the crowd to see Attalee.

He walked over to her. "The little girl was worried about you, and so was I." He looked worried. "Are you sure you can do this?" he asked her.

"What other choice do I have? If I didn't issue the Challenge, the war would continue and more of my people would die. It's time to stop the war and live in peace."

"You know this is for keeps. He will be trying to kill you."

"Yes, I know."

"Take him out quick, Chenee. When you see your chance, you must kill him. Just trying to injure him will leave you open for attack."

"With the Challenge, I have to kill my opponent, but thank you for the advice." Chenee smiled at him.

She pulled out the sword and walked toward Thom. He also stepped forward. "You can withdraw from the Challenge now if you wish," he told her.

"Only if you concede I am the leader," she stated. "Never."

Chenee brought her sword up so it was pointed at his throat. "You don't know how to use a sword, woman. Give up this farce."

Chenee's expression didn't change as she continued to move toward him. He lazily moved his sword up and tried to knock it aside. She deflected it and moved in for a strike to his chest. A look of fear crossed his face. Thom stumbled back and was just barely able to get a block up to force Chenee's sword away from his chest. The block knocked her sword to the right so she let it continue on its way and brought it around and up over for a head slash.

He blocked it and jumped back in surprise, but Chenee stepped in and feinted a cut toward his arm. When he overcompensated with his block, she twisted her sword downward and sliced into his leg, then had to jump back as he slashed sideways to cut her in half.

Thom glanced at the blood pouring from his wound and turned red with anger. Lifting his sword up over his head and screaming in rage, he advanced and began to swing wildly, hoping to catch her by surprise and then get in a fatal wound.

His first hit almost knocked the sword from her hands and she slowly retreated.

Instead of meeting his attack head on, Chenee used the technique Dav had used against the Warrior. "Soft way meets the hard way" as she called it. As the fight continued, she began to study his style. He was mainly open and unguarded, but she was inexperienced and wasn't sure how to take advantage of his clumsiness.

Dav had spent hours practicing with her on just such an attack. Most men would try to swing wildly and use this to psych their opponent out. The wild swinging finally began to wear him down. Whereas she was just staying back, relaxing and deflecting his blows, she was also waiting for an opening so she could slip in and deliver her own fatal wound. He stepped back to rest, but kept his sword up for protection. Cautiously, she moved slowly to the side and toward him so the sun was behind her.

Dav had taught her a trick and she hoped it would work. Thom watched as she moved closer and waited. He blinked his eyes as she inched closer and closer to him. He couldn't see her sword and the sun was causing a glare in his eyes. Chenee had moved so close to him, she began to wonder why he wasn't moving. *He can't see my sword,* she thought and took a chance. Pushing forward, she slipped past his sword and caught Thom in the throat.

His eyes went wide in surprise and shock when he realized her sword was just below his chin. Attempting to raise his own, he was too slow and felt the bite of her sword in his neck. Surprisingly, it didn't hurt and he thought it was only a scratch.

Swiftly, Chenee pulled her sword out, blocked his upward thrust and plunged it into Thom's stomach. He screamed in agony, dropped his sword and clutched at the blade, slicing his hands as he pulled on it. Chenee stepped back, pulled her sword free and let him fall to the ground.

Thom looked down at the ground and frowned at the blood pouring onto the soil. Slowly, he lifted his head to look at her and then the words of the hermit came back to him, "Chenee will win, Thom will lose." Falling forward, he began to travel his path to the Death World.

Whipping the sword through the air, she cleaned the blood off her blade and expertly returned it to her scabbard. Pausing to look at Thom, she then turned to her people. "Does anyone else wish to issue the Challenge?" The crowd was silent. She began to chant in the Oral Tradition, the Rite of Chief Initiation, and the crowd followed with her.

"I, Chief Chenee Messa the Sixth, of the Quranian Empire, will now answer your question, King Attalee of the Roman Empire." The crowd looked at her expectably. "Our hostilities against you are over. We will return to our lands and discuss retribution for the harm we have done. May we live in peace and create a better world for our children."

"Over my dead body you will," she heard someone say behind her and Chenee felt a curious pain in her back. The crowd was looking at her in horror. She looked down to see a sword sticking out through her stomach. She had a surprised look her face and turned to see who was behind her. Thom had crawled up from behind, risen to one knee and thrust his sword into her. Attalee screamed as he saw the blade rip through her and watched as Chenee staggered at the impact.

A team leader stepped in and with one cut of his sword, beheaded the former battle master. "How dare you attack the chief?" the man screamed as he struck the body over and over again.

Chenee fell toward Attalee and almost impaled himself on the end of the same sword as he caught her and gently lowered her to the ground on her side.

She looked at him without really seeing him. "Are you in pain? Chenee, please speak to me."

"No, not really," she whispered, but he knew she was going into shock. "I must get you to Caiisa," he said and stood to run back to Ka'an. A trumpet on the wall caught his attention. It was the attack signal. Had Cae lost his mind? A signal man was trying to send him a message, but his eyes were too full of tears to read it properly. He did manage to ascertain that the signal man was sending the attack message.

The front gate of Ka'an opened and Roman Calvary began to pour out onto the plains. The Quranians stepped back in fear, suspecting this to be a Roman trick. The horses turned as they came out of the gate and headed for the northeast canyon that led onto the Plains of Sorrow. Chenee lay moaning softly. Glancing up at the canyon, Attalee's blood ran cold. Eliam was marching with his troops and they appeared to be a well-equipped calvary unit.

"Attalee!" she screamed. The pain was beginning to spread throughout her body as the initial shock began to wear off. "As Chief of the Quranian people, I surrender them into your care."

"Nay, Chenee. I surrender the Roman Republic to you." She smiled. "You would do anything to make me happy."

The sound of battle began to reach his ears.

"Damn!" Attalee shouted. Looking at the man who had cut Thom down, he asked, "Who was Thom's second-in-command?"

"That would be me," he said grimly.

"We're under attack," Attalee said. "I propose we work together to repel the threat."

The man looked at Chenee and then back to him. "I guess we could do that, since we're no longer fighting," he said. "Now that Thom is dead, I guess that makes me the battle master." At the thought, his eyes flew open and he stood straighter.

"King Attalee, the Quranian army will work with you to repel the threat." Attalee was surprised at the transformation in the man.

"Good then," Attalee said, looking around at the collection of men around him. "Can you defend against cavalry attacks?"

The man brightened even more. "That's what we do best. I trained all my men to fight against your horses, so we do a good job." Pounding his chest, he turned to the other team leaders. "Pass the signal. Tell the men to ready the porcupine defense. We must fight against the horses coming out of the pass."

Attalee heard the trumpet sound from Eliam's army and their cavalry split up to hit the Romans and Quranians head on. He looked down at Chenee and noticed she was no longer breathing. A terrible rage filled his soul and he ran back toward Ka'an. General Cae broke away from the troops and headed toward him on horseback. Attalee was glad Cae was leading his horse behind him.

The king noticed his armor and sword were strapped to the horse's side. Quickly, he mounted his horse and guiding it with his knees, slipped the armor over his head. "We are vastly outnumbered," General Cae yelled at him as they rode into battle.

"You take our force and I'll try to coordinate the Quranians," he yelled back, as they split and raced toward their respective troops. Attalee was appalled at the Quranians. They had simply lined up and were waiting for Eliam's army to charge down on them. He couldn't believe this. He looked for the battle master and saw he was walking behind his men, yelling orders. Their archers had taken up position behind the wall of men and stood casually, as if nothing was happening.

"What the...?" Attalee yelled at the battle master, but his words were lost in the clash of the Roman and Eliam's cavalry. It sounded like a thunderbolt had slammed into the ground and cries of terror and triumph filled the plains. Eliam's men screamed in triumph as they saw the Quranians and the sun reflected off the sea of steel waving in the air. The ground began to tremble as the men spurred their horses faster.

The battle master grinned. "Ah, this will be glorious," he whispered to Attalee. The king shook his head. *It will be a massacre. I will have let Chenee down.* Something tugged at his mind though. *Why was the battle master so calm?*

Just as the enemy cavalry reached the Quranian line, the men bent down and picked up long poles, which they anchored into the ground. This made an effective barrier against the horses.

Eliam's troops ran into the stakes and their horses were impaled. The sound of frightened horses and dying men filled the air. The Quranian archers came alive and sent a steady stream of arrows into the following cavalry. Attalee and the battle baster smiled at the resulting confusion.

Attalee had to admire the defense. The men on horseback couldn't get past the stakes without impaling their horses or themselves and the savage archers were decimating the ranks within arrow range.

The battle master slapped the king on the back. "I told you we do good work against cavalry." They began to advance and menace horsemen with the stakes and Eliam's men had to retreat. It was working.

Part of Eliam's rear-guard broke away and headed off to the right side of the battle. "They are trying to flank us," Attalee screamed and the battle master agreed with his assessment. Screaming at the team leaders, he motioned for his men to turn and meet the threat. This thinned the ranks and allowed the enemy to filter through the porcupine defense and attack the archers.

As the archers tried to scramble out of the way, the right flank began to disintegrate. Attalee looked toward his men, but they were locked in battle by the wall. It would be up to them. Eliam shifted more of his cavalry to take advantage of the breech and Attalee groaned. But the Quranians rallied and attempted to close the gap. The long stakes were very effective in knocking down a man on a horse and the archers were still striking a blow against Eliam's troops. The psychological advantage of seeing a horse charging at them was more than most could take and again, the line began to break.

Offering a hand to the battle master, he let the man climb up behind him as they moved toward the thick of the battle. Team leaders were running everywhere, shouting orders to their men and attempting to reverse the tide of the fight, but slowly, they were being pushed back and defeat was only a matter of time.

As they neared the line, the battle master jumped off the horse and picked up a stake to join in the fray. Attalee pulled his sword and charged into the enemies' midst screaming his family's battle song as he cut and slashed his way through the enemy. The boy looked as if he were possessed by the evil demons and it was time for Eliam's men to retreat.

Seeing the king singlehandedly taking on the Calvary renewed the Quranians' morale and as they reorganized, the battle master sent men to outflank Eliam's motion. Even with their renewed energy, the battle was still being lost.

There was a momentary lull in the fighting around him and Attalee looked toward Ka'an. General Cae had retreated toward the wall. They were within range of the archers and Scorpios and these weapons were taking a terrible toll on the enemy troops. "Good job, Cae," he raised his sword in a salute and then turned to meet another assault.

The battle brought him closer to the battle master. "All is lost!" the man screamed, "we must retreat." Attalee shook his head in agreement. Then he heard a trumpet sound behind him. He frowned. Had Eliam moved his men up the southern passage behind them? If it was true, then the men would be cut down as they retreated.

Spurring his horse around, he decided he would try and slow the enemies' advance. He would order the Quranians to make for the city so they could retreat.

Turning to shout for the battle master, Attalee stopped dead in his tracks and let his sword arm drop down in surprise. Galloping across the plains was a collection of the Roman Families with their flags waving in the wind. It was a grand sight and Attalee almost cried in relief.

***

Eliam scowled as he looked over the battlefield. He was taking heavy losses on all fronts, but thought he could crush the Quranian resistance and then flank the Romans when he saw the approaching families. The tide of the battle was shifting away from him and regretfully, Eliam had his men signal the retreat. The intensive training he had subjected them to was evident as they closed ranks and broke off any battles with both the Romans and the Quranians.

General Cae and Attalee were amazed at the efficiency of the enemies' retreat and had to fight the urge to pursue and hazard their rear. Eliam's men left little opportunity for attack as they retreated in an orderly fashion. The battle master began to reassemble his men in case the enemy turned and attacked again, but Eliam's army quickly disappeared into the northeast canyon.

As the Families appeared, Attalee was surprised to see his mother leading an army. She smiled at him and noted her little boy had grown much in the months since he had left home. "I am very glad to see you, Mother," Attalee said as he looked over the Families assembled before him.

"We heard the king of the Romans needed some help," she said, laughing softly into her hand.

He thought for a moment. "The king thanks you for your thoughtfulness and..." He broke down in tears.

"What's wrong, my son?" His mother guided her horse closer to him. "This should be a time of rejoicing, not sadness."

He found he couldn't speak for a while. "I have lost someone very dear to me," he finally said.

"You are tired, my son. Let us return to Ka'an and we will attend to your friend's burial."

He shook his head no. "It is something I must do myself." The Quranian battle master walked up and Attalee clasped his arm. "You know, Battle Master, we fought well together all afternoon and I just realized I don't know your name."

The man smiled. "Forgive me for my rudeness. My name is Kaleb. Battle Master Kaleb."

"Battle Master Kaleb! You and your people fought bravely today and should be proud of your accomplishments."

Kaleb grinned. "Together. We did it together." Attalee nodded, "Together."

"We will tend to the wounded and feed your men," the Matron Ceran said to Kaleb. He thanked her and hurried off to organize his troops. She turned to her son. "Go to your friend," she said gently as he turned his horse sadly toward the late Chief Messa's tent.

The plains were littered with the tools of war, broken swords and bodies covered the ground. "The Plains of Sorrow," he whispered. The name had a new meaning for him now. He felt numb to the victory cheers around him as men rejoiced at still being alive and uninjured. For him, there would be no victory celebration, no laughing and drinking of wine. He had lost her.

CHAPTER ELEVEN

General Cae watched as the king made his way slowly across the plains. Just by the way Attalee's shoulders were slumped, Cae could tell the king was grieving his loss.

From the wall, Cae had seen Thom thrust his sword into Chenee's back. A small flame sparked across the plains and Chief Messa's tent began to burn. Attalee urged his steed into a gallop and arrived to find the Quranians piling their dead onto the fire for cremation. He searched for but couldn't find Chenee's body.

Jumping from his horse, he ran to one of the men and grabbed him roughly. "Where is Chenee?" he screamed as the wind shifted and thick, acrid smoke blew down on them. The stench of burning bodies filled their eyes and Attalee coughed. The man simply pointed at the fire.

Attalee had forgotten about the Quranian custom of burning their dead so the soul couldn't try to reanimate a dead body. He had hoped to see her one last time. Resigned, he climbed back onto his horse and returned to Ka'an. The front gate was wide open and Romans were spilling out onto the plains in celebration, but he didn't seem to notice.

He was deeply immersed in grief and mourning. At least his people would have peace. The Romans and Quranians alike formed a line as he went into the city and they cheered for the young king who had brought the war to an end. It took most of the afternoon for him to arrive back at the king's residence due to the crowds celebrating peace in the streets.

Attalee climbed the stairs to his room, then his attendants undressed him and began to clean the blood and grime from his body. It was then he found a bad cut on his leg. He thought about the promise from Zeus that he would never come to any harm. If he had known he could be injured, would he have fought so fearlessly against the enemy?

Changing into a fresh robe, he went to the table, picked up a glass of wine and walked out onto the balcony that overlooked the mountains. Campfires were beginning to dot the plains like the stars in the sky. Yes, at least his people would be happy, one thing he would never be again and he began to cry.

"Isn't it rude not to offer your guest a drink?"

He dropped his glass and heard it shatter on the stone floor. He knew that voice. He whirled around to find Chenee standing there with a frown on her face. Taking a step forward, he froze midstride. Was she a ghost, coming back to bid him a final farewell? She smiled at him and opened her arms.

"You're dead," he exclaimed.

Looking down at her body, she laughed. "I don't feel dead."

"But I saw you stabbed and fall to the ground. You stopped breathing. I…" he couldn't continue. It was too horrible to talk about.

"I don't remember any of that," she said innocently. "I awoke and found myself in your bed."

Attalee frowned. "It really is you then…?"

"Yes," she said.

He ran and held her body close and almost crushed her in an embrace. "I take it you forgive me?" she asked in his ear.

304

"Oh yes, my love, and I want you to be my wife," he whispered in her ear. "I would be honored," she whispered back and hugged him tightly.

"Are you hungry?" he asked. "Famished!"

He clapped his hands and requested dinner be served. There was a knock at the door and Attalee answered it. The hallway was filled with people and he invited them all in. First came General Cae and Dav, followed by Jupiter and the Matron Ceran, Caiisa and Hades. Bringing up the rear was Battle Master Kaleb.

"Well, this is quite a crowd," Attalee said and started to shut the door but a hand stopped him. He pulled back in surprise as King Attu and the Gentle One walked in.

"My goodness," King Attuicus said, "I can't remember the last time I've seen so many people in my room."

Attalee looked uncomfortable. "I am sorry, King Attu. We'll leave so you may be alone. Your arrival was…" he tried to think of a polite way to say it. "Unfortunate?"

"Ah, no, sir. That isn't it at all. If you desire, I will abdicate in your favor at once."

Attu looked at the Gentle One. "I told you I made a good choice in my successor."

He looked at Attalee. "The title of king isn't just a one time commitment to be abdicated on a whim. I believe this what you told a fellow human. But you, King Attalee, have done more for your fellow humans and by that, I mean the race of mankind, overall than I could have in a millions years. You are right, King Attalee. Humans should be ruled by one of their own and shouldn't be subjected to the will of the Gods, the Ones or any Eternal Beings.

"You should be able to make your own mistakes and learn from them." King Attu looked around the room. "I'm very proud of you all. Not many races make it as far as you have and when they do, it's always a pleasure for me to witness. Now, if you will excuse me, The Gentle One and I have a council meeting to attend," he winked at the Gentle One.

"Thank you for all your help, King Attuicus," Attalee said.

Attu looked puzzled. "If you only knew the half of it, King Attalee, you wouldn't be thanking me." He turned away as Attalee frowned. "And you, Captain Dav Vad. Now that you have found me," he chuckled, "would you like to return to your ship?"

Dav looked at General Cae and put her hand on his sleeve. "I believe I've discovered something I wasn't looking for, but I'm glad I found it. I'll stay here in Ka'an."

"Ah, you found love?" the Gentle One asked.

"Oh no, that's not it," General Cae and the whole room turned to look at her in shock. "I just want to explore the other side of the mountains..." Cae could see the devilish gleam in her eye. He began to laugh and the room joined in.

The Gentle One looked perplexed. "So, you don't want to stay?"

"Of course I want to stay," Dav answered and the room laughed again at the innocence of the Gentle One.

"Come, young One," Attu said with a laugh. The two Immortals folded time and space and disappeared.

"I still can't believe Chenee is alive," Attalee said to the room and he looked at Caiisa. "Were you somehow able to make it to the plains and heal her?"

"I didn't even know she was injured," Caiisa said. "I'm no longer a Priestess of the Goddess Athena."

"She's now the Goddess of the Death World," Hades finished for her. Attalee was mystified. *What had occurred in the past few days?* He knew Caiisa had been fighting with Hades, but here she was sitting beside him, holding his hand and had somehow become the Goddess of the Death World. *Had she won the battle?* This was a story he would have to hear, but he was interrupted as Jupiter came and placed a hand on the king's shoulder.

"Chenee's life was revived as a gift. A reward for the loyalty you've always shown the Gods." Jupiter looked at Caiisa. "I didn't think the new Goddess of the Death World would mind one less soul coming to her this afternoon as thousands were already making the journey."

Caiisa smiled. "The gift of life should never be held in bondage, King Jupiter."

Tears sprang from Attalee's eyes. "It is the greatest gift I have ever been given." He turned to Chenee.

"Thank you." She gave him a kiss.

"This is the special friend you were talking about?" The Matron Ceran walked up behind them.

"Mother, may I present to you, Chief Chenee Messa the Sixth of the Quranian Empire?"

Matron Ceran bowed to her.

"Chenee, may I present, Matron Ceran of the House of Ceran, my mother?"

Chenee went and gave her a hug.

"Shall we have a drink?" Attalee asked the room and sat down on one of the low couches. "Have you met my friends?" he questioned his mother.

"General Cae introduced us on the way over. It would appear you've made many new and interesting friends, my son."

Attalee looked around the room and had a faint grin on his face. "What are you thinking about?" Chenee asked him "Just how nice it is to be here among friends. Collectively, we have been through so much together."

"And this is just the beginning." General Cae added. "Yes, a new beginning," Dav winked at him.

"One thing I can't figure out," Attalee looked at Chenee, "is how you defeated Thom. It was like you had him mesmerized."

Chenee began to laugh. "A woman needs some secrets. I may have to use it on you one day." The room broke out in laughter.

He was still frowning.

"I'll tell you," she finally said. "It's a trick Dav taught me. You take the sword and point it so your opponent can't use their depth perception. If it's done correctly, along their line of sight, they won't be able to see the sword. I also surmised if I had the sun at my back, it would further reduce his vision. So I was able to walk right up to Thom and stab him through the neck. I should have done what Dav taught me, to kick the sword away from the body in case they have one last surge of adrenaline."

In the next breath, "By the way, do we need to tell our people we're no longer at war?"

As the room erupted in laughter, Chenee looked confused.

"You don't know what happened, do you?" Attalee said as everyone tried to speak at once.

Jupiter spoke up. "Chenee has no memory from the time she died to the time she awoke."

"Eliam attacked after your death," Attalee told her. "Your new battle master helped fight off the threat. We were losing when my mother showed up with a collection of the Families' soldiers and the tide of battle was turned." Chenee shook her head. "I can't believe all this happened."

"Believe me, it happened," Cae said.

She sat in shock. "I am glad we're no longer at war, but I feel like part of my life is missing."

"You're alive and with me," Attalee took her hand, "the missing part of your life is a time I never want to live again."

"That's sweet of you to say." Chenee melted into his arms.

"You know, you never did answer my question. A question I asked you several months ago above this very room."

"Is my being here not answer enough?" she teased him. "You are here, but will you stay with me forever?"

"Only if the marriage is publicly announced in the Baan of Marriage and the houses in question give their approval. I want you to know my intentions in this matter are purely ungentlewomanlike."

Attalee laughed at the amused looks they were getting and felt he needed to explain. When he and Chenee had first met, Attalee had extended the hand of friendship to her and she thought he was getting fresh. Haughtily, Attalee had told her that he, being a gentleman, would never dishonor his House by approaching a woman in that manner unless the Baan of Marriage had been publicly published. By this time, everyone in the room had imbibed quite a bit of wine and the laughter went on for some time.

"I will stay with you, always and forever," she whispered as the room continued to celebrate. "I would be proud to be your wife and queen."

He stepped away from her and shouted for everyone's attention. "May I present to you, my future wife?"

Chenee blushed as the room applauded.

The servants began to bring food and soon everyone was too busy eating to talk. General Cae was looking at the Matron Ceran. "May I help you, General Cae?"

"I was wondering how you knew to bring the Families to our aid? I mean it was quite an opportune time, or was it just luck?"

It was Jupiter's turn to blush and he cleared his throat. "I guess I must take credit for that," he looked sheepishly at the king. "I know Attalee had requested the Gods not assist you..." He let the words hang in the air.

"Yes," Attalee said, looking at the God with a frown.

310

"But you didn't specifically say I couldn't give other humans pertinent information."

Attalee looked from Jupiter to his mother. "Have you been teaching him old Roman Law?"

"No, just some of the tricks you tried to pull on me, my dear son."

"I think we should make you both part of the Senate. We would never lose a debate."

"You are offended?" Jupiter's face was beginning to cloud up.

"No," Attalee looked wistfully at the God. "If you hadn't helped us, we would have lost the war and I would be without my future wife. I am indebted to you in many ways, my Lord Jupiter. Someday, I hope I may be able to repay you."

"You've restored people's belief in the Gods and our temples, which give us our life force. As I told you before, her life is repayment for your kindness, King Attalee."

"Well, I appreciate everything the Gods have done for the New Roman Empire and I hope to continue our relationship in the days ahead."

Jupiter looked out into the night and back at Attalee. "King Attu spoke of humans and Gods relying on each other more. The Abomination is still out there, somewhere. It hungers. The Gods alone can't kill it, we must have help from humans."

"When and if it returns, we will work collectively to destroy it," Attalee promised.

"Will you be staying in Ka'an?" the Matron Ceran asked her son.

He sighed. "I had hoped to return to our House and rule from there, but with the threat Eliam is posing, I suppose I must stay here."

"Ah…the responsibilities of adulthood. When you can return, you will always be welcome. You and your new wife."

"Thank you, Matron Ceran." Chenee gave her a kiss. "What about you, General Cae?" the Matron asked.

He looked at Dav. "I want to explore the other side of the mountains with someone. I'm sure the king will require more information about Eliam and the army he has hidden there."

"Don't lie to us, General Cae. You're going to look for farmland." Cae raised his glass in acknowledgment. "Not a bad idea, really."

"You've found a way over the mountains?" Chenee asked and the room looked at her in surprise again.

"I'll explain all this to you later, my love." He tried to smooth over her hurt feelings.

As the night wore on, the party began to break up and soon, Attalee and Chenee were alone. He hugged his lost love to his chest and thanked the gods for returning Chenee to him.

***

Attu appeared on the pedestal of woe in chains. The Gentle One materialized beside him and looked at the Council of Ones. "I've brought the creature called King Attu."

"Where have you been?" the Angry One asked. "We ordered you to return eons ago."

"I had to go undercover and sneak up on this creature to capture him." The Council of Ones looked at each other. They weren't sure how the

Gentle One had done it, but he had. "We order you to destroy the creature called Attu."

"Why?" the Gentle One asked. "What has he done to you?"

"That creature is a threat to the Council, and therefore, a threat to the Ones."

The Gentle one began to walk around the pedestal. "The only threat I see to the Ones is this Council."

"How dare you speak blasphemy in our presence?"

The Gentle One turned and spoke sharply, "How dare you, the Ones, put yourselves above the other members of this universe?"

"We are called the Ones. We are above all others."

"The creatures in this universe were all shaped by the Creator to be equal and should be on the same level as the Ones. You have no more authority over them, than a moon has over the planet it orbits."

"The Council will deal with your insolence after we have destroyed this being," the angry One said with a snarl. Holding out his hand toward Attu, he stopped. "Wait, I have something else I must do," and opened his fist.

The Gentle One's universe appeared and the Angry One crushed it in his hand until the cosmic dust squeezed out of his finger. The Gentle One staggered as he felt trillions of lives snuffed out. He bent over with the pain of the psychological loss.

"No," the Gentle One gasped. "Can you not show some compassion?"

"Here is your compassion," the Angry One said as he stepped on the dust and ground it into the floor.

"And now for you," he said, looking at King Attu. Stretching forth his hand, he opened it and motioned for Attu to appear in his hand. The massive fingers closed over and crushed Attuicus until his body gave a satisfactory pop, then a small explosion as the creature's remains fell to the floor.

"So, Gentle One, will you suffer the same fate?" he returned to his seat. The Gentle One had recovered from the pain of having his creation destroyed and scattered to the cosmic winds. He stood tall and looked them in the eye. There was no look of fear on his face and he actually smiled at the Council of Ones.

"I asked you a question an instant ago. Have you no compassion for creatures beneath your station?"

"Compassion," the Egotistical One said. "In this universe, only the strong survive."

"On the other hand, what if you are the weak creature? Would you just accept your fate, or would you beg for compassion?"

The Angry One laughed. "We are strong. We are the Council of Ones and we pass judgment on the weak."

The Gentle One began to laugh. "I believe a lesson is at hand. Your judgment is about to be handed to you from a being more powerful than the Ones and I ask you again, will you now beg for compassion?"

The Council of Ones looked at each other and began to laugh. "You know our power better than any of the Ones, my child. Haven't we laid waste to your universe and King Attu this day alone?"

"No you haven't," the Gentle One said as he bent over and began to run his finger in the cosmic dust on the floor. Moving his hand in a circle, the dust began to swirl and glow. As pulses of energy flowed into the dust, the Gentle One and his universe reappeared beside the first Gentle One. Confused, the Council looked at the two Gentle Ones before them. Slowly, the first Gentle One began to dissolve until King Attu stood before them.

"We have been betrayed!" the Council screamed in terror as Attuicus collected them in his hands. He towered over the twelve members as they scrambled over each other and tested the boundaries of their imprisonment.

The real Gentle One came over to look down on them.

"What will you do to us!" the Scared One screamed in terror.

"Have compassion on us!" another One screamed in anguish and fear. Attu chuckled. "Did you show compassion to the trillions upon trillions of life forms you just crushed out of existence?" he asked with disdain in his voice. "As the Ones, you believed only in your own superiority and had no compassion for races of lesser abilities. And now you ask for a compassion that you, the Council of Ones, wouldn't give?"

"We are the most powerful beings in this universe," the Angry One screamed, "we will crush you and any others who stand in our way."

"For being what you consider superior, you sure are stupid. I hold you within my power—a power that pales only in the face of the Creator—and you mock me."

In response, the Angry One spit at Attu. The steely gray mucus worked its way down the boundary wall.

Attu closed his hand and the Ones' life force collected together and then blasted apart. The Gentle One shuddered as he felt the impact run through his One link and the other Ones mourned with him. It was the first time any of their kind had ceased to exist.

The Gentle One held his head in his hands and cried. To cease to exist was awful for his race and he felt the void within him fill with sorrow. It touched every One in their race and they were truly One.

Attu looked at his friend with concern and compassion. Then he smiled at the Gentle One.

Attu stretched forth his hand and extended it to the Gentle One. In his palm stood twelve new little Ones. "Unlike your Council, I am compassionate. They will retain their memories, but I have given them another chance to grow and learn how to be kind to other races. I give them over to you, Gentle One, to raise and teach them your gentle way."

Attu reached behind his back and pulled Sorti Ne and his children from another dimension. "Here is someone else I think would be an excellent teacher. Perhaps you and the human engineer can raise the Ones and babies together, in peace."

The Gentle One gently accepted the Little Ones from Attu and held them tenderly. "I will teach them," he put his arm around all of them—the Ones, the children and Sorti Ne—then he folded space and time and disappeared.

Attu looked around the chamber and caused it to fade to cosmic dust. Dust the Gentle One could use to build more planets, ah artistic balls of rock and life as he called it. Standing on the edge of the Universe, he felt proud of all he had accomplished. True, he hadn't understood the humans and had made many mistakes, but in the end, everything had worked out.

It was now time for him to leave, to return home and rest. He would miss the friends he had made in this universe, especially the Gentle One. He hoped the creature would evolve far enough to come and visit him one day. Time for him to leave? *I have been around the humans too long. I have all the time in the existence of eternity.* An opening appeared in deep space and he smiled at the sight of the lush garden beyond the doorway.

His family was waiting on the other side and with a feeling of deep compassion for their sadness at missing him, he stepped through into their arms. They overwhelmed him with feelings of happiness at his safe return. "By the Gods," he declared "I am home." Laughing, he thought *I really have been around humans too long.*

During the large welcome home party just as Attu began to shut the door, one of his children slipped out and went to look for food, life based energy.

EPILOGUE

5 years later "How are you feeling today?" Attalee asked Chenee, who was obviously with child. Brushing some of the scrolls off his legs, she sat down on his lap and put her arm around him.

"I feel very uncomfortable today. You Romans make strong babies and he's trying to push my ribs up under my chin."

Rubbing her belly, he made soothing sounds. She leaned against him and sighed.

"I have a surprise for you."

"You do?"

"We have special visitors coming today."

Chenee rolled her eyes. "We have special visitors every day." The king felt everyone who visited, from a pig farmer to the senators, was on the same level. Well, the senators were usually one step down the ladder from a farmer, but the king treated everyone the same.

"So who are the special visitors?"

He had picked up a flower and was gently smelling its fragrance. He acted like he was so absorbed in the enjoyment of its bouquet, he didn't hear her. It was a game he liked to play with her.

Chenee hit him playfully in the shoulder and he gave her a look of horror. He began to laugh as he saw her face. She hadn't been fooled.

"Cae and Dav have returned from the other side of the mountains." Chenee jumped with excitement and then regretted it as the baby pushed against her ribs. "Ow," she exclaimed as she pushed the foot back down.

***

When Dav and Cae arrived at the king's residence, a feast in their honor was given. They looked tired and worn out, so he had dinner held until they could bathe and change clothes. Chenee went to Dav's room to talk to her before dinner and was shocked to see her friend climbing out of her bath with a belly as large as hers.

She stopped and looked at Dav in surprise. "Why hello, little sister," she said as the girl just stood with her mouth hanging open. Dav continued to dry off.

"Dav," she exclaimed, "you're pregnant."

"Does it show?" she teased.

"But I thought you couldn't have children."

Dav looked at the scar across her stomach. It had been from a sword wound years ago and she had lost the ability to have a child. "Remember when Caiisa healed me after the battle with the Warrior? Well, before that time, I always had a pain in my side. When she touched me, the pain went away. I think that was when I grew back what had been lost before."

"I'm so happy for you," Chenee said and gave her a hug.

"So am I," Dav said. "I never realized just how much I wanted children until after the first one was born."

Chenee hadn't been listening. "You have another one?"

"Actually, two others, a boy and a girl named Attalee and Chenee."

"That's wonderful. Congratulations."

"Thank you," Dav said with a sparkle in her eye.

***

Cae picked up his wineglass and took a sip. "I've missed the luxuries of the Capital," he let the wine sit on his tongue and savored the rich flavor.

"I am glad to have you back. No one will even argue with me anymore. Not even the Senate puts up a fight when I ask them to do something."

"With the news I have for you, I'm sure the Senate will be calling for your head once again."

Attalee frowned. "What's wrong, my friend?"

"Eliam has regrouped his army and is preparing to attack once again." Attalee turned white. "We aren't ready for another prolonged battle."

"I know," Cae said, "that's why we destroyed his passage and came around the long way to escape his army and to keep our tunnel a secret. That's why it took us so long to return."

"Do you think he will find your access any time soon?"

"Doubtful. You have to climb down a cliff face and hang by your toes to swing into it." Cae recalled the experience with a frown. "Monte's description of the tunnel just opening up out onto the plains was a bit off target."

"How long do you estimate we have before he can find a way here?"

"It depends on how fast he can find another way under the mountains."

"We'll have to plan on it happening at any time then. I'll need someone with military knowledge to

320

get us started on a training plan." They looked at each other. "Dav," they said together.

"I hope you're not taking my name in vain," Dav said as she walked into the room.

"We were just discussing a new job for you," Attalee said.

"I'm retired. Anyway, I have several eighteen year jobs ahead of me as it is."

"You're right about that." Chenee looked on with a grin as she rubbed her belly.

"I can stay home with the kids," Cae said, "and you can go and conquer the world."

"Oh, just long enough to make babies and then off I go again, huh?"

"At least you'll get time to lay around at the beginning of the nine months and then again at the end." Cae laughed.

"You men are all the same," Chenee said in mock despair. "Only thinking about one thing."

Attalee grinned. "Getting out of work?" Chenee hit him.

Dav looked at Cae. "Yes."

Raising his glass, Attalee stood. "For now, let's enjoy our time together and worry about the future tomorrow."

"I agree," Dav raised her glass in a toast.

Walking out onto the balcony overlooking the city of Ka'an, they watched as the twin suns set behind the mountains.

***

Thirty years later on Earth

321

"Pluto Control, this is Moon Base twenty-three. We have an unauthorized vessel approaching."

"Roger that, Moon Base twenty-three, this is Pluto Control. I am attempting to raise the Control."

A long silence.

"Moon Base, this is Pluto Control. The Control is broadcasting on an old frequency. The Control reports it is the Pioneer Ship *New Beginnings* launched about forty-five years ago."

"Who cares! Tell it to head for the scrap yards like the rest of the returning pioneer ships. We'll begin to recycle her immediately."

"Roger, Moon Base this is Pluto Control. But the Control is saying something about it being hijacked and... Should I patch a feed into your line?"

"That's a negative. I have a shitload of metal to get down to Venus and this ship will help me meet the quota on time. Whoever hijacked it is probably dead by now and I have a hot date on Earth II, seventy-two light years from here and I want to be there by dinner.

"Send the scrapheap to the yards and stop cluttering up my lightwave traffic. This is Moon Base Out."

With a sigh, the Pluto Control informed the *New Beginnings* Control of her new berthing assignment inside the rings of Uranus.

The *New Beginnings* Control continued to send out her message of a hijack as she was towed into the yards. Almost immediately, the main drive was disconnected and with terrifying efficiency, the yard robots began to cut and tear her metal away, loading it on a space scow destined for Venus.

The red glow of the Control's main core grew silent and black as empty space surrounded it.

AUTHOR'S NOTE

I hope you have enjoyed the second book in the *New Roman Empire* series. It was really difficult for me to finish this book. The basic story line was done, but I had started a war between Caiisa and Hades in Book One and needed to set it up again in the sequel. While writing this part, my mother went into the hospital with pneumonia and later found out she had two blood-borne infections. The antibiotics shut her kidneys down and eventually, she went into renal failure.

As she was dying, I was writing about Thudder having to kill his own mother, which sets up a story in Book Three, but it was so hard having to write about it.

My mother had a liver transplant in 1984, that gave her another twenty years with us. To repay the young man who gave her a second chance at life, she became a Hospice nurse and helped other people start their journey to the Death World in a more gentle and loving way, before she was forced to retire for health reasons.

This is why Caiisa, who is a healer, can also emphathize with the dead and dying and why she made a perfect replacement for the God of the Death World.

In Mythology, the Gods are often portrayed as having no morals or values when it comes to getting what they want.

The battle for leadership of the Gods is an interesting one. One that was made even more so by the unexpected plans of Athena, but even Caesar's best friend ended up stabbing him to death. "Et tu, Brute", (Latin for You too, Brutus.)

This is my first attempt at writing a sequel, so I hope I did a good job. Thank you for buying this book. As in the past, I will give money to charity.

Fifty percent of the profits from this book will go toward the National Transplants Association in Memphis, Tenn.

The other fifty percent will go toward the Kramer Family College Fund, to be used to send children to school for nursing or related fields of study.

May God bless you and your families, Roger W. Kramer A very special thanks goes out to my editor, Chere'. She has had to put up with my very dry sense of humor and the psychoanalysis of Characters in the book. It has been great working with her and I look forward to many more Chapters returned to me in Red Lettering, indicating the items that need changed.